A DEATH
IN VENICE

BOOKS BY VERITY BRIGHT

A DEATH
IN VENICE

VERITY BRIGHT

bookouture

Published by Bookouture in 2024

An imprint of Storyfire Ltd.
Carmelite House
50 Victoria Embankment
London EC4Y 0DZ

www.bookouture.com

ISBN: 978-1-83525-536-0
eBook ISBN: 978-1-83525-535-3

To the city of Venice for providing us with the inspiration to write this book. It really is one of the most unique places on earth.

1

'Oh gracious, excuse me!'

Lady Eleanor Swift's fiery red curls bounced across her forehead as she lunged after her jade cloche hat. Having retrieved it, she bobbed down to help the stranger she'd bumped heads with to collect the spilled contents of her handbag.

'I mean... umm, *mi scusi*. We're in Venice, after all.' She smiled apologetically. The stranger nodded, the wide brim of her lilac sun hat obscuring her face. Eleanor shrugged. 'That's almost all the Italian I've had a chance to master so far because I've needed to say it so often. Given the crowds milling everywhere.'

She handed the woman a lipstick and compact, hindered by Gladstone, her bulldog, who was straining on his lead to reach under the young woman's hat and offer his best licky greeting.

Eleanor winced, feeling bad as the woman paused in placing the items hurriedly back in her handbag to rub at her temple. Aware she could only hope the woman would understand her in English, she continued genially.

'I've been trying to look where I'm going since I got here, but I'm simply too captivated and excited. To be here, that is.

And particularly in St Mark's Square.' She gestured around the colossal expanse of ivory white stone. The whole space was flanked on three sides with hundreds of colonnaded arches which ran down to the Byzantine basilica of St Mark's itself. 'It's all just too beautiful for words, don't you think?'

For the first time, the young woman looked up, revealing flawless olive skin and long dark lashes framing eyes so close to amethyst blue Eleanor couldn't help staring. Only nineteen, or twenty, Eleanor guessed, with her perfect heart-shaped face she would surely have been every Renaissance artists' favourite muse.

'Beauty has no point,' she replied unexpectedly, the melodic cadence of her Italian accent seeming at odds with her troubled expression. 'Not if one's destiny is forever to be looked at by the wrong eyes!'

Eleanor was taken aback by the enigmatic reply. 'Er, yes. Are you here for the Venice Carnival? I know it's officially banned in public, but there are still fabulous private masked balls, I hear?'

The young woman laughed mirthlessly. 'Everyone wears a mask in this city whether it is Carnival time or not.' She stiffened, as if she'd caught sight of someone.

Eleanor spun around but couldn't see anyone waving or making their way towards them. Turning back, she just glimpsed the young woman darting away into the surge of humanity in the square.

Eleanor grimaced as Gladstone nosed her leg with a soft whimper. She knelt down and cupped his chin.

'I agree, old chum. She seemed really quite upset that we'd collided. Even... agitated. Whereas I'd just begun to think it was an unavoidable element of sightseeing in Venice!'

As if on cue, someone's bag knocked into her shoulder. As she rose, she spotted an object on the ground just in front of her. Her pleated skirt had obviously hidden it. Picking it up, she swung around on tiptoe, trying to see over the heads of the crowd.

'I say!' she called in the direction the woman had disappeared. 'You forgot your...' she looked down at the item in her hand, 'your heart!'

The only reply was the continued ballet of Venetians impatiently dodging the hordes of tourists. Eleanor glanced down at her bulldog again.

'Goodness, she must be in a hurry to dash off like that without noticing her keepsake was missing.' She studied the palm-sized piece of glass in the shape of a heart, the strange look in the young girl's amethyst eyes troubling her.

About to call after the woman again, she heard a disapproving cough behind her. 'Clifford? Oh! *Mi scusi.*'

'Thank you, madam!'

She stepped out of the man's way and glanced around. But there was no sign of her butler, whose cough usually heralded a respectful telling-off over her myriad unladylike infractions. Not that she minded. Mostly. He was unwaveringly dedicated and her much-needed voice of reason, truth be told. And her beleaguered chaperone, as he would no doubt delight in reminding her many times during her weeks taking in the Grand Tour. She'd 'inherited' him, and the rest of the staff, along with her late uncle's extensive estate in the sleepy Cotswold countryside. And it was his life's aim, it seemed, to make her a proper lady of the manor. Her rather bohemian upbringing largely abroad having left her clueless when it came to the social etiquette of polite English society.

She scanned the surrounding crowds again, ears alert. But there was no cough. No tut. Not even a sniff. She patted her bulldog on the head.

'Remarkably, it looks as if we got away with that, Gladstone. An English lady of the manor yelling at the top of her voice in public like a common barrow boy! Tsk!' She frowned. 'It's unheard of for Clifford to be even a second behind schedule, though. Let's go and find him and tease him mercilessly about it.' She carefully slid the glass heart into the pocket of her tailored silk-tweed jacket. 'Mind you, I can't imagine even his unfathomable wizardry will allow him to work out who that poor young thing was, so I can return this. It might be precious, if only for sentimental reasons.'

She jiggled Gladstone's lead and struck out purposefully across the square, but her pace soon slowed. Partly because of her continued awe of this amazing thousand-year-old city and partly because of her new Venetian slippers.

Eleanor gazed in wonder at the sheer volume of people, young and old, crowding the square. Multitudes of children, dressed in ribboned caps and sailor-suited tops over navy britches or smart smock dresses, skipped around. Their parents' striking dark hair and eyes suggested they were local, or Italians taking in the sights. Snippets of conversations among the other passing groups sounded like Russian, Polish, Hungarian and German, with English and the occasional American voice cutting across them.

She looked up at the flutter of blue-and-white striped awnings with glistening tassels stretching out from the higher arches of the colonnades. Forcing herself to focus and stop dawdling, she pressed on in search of her butler.

Almost immediately, she pulled up short again. This time recognising the street artist whom she'd purchased a sketch from the day before. Yesterday, he'd been outside her hotel. She peered over his shoulder, once more entranced at how his jerky strokes so perfectly captured the waterway's hurly-burly against its backdrop of timeless grandeur. Perched on an upturned crate, he wore a collarless grey shirt and dark shorts. His sandalled feet were spread wide, his scrawny knees gripping the base of his easel, which was clearly nothing more than a battered case. Two brush handles propped the lid open, the inner compartment holding his slim supply of charcoal sticks. His works for sale were displayed on a sheet spread in an arc on the ground.

He hadn't delivered the sketch to her yet, as she'd asked for it to be framed. She thought of asking him now how long it would be, but hesitated. It had taken a while for them to understand each other the first time as he was a deaf mute and she was worried he'd think she was hassling him. Deciding she'd ask tomorrow if it hadn't turned up by then, her eyes fell on his sketch of two young lovers. They were staring adoringly into each other's eyes, perched on the wall of a picturesque stone bridge. She hadn't seen it yesterday. It must be new. Something about it pricked at her thoughts. She frowned. It not only reminded her how much she was missing her fiancé, there was something... else.

Shaking herself out of her reverie, she continued on, unable to stop peering back over her shoulder at the lovers' picture.

'Oh, *mi scusi!*' she mumbled for the umpteenth occasion, this time as she bumped into a smart black jacket.

'Still perfecting that one particular Italian phrase, I see, my lady?'

'Clifford, it's you!' She pulled back, catching the mischievous glint in her butler's eyes despite his otherwise inscrutable expression. Gladstone barked at the carpet bag hanging securely under his shoulder. 'There you are, finally.'

'Sincere apologies, my lady. But Master Tomkins is the reason for my regrettably unpunctual arrival.'

At his name, her ginger cat let out a jubilant meow as he poked his head through the padded hole at the end of the bag.

She tickled his velveteen chin. 'Any naughtiness on his part can be entirely excused as just excitement, Clifford. He's in Venice. Italy's most incredible island city!'

He shook his head. 'Perhaps. But Master Tomkins has been

feted so fervently by all the Venetians we passed that it is a miracle I made it even a yard past your hotel.'

'Well, that's your doing, silly.' She ran her hand over the carpet bag. 'I imagine they're as smitten with this darling kitty kit bag you made him as he is.'

'Actually, I'm minded to think it might be something else, given the eager crowds Tomkins delighted in playing up to.'

'Well, I shall still tease you interminably about being the one who was late. Given that, infuriatingly, it will probably be the only chance I ever get. We agreed to meet up ages ago.'

'Seven minutes prior, to be precise, if you will forgive the correction, my lady.' He pointed across the square at the giant cobalt clock face set between two ornate white pilasters. 'But perhaps the lady had not appreciated the clock's accuracy, given that it does not run on the indiscriminate timekeeping she favours?'

She hid a smile at his teasing and tried an unconvincing mock huff instead. 'I've been too caught up in my thoughts, actually. Besides, that clock is far too complicated to read with all those Roman and Arabic numerals, as well as the golden signs of the zodiac running around its face. The sun bounces off them and blinds one.' She held up a halting finger as her butler opened his mouth. 'Not now, Clifford. I promise you can bend my ears another time with your no doubt encyclopaedic knowl-edge about the clock's inner' – she waved a hand – 'gubbins and supposedly fascinating doodahs.'

He sniffed. 'Gubbins, my lady? Doodahs? That is the Torre dell'Orologio. A horological masterpiece, originally designed in 1490.'

'I'm sure. And I know how precious all things clock-related are to you. So tonight, with a sherry in my hand on my hotel terrace, I shall be your attentive audience for its every historical detail.' She ran her hands down her arms. 'Actually, maybe it should wait so I can at least do my best to listen properly.'

Clifford's brow flinched with concern. 'Is something wrong, my lady?'

'More perplexing, really.' Her fingers reached into her pocket and cupped the glass heart as she pulled it out to show him. As she turned it over, the sun caught the vibrant crimson and turquoise entwined swirls inside which she hadn't noticed before. 'I just have a funny tingle about someone I bumped into. Quite literally. This fell from her handbag. She was so beautiful and young, framed in her elegant lilac sun hat, she should be bursting with carefree joy. But it wasn't love in her eyes I saw, now I think of it.' She bit her lip. 'More like... fear.'

'Lilac sun hat?' Clifford repeated thoughtfully. 'Coincidentally, Master Tomkins and I passed a lady in such noticeable headwear several minutes ago. And I admit to feeling a tinge of discomfort at the male person she was with, given her reticent demeanour in accepting his arm. They boarded a covered gondola which headed out across the lagoon.'

She sighed. 'Dash it! Now she'll forever be without her heart.'

2

Eleanor really had intended to follow Clifford's suggestion of sightseeing systematically, if only to appease his intrinsic love of logic and order. But the excitement of being in such a unique and colourful city won over her best intentions only two minutes after she turned out of St Mark's Square.

'Really, my lady?' Clifford said, peering down the boutique-lined street, which was so narrow that in any other city it would be called a passageway. Its meagre width also meant the sun was little more than a pinched strip of light between the buildings on either side. 'And you intend to arrive at the Grand Canal whilst it is still spring quite how?'

She pretended to think that over. 'With my head swimming with Venetian wonder, plus umpteen shopping bags over each shoulder. And via a raft of those darling footbridges. I believe Venice has over four hundred of them. What do you say? Shall we skip along in the sun?' she ended with an innocent smile.

He eyed her sideways. 'Four hundred and seventeen, to be precise. And if I might respectfully decline to "skip" anywhere. However,' his tone softened, 'would that I am never the man to impede the spirit of exploration in another. Especially in my mistress, since I have observed it is a stronger urge than even the need for oxygen.'

'You're such a sport, Clifford!'

Before she could say any more, she was jerked forward by Gladstone as he set off on a lumbering charge. She allowed him his head, not having the heart to break it to him that the streets of Venice weren't paved with sausages.

The labyrinth of ancient thoroughfares they plunged into was continually dissected by the greeny-blue ribbons of the innumerable canals. The locals' adoration of her ginger tomcat, which she'd seen first-hand on trying to navigate the last of St Mark's Square, was less evident in the narrow, shadowy passageways. Mostly because there were fewer people, and he was harder to spot. Her distinguished butler, however, received a constant stream of admiring glances and waves from the women in and out of the shops, much to Eleanor's amusement.

She was still trying to grow out of her earlier lifestyle of travelling the world solo and into her new life as a lady of the manor. Much as she appreciated the blessings, she struggled with its formality and rules. Her butler's comforting presence and patient ear, however, she secretly adored. And never more than now as she wittered on to him over her fascination with the quaint shops and cosy cafés sandwiched between the petite houses she meandered them past.

Halfway down a particularly narrow street in front of a window display of exquisitely stitched leather gloves, her butler handed her a sumptuous-looking ice cream in a delectably caramelised sugar cone.

'A traditional Venetian gelato, my lady.'

She savoured the first taste, her eyes closing in ecstasy. 'Oh, that is sublime! Hazelnut and honey, I think. Very thoughtful, Clifford. It'll keep my energy up until we find a brunch spot.'

His lips quirked. 'It was rather more intended to soothe the lady's throat from barely pausing for breath in the last hour.'

She laughed. 'Now I understand! This is really your scallywag way of keeping me quiet for a few minutes, you terror.'

Treating Tomkins to the last lick of ice cream and Gladstone to the remainder of her cone, she set off again. And soon spotted a flash of jade-blue water at the end of the alleyway. A moment later they emerged onto the Grand Canal, teeming as always with traffic.

'Ha, what an unnecessary fuss you made, Clifford,' she said teasingly. 'Insisting we'd get lost!'

'If you say so, my lady. However, precisely where along the Grand Canal have we emerged?'

'Does it matter?' she said airily, shielding her eyes from the glorious sunshine. 'It's so breathtakingly dramatic, with that rainbow backdrop of painted buildings against the striking black of surely hundreds of gondolas. And the way of life so different, it would be nothing but enchanting wherever one was to arrive at it. I mean, there are no roads and no vehicles of any kind, and even a bicycle would struggle with all these stepped bridges over the enticing water.'

'Enticing, my lady?' He gave a disapproving sniff. 'If one might heed a slight paraphrasing of the words of the eminent Lord Byron from his "Ode on Venice". "He feels his spirit soaring, albeit weak. And of the fresher water, which he would seek."'

'Clifford, it's no use.' She clapped her hands. 'I've completely fallen in love with this incredible city. And that's that.'

'Heartening news, I'm sure.'

She nodded to each of her pets. 'Now Gladstone and Tomkins, old chums, all we need to do is find a gondola. But not just any gondola. One which meets the exacting standards my butler considers essential.' She steered her way through the flurry of pedestrians along the waterside, holding Gladstone back as she leaned out over the path's capped edging. Peering left, then right, she wondered how the scores of gondoliers ever managed to navigate their thirty-foot-long craft past each other in the congested canal. Particularly while needing to also dodge the faster moving, if fewer in number, powered taxis and delivery barges.

Clifford stepped up beside her, scanning the water. Without a word, he gave a commanding wave to one of the many red- or blue-striped shirted gondoliers waiting on the opposite bank.

'Lovely looking boat. And chap,' she muttered. 'But why that one, particularly?'

A few moments later, the tall trim gondolier, who had responded expertly, brought his craft to a stop up against the red-and-white striped poles next to them. He whipped off his straw boater, which made his dark curls flutter as much as his hat's shiny blue ribbons in the breeze.

'Good morning, Signor Clifford.'

He threw his hands out, revealing a silver monogrammed black silk cummerbund around his waist.

'My lady.' Clifford nodded at the gondolier. 'This is Angelo, whom I secured through the manager of your hotel.'

Angelo gave a deep bow, ending with a courtly flourish. He pretended to whisper behind his hand. 'But only after Signor Clifford made me answer many questions, Lady Swift!'

She shook her head. 'That is no small feat, I know from uncomfortable experience.'

'Angelo is the longest standing gondolier at our hotel, my lady,' Clifford said. 'Hence, I took the liberty of negotiating that he be at your disposal for the duration of your stay in Venice. Including the days of the Carnival.' He arched an admonishing brow at her. 'Albeit with the hope of keeping appointed times. If only for the household accounts,' he ended pointedly, slipping the gondolier several coins.

'Well, of course, it's just good manners. Tsk! If I'd known

you'd made an appointment on my behalf, Clifford, I'd have arrived on time! Besides, I seem to remember you were the one who was late?'

'Lady Swift, no problem.' Angelo eagerly pocketed the money. 'I think you and your *maggiordomo* like to argue, *si?*'

She laughed. 'It's called squabbling in polite society. But, yes.' She settled into the grand red velvet armchair he led her to, so incongruous on a small open boat, she thought. 'So *maggiordomo* is Italian for butler, is it? Clifford, that makes you seem even more distinguished to my mind. If that's actually possible.'

'Highly unlikely, my lady, given your menagerie—'

As the gondola tipped, he grabbed Gladstone, who had scrabbled up the side to hang his paws over, and placed the bulldog in the middle of the boat instead. Angelo nodded appreciatively and then spotted Tomkins marvelling at the world floating by. He knelt in front of the carpet bag and ran his sun-kissed hands reverently over the ecstatic tomcat's whiskers.

'Degno del doge!' he murmured.

Gladstone strained forward with an indignant snort and curled his tongue into Angelo's ear for attention.

'Agh!' The gondolier jerked to his feet, waving an amiable finger at the bulldog. 'You no fit for the doge!'

Eleanor looked from one to the other. 'The doge?'

Clifford nodded. 'The highest-ranking official in the Venetian Republic. Napoleon abolished the post on claiming the city for France in 1797. Though, the cat connection...?' He shrugged.

Angelo laughed. 'We Venetians love cats! And your cat reminds everyone, I think, of a famous doge, Francesco Morosini, who loved his cat so much he took it everywhere with him. Even into battle, it is said. And when he died, the doge had him embalmed!'

Eleanor covered Tomkins' ears. 'Don't you worry. We're not going to have you embalmed!'

Angelo patted Clifford's shoulder on his way past. 'Sit, sit. We go!'

Eleanor tutted at her uncomfortable-looking butler. 'You'll have to break your precious rule of never sitting in front of your mistress. We're in a gondola, for heaven's sake.'

He looked askance at the two identical inward-facing seats, then sank stiffly into the opposite one. This tickled her since neither was any less throne-like than the one she occupied.

As Angelo pushed them away from the poles and started rowing, Eleanor leaned back in her seat.

A gondola ride on the Grand Canal in the sunshine, Ellie? Does it get any better than this?

3

The first thing that struck Eleanor as their gondola reached the middle of the congested waterway was how little it rocked now Gladstone was cuddled beside her. He sat on the double seat as still as a bookend, eyes wide with wonder.

Angelo rowed them further along the bustling canal, expertly steering through the stream of traffic, often inches from another boat and with many a shouted greeting to the other gondoliers they passed. A moment later, they slid under the renowned Rialto Bridge, which was teeming with tourists hanging over the stone balustrading.

'Yoo-hoo, m'lady! Up here!' Four familiar and overexcited voices hailed.

Eleanor looked up. 'Clifford, it's the ladies!'

She waved enthusiastically to her staff, who were semaphoring wildly with their hats.

'Indeed,' he tutted. 'As, disgracefully, all of Venice is now aware.'

She smiled impishly. 'Just so you know, Clifford. For every occasion you tell them off, I shall simply commit some far worse misdemeanour to deter you from plaguing their well-deserved holiday with unnecessary admonishments.'

He stroked an imaginary beard. 'Mmm. And the unusual aspect of that is?'

She hid a smile and turned back to Angelo. 'You know, I'm positively hankering to be a gondolier. How do I go about it?'

He shook his head. 'Of course, Lady Swift. It is a wonderful thing. But it cannot be. You must first be a man. There are no woman gondoliers. It is tradition. And tradition means a lot in our city.'

She opened her mouth, then closed it.

This is no time for a tirade about women's rights, Ellie. Besides, it's not your city. Or country. And you're on holiday, remember?

She smiled sweetly. 'So how did you become a gondolier?'

'Because I come from a long-time family of them. Like every other gondolier, the right is handed down through generations. We work hard to keep our city like our ancient fathers who built it from the beginning.' His face darkened. 'Although some on our city council want only change and to destroy our heritage!' He waved with one hand at the rows of magnificent buildings on either side. 'One thousand years ago, there was only sea with a hundred tiny patches of... swamp, you English say, I think. That's when our forefathers work out how to make this whole beautiful city on the foundation of just wood.'

Her jaw fell. 'Wood?'

He nodded. 'Many, many wooden poles they hammer down, down, down into the mud.'

'Poles? Made of wood?' She shook her head in disbelief. 'But most buildings in Venice are stone. And simply enormous. Like St Mark's Basilica. Clifford said it's two hundred and fifty feet long.'

'And almost as wide, my lady.'

'Exactly. That must be unbelievably heavy!'

Angelo nodded proudly. 'Yes. But still the whole city is built only on wood. To be the Venetian means to always use your head. Like the... the fox, I think you say in England.'

She looked with new awe at the rows of buildings lining the Grand Canal.

'Well, if I can't be a gondolier, you can at least tell me something about your intriguing craft.'

Having been brought up as a child on the sea, she was used to the traditional method of rowing with two oars, facing backwards from the centre of the boat. But, despite the gondola being longer than any rowing boat Eleanor had been in, Angelo was standing up at the rear. Rhythmically easing his body back and forth, his wrists lightly twisting against his long single oar. 'It's incredible how you make this thing move! I'm looking at the other gondolas and there can't be more than six inches of the boat actually in the water.'

He puffed with pride. 'I tell you, this is the best gondola in all of Venice! But each gondola is unique and especially built for a gondolier to his exact weight, otherwise it will not steer properly.'

Clifford threw her a mischievous look. 'Still harbouring a yearning to join the profession, my lady? Rigidly following a routine meal schedule and indulging in only lady-like portions?'

She shook her head in horror. 'Not a chance, Clifford. What a hideous idea!'

Even though she was still blessed with an enviably svelte figure it belied her healthy appetite.

Angelo chuckled, his brown eyes shining as she turned back to him.

'So, every one of these beautiful boats has been made to measure?'

'Si. But this one was made for my father who was lighter than me, so until I lost a little weight, it steer badly.' He sighed. 'When I first become a gondolier, I inherit the boat from him, because he become too old to carry on. Then he die.'

She winced. 'I'm sorry.' She pointed to the prominent ornamental S-shaped emblem glinting on the bow, which curved all the way down to the water. 'And that?'

'The name is *fero da próva*. It is the symbol of Venice. The whole shape is like the Grand Canal. The top, see how it sweeps down at the back but is straight and short at the front? This is the mark of the doge's hat. The six square fingers below point forwards. They mark the six *sestieri* of Venice. Like... the... how you say?'

'Districts?'

'*Si*, Signor Clifford! And the one at the back is for the island of Giudecca. But the whole *fero* has more purpose also. It works as the weight to keep the front of the gondola in the water.'

'And what of the increase in motorised vehicles on the canals?' Clifford said. 'Has this not created problems for you?'

Angelo threw a hand out. '*Si*! It is much harder for us now. People buy motorboats to use as taxis and for themselves.' He shook his head. 'Always nowadays people are in a hurry. They do not want to get there elegantly, only fast, fast, faster!'

She nodded, feeling guilty of this herself. 'It's the same in England. Only with cars replacing horses.'

He shrugged. 'It is the same everywhere, I think. Here, many are opposed to it, but those in charge always shout progress, progress! Everything must bow before progress! There is one councillor who shouts the loudest. So, now every year, there are less and less gondolas... and gondoliers! Maybe one day there will be none and then a thousand-year tradition will be lost!'

With a quick flick of his oar, he brought the gondola to a stop as a motorised taxi sped past. He gesticulated after it. 'You see! Last month, one hit a gondola and the gondolier was killed. But will our council do anything about it? No!' His face clouded as he stared after the speeding boat. 'If we gondoliers catch him, he does not do this dangerous and disrespectful thing again!'

Eleanor's reply was interrupted by the sound of two angry male voices. From a narrow side canal, another gondola was turning into the main waterway's thoroughfare. On board, the gondolier and his heavyset, pale-blue-suited passenger were in the midst of an altercation. Or so it seemed to her. But she'd already learned that when the Venetians were merely having a polite exchange of opinions, it often sounded to English ears as if they were having a full-blown row. She glanced at Angelo, only to see him frown and shake his head, as were several of the other gondoliers around.

So it seems the two men are arguing, Ellie.

The disagreement grew louder as the gondola pulled level with their boat. With the man now standing, the gondolier and his passenger were arguing face to face. As if to emphasise what Angelo had just been saying, a delivery barge ploughed past, leaving the surrounding gondolas pitching and rolling wildly in its wake.

'Whoa!' Eleanor waved a fist at the pilot of the barge, then clasped Gladstone tight into her side as the gondola lurched in the billowing swell. Clifford pressed Tomkins' carpet bag tightly to his chest, where he was now braced in the bottom of the boat. All around them, people were crying out as they hung grimly onto anything to hand. Even Angelo struggled to keep his craft upright.

The rolling swell pushed a nearby motorboat into the gondola with the arguing men on board, the collision then knocking the gondola's bow into the boat she was on. The two arguing men were thrown together, their arms flailing to keep their balance. The passenger stumbled backwards. For a moment Gladstone, standing up on the seat and barking urgently, distracted her. Tugging him back down, she looked up as a frothy white-green arc rose out of the water and soaked the gondolier. She blinked.

There's only one man on the gondola, Ellie. The passenger's fallen in!

She stood up and scoured the water.

'My lady, no!' Clifford called as she swiftly tucked Gladstone between his knees, so she was free to leap to the man's rescue. She hesitated, then noticed the man resurfacing.

'But he's face down!' she cried. 'He must have hit his head on something.'

Before she could act, the two nearest gondoliers leapt in to grab the man before the motorboat struck his helpless form. The pilot seemed aware of this, however, as he quickly steered away from the other gondolas and the man in the water.

Angelo steered his gondola in close so they could heave the unconscious man's top half over the side of his boat. Eleanor instinctively reached over to help, but immediately recoiled, her hand flying to her mouth.

'Clifford! What... what on earth is that sticking out of his back?'

4

Life on the Grand Canal had seemed delightfully busy before. But in a split second, Eleanor now found it frustratingly frenetic. Emphatic Italian voices yelled over each other, a sea of arms gesticulating from nearby gondolas rapidly bearing down on them.

'We don't need onlookers!' she cried, dropping to her knees to reach the man's body, which the gondoliers in the water were valiantly bracing against the side of her gondola.

'They are not onlookers, Lady Swift!' Angelo said. 'Us gondoliers take charge. The canals are our home. You watch.'

'But what about the one who was fighting with him? Supposing he gets away?'

'He will go nowhere!' Angelo said grimly, stepping down beside her. He pointed over at the fatal gondola which she now saw was filling with striped-shirted gondoliers, all encircling their colleague. It was only then she realised their own boat was being held on the spot by an arc of eight others' bows. The glinting *fero da próvas* looked like a cavalry of highly trained horses. The riders, the gondoliers themselves, adjusting the position of their craft with a barely discernible twist of the wrist.

'We will pull him in with us.' Angelo gestured at the body. He caught Clifford's sharp look. 'You tell the lady not to help. She does not take any notice of me.'

She shook her head. 'It will need the three of us. He was a sizeable fellow.'

Clifford and Angelo each gripped an arm while Eleanor hauled on the man's waistband. With the two gondoliers treading water shoving hard on a leg each, the body was finally heaved aboard and laid on its side. Her war nurse's training kicking in, she felt for a pulse, already knowing it was a forlorn hope. A moment later, she glanced up at the waiting faces and shook her head. Gladstone let out a whimper and nuzzled the glassy-eyed man's cheek.

'Poor fellow, it's too awful, I know, old chum,' she murmured, burying her face in her bulldog's wrinkled forehead. She felt Clifford press a handkerchief into her hand. As she looked up again, he covered the top half of the body with his jacket. As much to obscure her view as a mark of respect, she acknowledged with a grateful nod.

Angelo rose with what sounded like a long series of instructions, addressing first those securing his gondola mid-stream with theirs, then the others guarding the gondolier who had been arguing with the dead man.

Released from the hold of the flotilla and with Angelo back at his rowing station, their gondola began the sombre journey across the Grand Canal towards the bank. It was followed a short distance behind by the convoy accompanying the boat of the captive gondolier. As the other traffic paused to clear a path, Eleanor bit her lip.

'It never struck me before, Clifford, that Venetian gondolas are painted a funereal black.'

He scanned her face with concern. 'Just as it should never

have, my lady. It is beyond grievous this incident occurred in your presence.'

'Not as much as for our poor friend here. Whoever he is.' She leaned forward and brushed a scrap of old yellowing cloth with what looked like a black and white sweet wrapper stuck to it from the man's clothing. 'And his dignity in death isn't helped by all this old rubbish from the canals.'

Clifford nodded sombrely. 'Although I have observed they have been mostly free of general waste and surprisingly clean.'

As they neared the bank, the hubbub from the sizeable crowd that had already gathered increased. She ignored it and concentrated on the next step.

'Angelo! I assume the idea is to lift our deceased passenger ashore?'

He nodded and manoeuvred the gondola alongside a stretch without any of the striped posts. 'Only if I stop longways against the side can we lift him out.'

He brought them to an expertly executed stop against what she would have called the quayside, though there were no mooring rings or posts. As the excited bystanders surged forward, jostling for a ringside view, Clifford alighted and stood facing the crowd.

'Signore e signori, per favore!' he called in his distinguished, clipped tone. 'Ladies and gentlemen, please step back and clear a path.'

But far from his commanding bearing bringing a hush, as Eleanor had seen it do countless times before, it had the opposite effect. The crowd grew more animated, making him cover his ears as he retreated.

'As I suspected, my lady,' he said apologetically. 'The Venetian temperament is a trifle more... lively than one is used to back home. And I'm afraid that is pretty much the full extent of my command of Italian.'

'Well, good try, Clifford.'

Angelo appeared next to her. 'This is the work for us gondoliers now, signore. Please take Lady Swift off the boat.'

'Willingly,' he replied. 'Please inform the police of the hotel name where—'

Angelo waved him down. 'Signor Clifford, it is better for you and Lady Swift to wait. Believe the man who has lived all his life in Venice. You need to be here when the police arrive.'

A moment later, Eleanor was standing beside her butler on the stone walkway, quietly grateful for his comforting presence. She ran her hand over Gladstone's ears where he lay in Clifford's arms. Tomkins stretched his paws out of his padded window for her to stroke as well, offering soft meows of solace.

She watched the eight gondoliers who had held Angelo's gondola fast mid-channel struggle along with him to hoist the body's deadweight up onto the quayside. She wondered just how the five of them had managed to lift the man out of the canal and into the boat at all. Fleetingly, she realised that her shoulders were rapidly stiffening up from the effort. She shook the thought away, concerned only with the forlorn victim, still draped in Clifford's jacket, now lying in a growing puddle on the ground.

A renewed clamour broke out from the crowd as the suspect gondolier was herded ashore, flanked by a grim-faced army of his peers. It was only now she noticed the livid scar on his left cheek. His previous enraged indignance had changed to pleading protestations. She guessed it was still falling on deaf ears, however, from the other gondoliers' collective headshaking and barked retorts. But frustratingly, she couldn't understand a word of the exchanges. She caught Angelo's eye with a questioning shrug.

'They tell him not to try and make a run for it,' he said. 'But he tells them he had no reason to be killing this man. That he has no idea how it comes this man is dead.'

She glanced back at the gondolier and his captors. Much fist waving was now accompanying their collective artillery of words. A phrase kept being repeated.

'Angelo, what is it they keep saying to him?'

'They say that the weapon that killed this man is the tool of a *squerariolo*, the respected men who make our gondolas. And they are right. I think this too when I first see it sticking out from the body.'

She frowned. 'So is he a... what was it... *squer*-something, as well as a gondolier then?'

He shook his head vigorously. 'One man can never be both! A *squerariolo* takes a lifetime to learn and perfect his craft.'

Before she could reply, tempers flared behind her. The accusers and the accused seemed close to blows, with everyone now shouting and waving their fists.

She spun back to Angelo. 'I say, I do think someone ought to intervene before it's too late.'

He shrugged. 'For what, Lady Swift? No one is fighting. This is Italy, not England. The men shout he is guilty, he shouts he is not.'

'All the same,' she muttered, 'let's hope the police get here before this escalates into a lynching party!'

5

The sound of a ringing bell cut across the hullabaloo. Eleanor peered through the crowd, but there was no sign of uniforms trying to part the throng. Clifford gestured out into the Grand Canal where a motorboat was speeding towards them.

'Goodness, I forgot the police would arrive by water.'

'There being no other way, my lady, with the waterways sufficing for roads.'

The boat slowed as it approached the bank, the half-dozen men on board stepping ashore before it had stopped.

The police's arrival made the captive gondolier even more animated and vocal.

'He says this is no way for gondoliers to treat one of their brothers,' Angelo translated before she could ask. 'But to be a gondolier is the greatest honour of our city. When he killed that man, he dirtied that honour.'

Eleanor watched as the policemen parted the crowd. Universally tall with broad shoulders and trim waists, their fitted blue jackets had a white leather strap running diagonally across their chests and around their middles. It ended in a clasped pouch on one hip and a holstered gun on the other. A white-peaked cap finished off the uniform.

'Gracious, our English police never carry anything more than a wooden truncheon,' she murmured to Clifford, thinking even her fiancé, a senior chief inspector back in England, only carried a revolver on the rarest occasion. And always as a last resort.

'Quite. Those are Beretta pistols, my lady. Not surprisingly, since the Beretta company rose to prominence back in 1526 through its production of the long-barrelled *harquebus* gun for the Venetian Arsenal, no less.'

Knowing he was trying his best to distract her from the awfulness of a man lying dead at their feet, she nudged his elbow. 'Careful. Your history lesson might take us way into the small hours at this rate.'

'Or through to breakfast preferably, my lady. Since I fear you will not sleep after this distressing event.'

A barrage of orders erupted from one of the policemen. Standing legs wide apart, hands behind his back, he was obviously in charge. Two of his men stepped smartly to each end of the body, while the others replaced the gondoliers in guarding the accused. The tallest policeman pulled Clifford's jacket from the dead man's face and stiffened.

'Capitano! Per favore?'

She didn't need Angelo to translate that there was something unexpected about the deceased. His superior strode over. Glancing down, his jaw tightened.

'Signor Vendelini! Che spreco.'

'He say this death is a great waste,' Angelo whispered. 'The signore was an important Venetian businessman on the council.'

'You recognised him?'

'Yes. His name is Benetto Vendelini. I mentioned him to you.'

She frowned. 'The councillor who was always demanding progress?'

He nodded and whistled quietly. 'His family will not take this easy. The Vendelinis have been important in Venice for always.' He looked over at the accused and shook his head. 'So it starts again,' she caught him mutter.

Before she could ask him what he meant, the man she assumed was the chief of police marched up to face the captive gondolier. He released a stream of Italian which sounded like a mixture of accusations and threats, to her ears. Whatever he said, it was clear the gondolier was refuting it, although he seemed to tread carefully in doing so. She frowned.

Is that because the police don't take kindly to being challenged, or because he's trying to get his story straight, Ellie?

Clifford's arched brow told her he'd had the same thought.

A furore of shouting and fist waving broke out from the other gondoliers, Angelo included.

'Whatever's happening?' she said.

'He says he never seen before the tool of the *squerariolo* that kills Signor Vendelini. But he makes a bad mistake. That is why we shout.'

'What mistake?'

'His uncle is a *squerariolo*, a gondola builder.' His face clouded. 'So it is easy for him to lay his hands on such a tool. And this gondolier is known by us all for his quick temper.'

With an imperious flick of one hand, the gondolier was marched away and unceremoniously bundled on to the police boat.

The captain turned slowly on his heel and regarded the dead man dispassionately. Meanwhile, the other policemen began taking statements from each of the gondoliers.

'Finally,' she heard Clifford murmur to Gladstone, who was still in his arms.

She stood straighter. 'Angelo, if I'm to be questioned, please can you translate for me?'

'Why do you assume I do not speak the English, signora?' the captain said before her gondolier could reply. He strode over and graced her with a stiff nod.

'Forgive me,' she said contritely. 'All of this has been rather distracting.'

'Really, signora? Death in Venice is not what you are here to see? This is what you wish me to believe, of course. But I am not the simple fool, so I warn you—'

Clifford interrupted with a sharp cough. 'Captain, if I might introduce Lady Swift. Of Henley Hall? Also Baronetess Derry of Ross.'

She tried to keep her features neutral. What bearing could her obscure Irish baronetcy have here in Italy? She caught her butler's cautioning look as he continued. 'Needless to say, her ladyship is here to take in the sights of your city. This incident, sir, is a travesty at the very least.'

The captain's eyes narrowed. 'Baronetess, you say? Like our Italian *baronessa?*'

He hesitated for a fraction of a second. 'Yes. To all intents and purposes.'

The captain rubbed his chin. 'Mmm. Now I see. You are the *maggiordomo*. The butler, I think?' Turning to Eleanor, he nodded again, this time more courteously. 'You know someone in Venice? Someone I can ask to check you are truly who your man says you are?'

She shrugged. 'I can assure you I am who I say I am. However, perhaps you are acquainted with Contessa Eugenia Contarini?'

The captain's left eye twitched. 'You know the contessa?'

'Yes, we met in London earlier this year. She graciously asked me to visit her when I came to Venice. I'm going to her party this evening.'

He took a step back. 'Then Baronessa Swift, excuse me. No more questions.'

She frowned in confusion, having expected only a more polite attitude from him, not that she be dismissed altogether.

'But wait. Surely you need to hear what I saw? I was on the gondola next to the one where this poor dead man was murdered.'

'No. Thank you. The statements from the gondoliers and other witnesses are sufficient for now. If we need to take your statement, we will contact you at your hotel. For the moment, I have the body. And the murderer.' He smiled thinly. 'Please enjoy your time in our city, Baronessa. And your party with the contessa.'

He strode off to the boat, leaving Eleanor shaking her head at her butler's respectful urging that he escort her immediately to her hotel.

'Thank you, Clifford. But for there to be any chance you might catch even a hint of sleep tonight, I just need to ask Angelo one thing when the police are done with him. I'll only witter on interminably to you with questions you can't possibly answer otherwise.'

He held up his hands in surrender, then whipped his jacket from over one of the policemen's arms as they lifted the body and made for a second boat that had drawn up a moment before. A waterborne hearse, she assumed. She bowed her head and offered a final prayer for poor Benetto. As she finished, an uncomfortable feeling crept over her. As if someone were watching her intently. She looked up sharply to see a man with close-cropped dark hair turning away and fading into the crowd.

Once Angelo had been waved off by the policeman who was taking his statement, he glanced around before spotting her and hurrying over.

'Lady Swift. Are...' He paused. 'But apologies, I need to call you Baronessa now.'

She laughed. 'Oh gracious, no. It's true I am one, but it was just my scallywag butler's way of ensuring the captain treated me with the proper courtesy. But, Angelo,' she pleaded, 'please settle my thoughts by telling me what you meant when you were explaining who poor Benetto Vendelini was. You said, "So it starts again." But what?'

His expression turned grave. 'The feud. The gondolier they put under arrest is Gaspo Secco. The Seccos are related to the Marcellos, a family the Vendelinis fought with for many centuries until they made a truce. Much bad blood they had between them. And much was spilled. I tell you, it was famous throughout all of Venice! If not all of Italy!'

'Goodness!'

He scratched his head. 'But I also tell you, I do not understand. I was sure this feud was ended a long, long time ago.' He reached over and cupped Tomkins' chin. 'But, little *gatto*, maybe I was wrong about this!'

6

Eleanor allowed Clifford to guide her through the crowd, keen to be anywhere else. But her arm was tugged sharply back behind her. 'What the...?'

She turned to find her bulldog pulling violently on his lead in the opposite direction. He let out a flurry of barks, Tomkins meowing in support.

'Mutiny definitely not required at this moment, thank you, Master Gladstone!' Clifford commanded.

Nose in the air, her bulldog uncharacteristically ignored him and sat down, his back legs thrown stiffly out sideways.

Eleanor shook her head. 'Waywardly naughty doesn't begin to cover the cheeky delinquent you insisted we brought along, Clifford.'

He eyed her sideways. 'I seem to remember, my lady, the idea of bringing your two companions was entirely down to your decision to—'

'Yes, we jolly well can, my girl!' a forceful voice exclaimed.

Clifford's lips pursed. 'To your decision to bring your equally delinquent staff!' He beckoned a white-gloved finger over several rows of heads in front of them, his extra height giving him a view she didn't have.

'On this singular occasion, ladies, yes, you may!' he called.

She looked down at her bulldog. 'So that's what you were trying to tell us, old chum.' She ruffled his ears as he lumbered up her legs. Then she had a thought. 'Oh, Clifford! Not a word about the poor dead fellow, though, yes?'

'Most assuredly, my lady.'

Her face lit up as her four female staff broke through the throng, dodging under the elbows of the people still gawking at the fatal spot.

'Ladies! What a treat to see you again so soon.'

Beaming as Clifford marshalled them into a line, she marvelled, as she often did, how their ages and heights varied as much as their personalities. Yet they were a staunchly close-knit group who would rally for each other in a blink. And even more determinedly so for Clifford, she'd delighted in seeing for herself, despite the firm hand he valiantly strove to keep them under as the head of her staff. But what had warmed her heart most was her staff's collective devotion and loyalty to her, right from the start of inheriting her uncle's estate.

She came back to the moment as the ladies all curtseyed in unison. Heading up the line was her diminutive housekeeper, Mrs Butters, with her motherly curves. The oldest of the four, as her soft greying curls bore witness to, she still had a strong sense of fun. Next was her straight-talking, English-pear hipped cook, Mrs Trotman, the ringleader for saucy mischief, much to Eleanor's secret delight. And Clifford's dismay. Beside her was one of her young maids, Lizzie, as sweet-faced as she was natured. A fairly recent addition after Eleanor had rescued her from an unhappy appointment in her native Scotland. She was the only one among them who hadn't been in service when Eleanor's beloved uncle had owned Henley Hall. And lastly, there was the youngest, Polly. A charming gangly streak of relentless, wide-eyed wonder and innocence. And clumsiness. Clifford regularly lamented that the household budget he kept such a fierce hold on was chipped away every month by the amount of crockery Polly's well-intentioned but uncoordinated efforts broke. Eleanor knew underneath all his chidings, however, he cared for the young girl's welfare enormously. She had other staff: Joseph, her gardener, and Silas, her gamekeeper-cum security guard. But they'd gladly stayed behind to keep an eye on the Hall, neither caring for travel, nor for the high jinks the ladies were bound to get up to abroad.

'Ladies, I am mystified,' Clifford said playfully. 'Inexplicably, it seems her ladyship is pleased to see you.'

Far from the shared giggles Eleanor knew he'd intended this to rouse, Mrs Butters bustled forward with an anxious expression, mirrored by the others.

'Not as much as we are to see you, Mr Clifford. Nor you, m'lady. We were all fretting like jellied eels, watching the to-do. And that was afore the police arrived. Oh my stars!'

'Ah! Too late,' Clifford muttered to Eleanor.

She floundered for a way to move the conversation onto lighter ground. 'I thought you had dallied up on the Rialto Bridge after treating us to a wave down in our gondola. Any window shopping in all those beautiful little boutiques in the central arcade, perhaps?'

'We was planning to, m'lady,' Mrs Trotman said. 'But then the two young 'uns had the idea of us scampering along to surprise you again.'

'Scampering, ladies?' Clifford said disapprovingly.

''Twas only meant to be a bit of fun for the mistress, Mr Clifford, to wonder how we'd gotten ahead like magic. Lawks knows, a bit of fun wouldn't have gone amiss after what we saw, mind!' Mrs Trotman reached along the line to pinch Polly's cheek gently. 'This one was in need of a week's worth of your largest hankies, Mr Clifford. You should have seen the waterworks when we thought her ladyship was going to jump in after that gentleman. Fit to fill that there ditch.'

'Venice is not served by "ditches", Mrs Trotman. They are canals. And incredible feats of civil engineering.'

'If you say so.' The cook shrugged. 'But I bet the stream o' words that flew out of that man's mouth afore he went underwater weren't very civil!'

Polly edged her hand up. Clifford nodded, giving her permission to speak up.

'But how lucky was he that you and Mr Clifford was so quick to save him, your ladyship!'

Lizzie nodded. 'And that wee boat whiskin' him away off to hospital like that.'

The four of them leaned forward, clearly seeking reassurance.

'Well, umm...' She deferred to her butler with a pleading look.

'The gentleman will be seen by a doctor, ladies,' he said in a kindly tone, whipping two pristine handkerchiefs from his inside pocket and holding them out to Polly. 'But regrettably, not for treatment. Despite everyone's sterling efforts, unfortunately it was too late for him. But' – he held up a halting hand as the four of them gasped – 'rest assured, the gentleman passed instantaneously. I sincerely doubt he was even aware of what happened. He is at peace now. The police have apprehended the reprehensible party they believe responsible, so there is nothing to worry about.'

'Responsible?' Mrs Butters breathed. 'You mean, that poor man was—'

'Please don't dwell on what you saw, ladies,' Eleanor said quickly. 'Being sad on his account won't turn the clock back.'

'Poor man, all the same,' Mrs Butters said. 'Especially as someone up and done for him, it seems. Well, fancy that. Some folk just don't know how to sort their differences peacefully.'

Mrs Trotman nodded. 'Butters, I told you it was rummy the police left him lying there a while, talking to everyone first.'

'Including you, m'lady,' Lizzie said tentatively.

'Has your holiday sunk to the bottom of the dit— canal like a sack of rocks now, m'lady?' Mrs Trotman said anxiously.

'If you're fretting that I'm about to get caught up in the investigation?' They all nodded. 'Well, absolutely not. It's a matter for the Venice police, who have made it clear I am not required at the moment, even as a witness...' Her brow furrowed, the conversation having brought back the memory of that morning. She'd been grimly hanging on in the wash of the speeding barge, which had... her frown deepened... thrown the two arguing men together... and then their gondola hit hers...

She shook her head. *Something isn't right, Ellie. Something's missing.*

She realised Clifford and the ladies were staring at her.

'Sorry. Where was I? Oh yes. So, we are still all here on holiday, and that is how it is going to stay.' She turned to Clifford, who was eyeing her guardedly. 'Now, I'm positively parched. As the troops must be, after their delightful efforts to surprise me, so...'

Clifford gestured forward like a shepherd mustering sheep. 'Ladies, shall we to tea and cake?'

7

How her butler had led them all to such a darling, tucked away café in a side street she had never seen before, Eleanor couldn't begin to work out.

'Clifford, it's perfect. Thank you.'

She settled against the pretty lace cushion nestled into the painted pistachio-coloured seat he was holding out. 'I love the rogues' gallery of portraits running around the walls.'

'A family-run establishment for four generations, I understand, my lady.'

'No wonder it feels so cosy then.' She drank in the colourful decor with delight; sunshine-yellow walls, rainbow-coloured lamps and potted pink oleander trees under each of the glass roof panes. It was spotlessly clean and smartly presented enough not to entirely contravene the rigorous standards her butler insisted on for her. Equally, it was modest enough for her ladies not to be too overawed. A delicious-looking array of nibbles filled the long, polished glass cabinet which served as the counter. She found the relaxed atmosphere enchanting.

As her staff took their seats around the table, she smiled. They had made her believe she could finally feel she belonged somewhere and that thought whisked her back to some of her most treasured times of the last few years.

'Uncannily akin to flouting the rules with your staff in the kitchen at Henley Hall, my lady?' Clifford said mischievously, obviously having read her thoughts.

'A little.' She winked at the ladies. 'Do you think they serve lethal home-brewed concoctions, worthy of Mrs Trotman adding to her collection?'

He shuddered. 'Thankfully not. "Tiddly in Venice" is not a fitting title for one's collective memories in this incredible city.'

Mrs Trotman gave him a cheeky glance. 'Butters, was it my apricot rum or the gooseberry gin as had Mr Clifford looking rather glassy-eyed the last time?'

Her housekeeper pretended to think it over. 'I do believe it was your rhubarb brandy, Trotters. Or maybe as that was the time afore.'

Eleanor chuckled with the others as she jerked a teasing thumb at him. 'I remember it being the carrot and turnip tipple which had my supposedly impeccable butler almost in his cups.'

Before he could reply, their food arrived, Clifford having ordered as they entered. Three aproned women bustled over. Eleanor thought they must be sisters, their ruddy faces were so alike. As they set down a raft of wooden platters with feet in the shape of lion's claws, Eleanor beamed in delight. The atmosphere felt more like being invited for a family lunch than a restaurant.

'Grazie!' She turned to her butler. 'I say, top-notch choosing, Clifford. However you managed it.'

He eyed her sideways. 'To ensure sufficient, if unladylike, proportions for a certain party, last evening I mastered the Italian for "lots of everything".'

She rolled her eyes good-naturedly as she cupped her bulldog's chin where he had hurled his top half into her lap at the arrival of the food.

'Tsk, mischievous whatnot! Back to butler school for him, hey, Gladstone?'

At his friend's name, Tomkins meowed to be let out of his kitty kit bag, which drew the waitresses bustling back over to make a fuss of him. As if parading for his adoring fans, he leapt nimbly up and paraded slowly around the ring of laps before curling up on Polly's.

'It is your turn to be honoured by the ginger menace,' Clifford said to the delighted young maid.

''Tis already too much of a wonder just to be here, sir. Thank you to the moon, your ladyship,' Polly breathed, her eyes swimming with joy.

'You're very welcome. All of you. Now, Clifford, how do I officially start off a buffet meal like this in Venice?'

He arched a disbelieving brow. 'Does your normal style seem too boorish in this oh-so-elegant city?'

'Not a bit, actually.' She turned to her staff. 'We're on holiday, so dig in!'

After a few minutes of silent munching, she moaned with pleasure.

'I say, these little round toasts topped with all manner of delectableness are as sublime as those miniature triangular sandwiches.'

'*Crostini* and *tramezzini*, as I believe they are called,' Clifford said. '*Cichetti* is the umbrella term for all these small bites. Perhaps you might manage the more detailed introductions, Mrs Trotman, from your expert view?'

Puffing with pride, Eleanor's cook cast an appraising eye over the platters. 'Grilled sardine strips with sea salt, and the good kind it is too. Air-dried beef slices, you can always tell when it's done proper like. Cured pork... cheek, I'd say. And these are' – she inspected one more closely – 'cod mousse with olive oil, garlic and parsley, if I'm not mistaken. Plus pointy tomatoes stuffed with capers. Olives like they was going out of fashion, shrimps on some clever baked... cornmeal porridge fingers, I think. And anchovies' – with a nod from Eleanor, she took a bite – 'with the fiercest blue cheese ever left to run riot.'

Eleanor laughed at the last description, catching Clifford's eye. 'It could be marvellous fun back home if the rules might stretch to us having a Venetian supper together once in a while so we can reminisce over this holiday?'

He nodded. 'Most assuredly, my lady.'

She spotted Tomkins quietly pawing one of the sardine nibbles off the table for himself and a pork one for Gladstone. She put her finger to her lips as Polly caught them, too. The young maid giggled but said nothing.

A large pot of coffee and a jug of fruity-looking cordial for the maids arrived, together with a plate of irresistible citrus-smelling button biscuits. As the empty platters were cleared to make room, Eleanor wiped her mouth with her napkin and turned to the ladies.

Before she could ask what they had been up to, however, she froze. A man with close-cropped dark hair was staring through the nearest window. *The man from the crowd, Ellie.* For a moment, he locked eyes with her and she had the most uncomfortable feeling that he was somehow... judging her? She shook her head.

Don't be silly, Ellie. He's probably just a street gawker.

She looked again, but the man had gone.

Clifford gave her an enquiring glance, but she waved a dismissive hand. She was there on holiday and there were treats to enjoy.

'So come on, ladies,' she said. 'I'm itching to know what you've been up to today?'

'What wonders haven't we seen might be a quicker answer, m'lady,' Mrs Butters cooed. 'We'll all sleep for England tonight in our beds and no mistake.'

'So your accommodation is comfortable enough?' Eleanor

had left all the arrangements to book a suitable boarding house to her trusty butler.

Her housekeeper spread her hands. 'Lawks, m'lady, you should see our rooms! You'd think we were royalty with all the pretty cotton upholstery, matching curtains and little sets of drawers. One each, as well. Trotters and I have got the blue and cream 'un and the young 'uns are in the pink and green 'un t'other side of the archway.'

'The east and west wings we calls them,' Mrs Trotman chuckled.

Lizzie nodded. 'And there's a wee sitting room down the stairs, m'lady. With a basket of games we're allowed to play.'

'Which Trotters has already started making the rules up for as she goes along,' Mrs Butters said with a roll of her eyes.

Mrs Trotman's mouth fell open in mock indignation. 'I have not, Butters. I'm just the better player and you know it.'

Mrs Butters laughed as Clifford finished setting out the cups and poured for everyone. 'There's been that much to see with every step we've not got far round, in truth. Polly and Lizzie can't be moved for staring at the ladies' dresses in the streets. Beautifully made they are, mind.'

'Ach, it's the colours, m'lady,' Lizzie said. 'We've ne'er seen the like.'

'And the men's suits too. Rather like looking through an exquisite kaleidoscope, isn't it?' Eleanor said.

Polly looked confused. 'If a kal... one of those is like dreamin' in rainbows, yes, but prettier still, your ladyship.'

Lizzie snuck a peek at the cook. 'And Mrs Trotman likes lookin' at the boatmen.'

Mrs Trotman tried to shoot the maid a stern look, but failed to hide a grin.

'There's a surprise,' Clifford said drily, much to everyone's mirth.

Eleanor shook her head. 'What else has entertained you, Mrs Butters?'

Mrs Trotman poked her friend in the arm. 'Butters has been studying the washing, of all things!'

Eleanor looked enquiringly at her housekeeper. 'That's very conscientious of you, Mrs Butters, but you're supposed to be on holiday.'

Her housekeeper flapped a hand. 'She means the laundry, m'lady. 'Tis a special way to do it here, I realised. Mr Clifford will be instructing me to do the same back at Henley Hall, I shouldn't wonder.'

He nodded. 'Perhaps. Taking another's custom home to adopt is often the best form of souvenir.'

''Tis on account of the washing lines being strung across the alleys and the narrower canals. From building to building, you see.'

'Which must work on a simple pulley system, usually of two or three lines per household, I imagine,' Clifford said. 'The first item is pegged and then the line behind is pulled, which moves that item forward enough to hang the next. And so forth.'

Mrs Butters nodded. 'Which means half of whatever I hang out ends up hanging under the window of my neighbour across the street or canal, Mr Clifford.'

'What of it?' Eleanor said. 'I can't imagine people pilfer each other's laundry?' She tuned in to the fact her butler was throwing her an imploring arch of one brow. 'What am I missing?' she whispered.

'Everyone's underfrillies swinging in all their glory under the nose of the man who lives opposite!' Mrs Trotman said in an innocent tone. 'Fancy that, Mr Clifford.'

He pinched his nose. 'Not personally, Mrs Trotman, no.'

Eleanor hid her smile. 'So what is the Venetians' "special way" to alleviate that, then?'

'Easy, m'lady. All the intimate... the bits Mr Clifford doesn't want to hear about, are hung in the middle with sheets or at least shirts or skirts hiding the—'

'Unmentionable items.'

'That's them, Mr Clifford.'

Eleanor laughed. 'Ingenious. But why would we implement that at Henley Hall? The estate is so vast, our nearest neighbour is almost two miles away.'

Mrs Trotman chuckled. 'So Mr Clifford can leave the house on wash-day Mondays without having to close his eyes like he does now.'

Clifford pretended to ignore the ladies giggling, busying himself with consulting his pocket watch.

'I believe, my lady, we need to leave the... ah, unruly element of your staff to their own devices. If, that is, you are to have sufficient time to prepare for the contessa's party this evening.'

She groaned. 'Dash it, Clifford. Why did I say I would go? I know I'll love it once I'm there, but it suddenly seems a little... daunting, meeting all those new people. Especially as most, if not all of them, will be Italian and I only speak English.'

Her cook tutted. 'You shouldn't worry about that, m'lady. It's them as is foreign, not yourself.'

She opened her mouth to reply, but decided it was best left.

Having said goodbye to the ladies outside the café, she set off back to her hotel, idly watching a gondola glide past on the nearby canal.

'It is an honour that you have been invited to the contessa's party, my lady,' Clifford said gently. 'The contessa is obviously well-respected in Venice, given the reaction of our captain of police earlier. And what else have you planned, if I might be so bold?'

She sighed. 'You're right, as usual.'

After all, Ellie, whatever poor Benetto Vendelini had planned for tonight, I'm sure it didn't involve spending it on a mortuary slab!

She paused, Clifford almost running into her, as a barge passed the gondola a little too fast, its bow wave causing the gondolier to shout a rebuke. She frowned. 'Barges? Barges and waves?' She rubbed her forehead. 'Dash it! What is it?'

Gladstone, who'd also been brought up short, shot her a confused look.

'It's quite alright,' Clifford said soothingly. 'Her ladyship is not ill, Master Gladstone. Merely trying to think. A distressing event to witness, I confess, but you need not worry yourself.'

She rolled her eyes. 'Very funny! But this is important. I've got a niggle about what I saw when...' She gazed at the receding barge, willing the thought to form coherently. 'Oh! I've got it!'

She spun around. Her bulldog regarded her with a disapproving stare. Was he being taken for a walk or not? Deciding not, he plumped down on the ground next to her.

She bent and patted his head distractedly.

'Clifford. When that barge drove past too fast earlier today, creating all that wash which had us, and everyone in the boats around us, hanging on for dear life, I was concentrating on Gladstone. To make sure he didn't fall out.'

'And myself on Master Tomkins.'

'Exactly. And I was sitting in my seat, rocking all over the place. But just before I dragged my gaze away from the men arguing in the other gondola, who we now know were Gaspo Secco and Benetto Vendelini, a boat was pushed into it by the wave.'

'As were we,' Clifford said.

'Yes. But it was just before we were. A small motorboat. And the pilot was...' Her eyes widened. 'Of course! That's what was odd. He was standing up! Despite everyone else sitting down and hanging on. In fact, only Benetto and Gaspo were also standing – and that was because they were arguing so much they were oblivious to anything else.'

Clifford looked thoughtful. 'I admit I cannot recall such an image. But your memory has proven uncannily accurate on previous occasions. Assuming you are correct, why is it of importance?'

She shook her head. 'I don't suppose it is. It just made me think for a moment. When Gaspo was protesting his innocence, I know it was in a foreign language, Italian obviously, so I didn't get exactly what he was saying, but he sounded sincere. He sounded...'

'Genuine?'

'Exactly.' She bit her lip. 'And if by any remote chance, and it probably is a remote chance, Gaspo didn't kill Benetto...'

Clifford nodded slowly. 'Then the man standing up in the motorboat that collided with his gondola just before ours may have had an equal opportunity and—'

'Could be the real murderer!'

8

A salt-tinged breeze wafted a tantalising hint of the Adriatic into Eleanor's bedroom, rustling the embroidered gold-winged lions prowling the hemline of the ivory silk curtains. She caught her butler clearing his throat from somewhere unseen.

'Rather uncharacteristic procrastination, if you will forgive the observation, my lady.'

She gasped and hurried into the main room of her suite, the 'receiving room' Clifford had called it. But it was empty. The hem of her emerald gown caught on the frame of one of the Gothic arched doors. She tutted, reminding herself that elegant gliding was required if her dress was going to end the evening in one piece. Gathering up the yards of silk behind her, she marched into the next room where her butler's suited rear view greeted her. She put her hands on her hips.

'No, Clifford, I won't forgive the observation. First, because you couldn't "observe" anything as you've holed yourself up in the safety of this butler's pantry here since we got back. Lest you catch the merest glimpse of so much as my ankles, I imagine. On which note, Mr Chivalrous, I am now fully dressed.' As he turned, tentatively lifting his fingers from his eyes, she gestured around her. 'And second, I've not been procrastinating. I've... simply been so keen to see the wonders Venice had in store, that I haven't truly had time to appreciate my... my suite properly.'

'If you say so, my lady.'

She opened her mouth to protest again and then sighed. 'Dash it, Clifford. Alright, I admit it. I might feel the teeniest bit nervous about meeting Venice society's elite. I know I've met plenty of aristocratic types around the world, but that was mostly when I was a child with my parents. Or later, travelling alone, just a bicycle and me. I was no one, really. Now, through a quirk of inheritance, I'm an English lady. With an estate and staff. Wonderful staff, actually. But I still don't feel at all like the society lady I'm supposed to be, as well you know. Even though' – she spun around – 'here I am living in sumptuous luxury, like an actual Venetian princess.'

He bowed. 'Entirely as it should be. This is everything his lordship, your late uncle, wished for you.'

Her shoulders fell. 'If only he were still with us.'

'In spirit, his lordship always is,' Clifford said gently.

Feeling the all too familiar lump in her throat threaten whenever family was mentioned, she hurried on. 'Well, I'm sorry that you are losing the last ounce of starch from your impeccable shirt collar over how late I'll arrive at the contessa's party. I'll try to speed up, but it took a while to report what I'd remembered to the police about the motorboat. For all the good it did!' she muttered.

He shook his head. 'You did your duty, my lady. Now, it is up to the police to follow up or not.'

'"Or not", for sure! They showed no inclination to pursue the matter.'

Which doesn't mean you won't if you get the chance, Ellie.

She sighed. 'But I admit, it seems most likely the gondolier was responsible, so all I've done is made us late.'

'Actually, my lady, you still have sufficient time to enjoy a brief appreciation of your suite as the contessa is sending a private launch.'

Her shoulders relaxed. 'Wonderful!' Taking the slim tulip glass of golden liquid he was offering on a silver tray, she savoured a sip.

'Ah! Not brandy, as I expected. Nevertheless, it's delicious, like toasted almonds, dark chocolate and marzipan.'

'It is grappa, my lady. An aged distillation of exceptional pedigree from Venice itself. For Dutch courage and as a digestif after the unladylike quantities of tea and *cichetti* consumed recently with your band of elves. Hmm, and with the terrible two!' He waggled a white-gloved finger at her ginger tomcat as he skittered in with her bulldog in lumbering tow. 'Masters Tomkins and Gladstone, be aware, upon depositing you both with the concierge this evening, I shall give him full warning regarding your thieving proclivities.'

'And,' Eleanor whispered in her bulldog's ear, 'the bag of treats waiting here on the countertop, because he's a hopeless softie underneath.' She straightened up. 'Now, Clifford, as we unexpectedly have time, please give me the tour.'

He bowed. 'The hotel itself, my lady, was built in the fifteenth century as an actual palace. It has been much refurbished since, but the ceiling frescos, gold fireplace reliefs, marble floors and pillared entrance hall all date from the Renaissance, I believe.' He led the way on through her expansive sitting room which, like everywhere else, was dotted with fresh floral displays. 'In here, gracing the walls is a series of replicas of old Italian masters; Botticelli, da Vinci and, of course, Michelangelo.'

She looked around, shaking her head. 'It's like the most lovingly curated art gallery and museum, yet it's not at all stuffy. So many beautiful little details, such as these delicate figurines and lace divider screens. And the darling recessed library in the alcove there, with its quaint quill writing set and leather journal to capture one's memories of Venice.'

'Perhaps a nod to Lord Byron who often stayed here?'

'Byron? The eighteenth-century English romantic poet?'

'Yes. Although he was equally, if not better, known for other... er, less literary pursuits.'

She laughed as she ran her hand over a plum ottoman, the tassels of which Tomkins was playfully batting with his paws. 'Clifford. Not speaking of Lord Byron's other activities while here, of course, but you simply must run the gauntlet of my untidiness just once to peep into my bedroom. It's got a domed centrepiece of coloured glass cherubs in the ceiling. Plus a divine four-poster bed, ruched in acres of turquoise and silver silk.'

His ever-impassive expression faltered. 'If I might respect-fully decline from doing so?'

She laughed again. 'Alright. Lead me on, then.'

They stepped out onto her full-length private terrace, which was a haven of flourishing potted citrus trees among plush azure cushioned seating, all set on more intricately patterned marble flooring. She leaned her back against the white stone balustrading, thinking the interior looked no less captivating from outside than in. As she did so, he nodded at the view.

'An unrivalled vista of the Punta della Dogana and the Santa Maria della Salute Basilica across the Grand Canal where it exits into the lagoon.'

She took in the vast domed edifice of white stone he was pointing to at the end of the triangular spit of land on the Grand Canal, very different from the eclectic mix of buildings of two to six or more storeys lining a lot of its length. Almost opposite, a small hotel that looked as if it had seen better days caught her eye, its faded pink façade and peeling green shutters giving it an air of careworn neglect. That was another thing she loved about

Venice, its vibrancy. Buildings were often multicoloured, painted orange, green, yellow, pink, blue or a shade of each. Even the bare brickwork was an earthy red.

The melodic tinkle of the telephone interrupted her reply.

'My lady?' Clifford called a moment later from the doorway, eyes bright. 'A faint line from England. On which a certain Detective Chief Inspector Seldon is hanging in eager anticipation for his betrothed.'

She darted forward at the unexpected chance to speak to her fiancé.

'Hugh!' she cried into the receiver.

'Eleanor? Oh, thank heavens.' Seldon's deep voice tickled her ears with delight, as it always did. 'I thought this infernal apparatus had cut me off again. This is my third attempt to reach you.'

'Well, you've got me now.'

'Really? After a shamefully long time dredging up the courage to propose, I hope I still have.'

'Hugh, whatever do you mean?' She shrugged at Clifford as he glided past to answer a knock at the door. 'I'm just busy swooning around Venice being courted by—'

A quiet groan interrupted her. 'As I feared.'

'Feared? Hugh, that's not like you.' The line crackled, then went silent. She waited a moment, then spoke. 'Look, I'll just talk in the hope you can hear me, Hugh. I was saying I'm being courted by the romance of this amazing city. And for once, I've even dressed up elegantly enough for my stickler of a butler's approval. Can you picture that?' She paused, hoping to hear his familiar chuckle. She didn't.

'Romance, I see.' Seldon's voice suddenly came through clearer than before. 'Dressed up too. So, even more captivating than ever. And in a city of Casanovas!'

Her shoulders rose with happiness. 'Flatterer!' She turned away from the receiver. 'Oh, for me?' She tugged Clifford to a halt by his jacket sleeve as he tried to skirt back past her, carrying a floral bouquet with both hands.

'Blast... Eleanor? What's that?' Seldon said.

'The most beautiful bouquet,' she gasped, flapping her hand at Clifford to stop him hurrying the flowers away. She scooped up the printed envelope from the centre and began tearing it open. 'I don't know how you managed to time them to arrive so perfectly while we're talking, though, Hugh. That's the most romantic thing any chap could do for his girl. You must have colluded with my butler again!'

There was no missing his sigh. 'No, Eleanor... Because they aren't from me.'

'As I attempted to tell you,' Clifford murmured.

Her hand shot to her mouth. 'Er, it's... it's enough you've telephoned as a surprise.' She tried to hastily think of another topic of conversation. 'Hugh, tell me you've eaten something at least? And you're not working every single hour?'

'Instead,' Seldon's voice came back drily, 'perhaps you might tell me who the flowers are from?'

She glanced at the card. 'They are from... Ah, the hotel! But... Hugh? Hugh? Dash it!' She groaned as her butler reappeared. 'Clifford, he's been cut off.'

'At a most inopportune moment, my lady.'

'Why? Because of the flowers? Anyway, the card said "Compliments of the management". No, Hugh knows me better than that.'

'But does the gentleman know himself better?' he said sagely.

She frowned. 'I'll buy him something tomorrow. Though he won't get it until we're home, of course. But still.'

His brow flinched. 'As you wish. Then, if I might inform you, from the balcony I have just noted a rather fine motor launch turn in from the eastern side of the lagoon.'

'Alright, lead on, Clifford.'

He shook his head. 'As your butler, I will take the staff stairs and meet you in the main reception area as usual.'

As she descended the triple-width stone staircase to the grand lobby, the early evening sun cascaded in through the cathedral-esque windows. Clifford was waiting by one of the many classical statues.

'Your menagerie is safely ensconced with the concierge until your return, my lady.'

'Thank you. Oh no, I forgot my...' She tailed off as he held up her beaded silk wrap for her to slide into.

'The weather forecast is beyond favourable, my lady. A fine evening with no change anticipated tomorrow, according to my travelling barometer.'

She smiled that her gift a while back was precious enough for him to have brought along.

Clifford gestured out the front entrance.

'Your launch awaits.'

'I say, is that marvellous boat out there yours?' a youthful voice called.

Eleanor turned to see a bouncing head of straw-blond hair. She took in his high-waisted cream suit bottoms and matching ruff-frilled shirt, the collar of which seemed to be squabbling good-naturedly with his happy-go-lucky blue neckerchief. Together with the short black jacket ending at his ribs, he looked like he had stumbled out of a Regency novel. Altogether, he was too incongruous for a young man in his early twenties. Especially one clutching a stuffed bear cub under his arm. She was itching with curiosity as he stopped in front of her.

'What ho! You must be one of us,' he said.

'Categorically not,' Eleanor caught Clifford mutter to himself.

She laughed. 'That rather depends on what *you* might be one of?'

'I mean English.' He flapped his jacket sides. 'Oh, and don't mind this get-up of mine. It's all part of it, you see?'

'Not a bit. But I confess, I'm dying to know.'

'Perhaps I might, sir?' Clifford said. At the young man's nod, he continued. 'A reliving of Lord Byron's adventures in Venice, perchance?'

The young man nodded vigorously. 'And how, by jingo!' His cheeks coloured as he turned back to Eleanor, seeming to take in her gown for the first time. 'Oh wickets, I've clearly bolted out of my room without my manners. Forgive me. You're obviously on your way to somewhere totally scintillating and I've pinned you on the spot to hear my wafflings. Apologies.'

She smiled. 'Not a bit.'

'If, sir, I might introduce Lady Swift?' Clifford said pointedly.

His face split into a wide grin. 'Delighted. I'm Kip.'

She cocked her head. 'Just Kip? Pithy and to the point. Must save you acres of time.'

He laughed. 'My full name is Casper Theodore Allegro Fitzmorton Kipling.'

'Ah,' Clifford said. 'Son of Lord Melchester Kipling, sir? Earl of Saxborough?'

'That's Father, alright! Although it might as well be Earl of Never Never Land, as it's a defunct title these days. Which is spiffing.'

Eleanor looked doubtful. 'Really?'

He nodded. 'Absolutely. Pater freely admits he wouldn't be up to scratch to be an earl. Total dreamer, you know. Artistic type. And he's the last one left. Apart from me. An inferior chip off his wonderful block, mind. But the poor old trout's ticker isn't up for much in the way of capers any more. That's why I'm in Venice. He's an amateur poet and always dreamed of emulating his hero, Lord Byron, in verse and deed! So I'm here to live out his last unfulfilled yearning and write home with all the scandalous detail!'

She shook her head. 'That sounds wonderful. And, by coincidence, Clifford mentioned Lord Byron just before we met. Perhaps I shall bump into you, and, for whatever his purpose is, your bear, again?'

'The story goes that Lord Byron used to own a real bear, my lady,' Clifford said with a barely disguised sniff. 'When he entered Cambridge University in 1805, he was informed that students were not permitted dogs. As a dog lover, he was infuriated by this ruling, and subsequently bought a bear. The university, having no ruling specifically against bears, was forced to allow him to keep the animal.'

Kip nodded dolefully. 'Only mine isn't real. And I know he never had one in Venice. But I thought it would add a touch of...'

'Theatre?'

'Exactly, Lady Swift! But they're harder to come by than I imagined. Taxidermists in Venice, I mean. I was going to get a stuffed one. And that was already a cowardly compromise. Because, well, frankly, the idea of traipsing everywhere with a real live bear made a chap question if he'd make it to his hotel bed with his head still attached!'

9

Outside the hotel, the red-jacketed pilot of the contessa's launch awaited Eleanor on the hotel's landing jetty. Beside him was one of the sleekest, most beautiful motorboats Eleanor had ever seen. Open-topped with exquisitely stitched leather seats, a row of silver-bezelled dials and a half-moon windscreen, the highly varnished wood of the arrow-nosed craft shone like a mirror. She marvelled that the bow accounted for almost half of the boat's length, the hull itself tapering in an extravagant 'V' as it disappeared below the waterline.

'Gracious, is that a thirty-foot speed launch?'

'Si, Lady Swift.' The pilot nodded appreciatively. 'It was especially built for the count and contessa.'

She admired the lines again. 'My father told me as a child of his dream that one day such designs might be realised. He used to draw similar things from his imagination at the galley table of our yacht, saying they should positively fly.'

'And,' Clifford said, 'wrangle with your late uncle over the intricacies of precisely how. On the all-too rare occasions your parents were in the country to visit, I recall.'

Having helped with the train of her gown as she stepped in, he sat in the row behind her and their pilot.

As they roared away from the jetty, she noticed a form standing unmoving in the shadows directly opposite the jetty. Prickles ran up her arm. She shook herself.

What's wrong with you, Ellie? It's just someone... standing there minding their own business.

She settled into her seat, arm resting along the side of the sleek craft, drinking in the warm evening air. But the image of the stranger in the shadows stayed in her thoughts.

A few minutes later, after weaving a path through clusters of powered and unpowered boats dotting the water, the launch spun left. Clifford leaned forward.

'We are just clearing the most south-easterly end of the main island of Venice, my lady. Into the mid-waters of the lagoon, and her archipelago of smaller islands.'

She half-turned. 'That first one is tiny. What is it?'

'A monastery until the Napoleonic invasion, I believe. But now, of no interest at all,' he said dismissively.

They continued across the aqua-green water until the pilot pointed at a larger island.

'That is Murano island, Lady Swift. Where the famous glass of Venice is made for many centuries. Perhaps you will visit?'

'I can't imagine I'll have time. Not with the Carnival starting soon. But maybe I'll find time. I think glass-blowing is so clever.'

Their journey continued, the pilot furnishing information on the myriad islands they passed. The few that were heavily populated soon gave way to many with only a church and a few clusters of houses. Then the islands became little more than tiny atolls, home only to low-lying grasses and tufted reeds dotted with slender white egrets.

Finally, he pointed ahead at the largest island of the last half hour by far. Along the shoreline, lush trees had been planted, shrouding the interior from prying eyes. As the pilot slowed to turn into a narrow channel, Eleanor glimpsed her hosts' home for the first time. Resplendent in soft coral pink, the villa rose four floors to a red-tiled roof, part of which incorporated a vast bird's-eye view terrace.

The driver stopped alongside a long wooden jetty next to eight other similar, but smaller, launches. A cream-liveried footman was waiting to help her alight.

'Lady Swift, welcome to Villa Isola. This way, please.'

Eleanor thanked the pilot, much to his seeming confusion, then wrangled with her gown train as she set off after her welcoming party.

'Here goes,' she murmured to Clifford, feeling her confidence waver. 'Into the vast unknown of Venetian high society.'

'None of whom actually bite,' he whispered back with a wink.

In a blink of his suit tails, he melted away to the staff entrance.

Eleanor took a deep breath and started up the imposing steps. Inside she was met by acres of marble, cream and gold upholstery and bold, modern geometric patterns. In the centre of the hall was an ornate fountain, ringed by statues of what looked like Greek or Roman gods and goddesses. Whoever had designed this villa knew exactly what they wanted. And made no excuse for getting it.

'Lady Swift,' a musical voice tinkled. 'So delightful that you came.'

Contessa Contarini glided across the marble floor, the epitome of style and grace. Like her flawless English wrapped in an irresistible Italian accent, she emanated a confidence only the truly cosmopolitan could manage. Fine bronze silk pleats hung from her shoulders, highlighting her delicate collarbone, and around her swan-like neck a string of pearls shimmered.

She had the poise of a ballerina and the sophisticated air of a woman born to great wealth. However, her rigidly held shoulders hinted she was less relaxed than she wanted to let on. Since hosting any social event, large or small, filled Eleanor with dread, she offered an extra warm smile.

'Contessa, so kind of you to invite me. And to send your launch too.'

'Nothing of the sort, my dear.' She reached out and took Eleanor's hands in her silky soft ones. 'Everyone is eager to meet you.'

Eleanor laughed nervously. 'Gracious, I am going to be busy.' She waved a hand around the hall. 'Such a beautiful home you have.'

'Thank you. We like it.' The contessa led Eleanor on, scooping up two glasses of something bubbly from the hovering waiter. 'Our spring only residence, of course. However, each of our homes must be the absolute reflection of one's personality. On this I never compromise.' She wafted an understated diamond-banded wrist above her coiffure, which made Eleanor look up. Gracing the ceiling was a remarkably lifelike fresco of the contessa herself, head-to-toe in swirling folds of crimson surrounded by a garland of pink roses. 'My husband's idea.'

Eleanor gazed at it, rather lost for words. 'It's... wonderful. I'm looking forward to meeting the count again. We barely even had time for introductions back in London before he was called away on business.'

'As he was again at five o'clock yesterday morning. To Switzerland.' She pointed a manicured nail at a nearby floral display. 'Hence the orchids. My husband *never* neglects me.' She ran a sisterly eye over Eleanor's gown and nodded. 'So perfectly English. Like you, my dear. Come. We shall start with the family and the one who will not wait first, naturally!'

'Naturally,' Eleanor murmured, having no clue who that might be.

A moment later, steel-grey eyes framed by a head of lustrous ivory hair met hers. Rising slowly from the chair, the mustachioed man rolled his shoulders back to stand as straight as a board, belying the seventy or more years his deeply lined face suggested. The regal burgundy velvet of his jacket and bow tie were a fitting accompaniment to the elaborate silver-handled cane he rested both hands on.

'Nonno,' the Contessa said. 'This is—'

'The English aristocrat lady. I can see that for myself, Eugenia.' Far from the reedy croak Eleanor expected from someone his age, his voice was an arresting rich baritone, his words delivered in an uncompromising tone. He nodded, his lips seeming to think of smiling, then deciding not. He drummed his jacket breast with a sun-spotted hand. 'Lady Swift, I presume it is not business that brings you to Venice?'

'Not this time,' she replied, feeling as if she were a naughty schoolgirl and had just been told off.

The elderly man grunted and tapped his cane sharply on the floor. 'Yet all you will sightsee here was built over the centuries from business. Commerce, young woman, is the lifeblood of this city!'

Eleanor's independent spirit resurfaced with a bristle at being told what to think. 'I was led to believe that love was the beating heart of Venice?'

The contessa's eyes widened. Eleanor thought the old man would erupt, but instead he snorted with laughter.

'How right you are, young woman! Us Venetians are equally obsessed with both. Now, leave me to study the trade papers. Once a merchant, always one!' He flapped them away with his cane.

The contessa led Eleanor off, shaking her head. 'Never before have I heard him accept a different opinion to his!'

'I hope he didn't think me rude,' Eleanor said. 'He's a... a delightful gentleman. Who, exactly, is he?'

'My grandfather. Nonno, as we say in Italian. The whole family's Nonno, in fact!' she added a little theatrically. 'And never for a moment does he let us forget it!'

Eleanor frowned. 'The whole family's grandfather?'

The contessa nodded. 'Nonno rules everything. And everyone. We have hundreds of family members, but only one Nonno!' For a moment, her slender hands balled at her side. 'He is always right. And all others wrong!' Her smile flickered as she shrugged. 'But as head of the Marcello family, he must be as he is.'

'Marcello?'

Marcello, Ellie! That's the family Angelo said are related to the Seccos. The ones who feuded with the Vendelinis.

'So you are Contarini by marriage?'

'Yes. But I am Marcello through and through.'

Eleanor was desperate to ask if she knew about Gaspo the gondolier's arrest, and her opinion on his guilt. But she hardly knew the woman. And in the middle of a party she'd kindly been invited to it seemed beyond rude to pry. Before she could stop herself, however, her tongue overruled her manners.

'Do you know Signor Gaspo Secco?'

Her host tilted her head. 'Mmm, the name doesn't ring a bell. The Seccos are related to us, of course, but we are a very large family, just us Marcellos.' She smiled at Eleanor. 'Family is everything to us. It must be the same for you?'

Eleanor shook her head. 'I have no living family that I know of. My parents went missing when I was nine and I never met any of my grandparents. I did have one very beloved uncle, who I saw little of until he too, unfortunately, died.'

The contessa looked horrified. 'Then I am so sorry for you, my dear.' She looked at Eleanor quizzically. 'But how did you know about the connection between our families? You have only been in Venice a short while.'

She groaned inwardly. *Now what are you going to say, Ellie?*

She was saved by a flurry of chestnut-haired children skipping over to them. The boys were dressed in beautifully tailored blue jackets with white linen shorts and the girls in the finest matching ribbon-waisted and frill-hemmed dresses.

'What a treat.' Eleanor smiled around the unexpected arc of thirteen excited faces, which had bounded to a halt in front of her. 'You're all allowed to join the start of the party, I see.'

The eldest of the boys frowned. 'And stay to the end, Lady Swift. Why would we not?'

Not knowing how to enlighten him that children in England were still very much neither seen nor heard at formal events, she nodded.

'No reason at all. And how fortunate for me that one of you speaks English, because I'm afraid I don't know any Italian.'

The tiny doll in the middle slapped her hands on her hips. 'I'm Bella. And we all know English. And French. And German.'

Firmly put in her place, Eleanor bobbed down into the little one's eyeline and whispered, 'Then, Bella, maybe you can teach me a few Italian words this evening, please? So I can be clever like you all are.'

'You can try, I think.' Bella giggled, sliding her hand into Eleanor's.

'Not now, Bella. I need Lady Swift to meet lots of people.' The contessa held her hands up at the collective groan from the children. 'But how would we like to invite our special guest to come with us shopping and to the Lido the day after tomorrow?'

'Would you really come?' the oldest of the girls asked, stepping forward, adding, 'I'm Justina.'

'Justina, Bella, all of you, I would love to,' Eleanor said genuinely, thinking it might also provide an opportunity to ask her hostess more about the connection between the Marcellos and the Seccos without seeming so impolite.

She turned to her hostess with an enquiring look as the children scampered away.

'Nieces, nephews, cousins of cousins and some are even my own treasures,' the contessa said, scanning the room.

Eleanor followed her gaze, seeing nothing but an alarming number of faces she'd need to learn the names of before the evening was out.

'Ah, perfect,' her hostess cooed as they were joined by a kindly faced man in his fifties with a fulsome black beard. He wore his jacket unbuttoned over a crisp white shirt. The ends of his dove-grey tightly wound neckerchief were tucked into his collar, a soft black cap covering the crown of his wiry ebony hair.

'Lady Swift, this is Doctor Pinsky.'

He slid his hands behind his back and nodded politely to Eleanor. 'Simply delighted, Lady Swift. How fortunate I am to meet you.'

She hesitated.

You're on holiday in another country, remember, Ellie? If he doesn't want to shake hands, that's his business.

'Likewise, Doctor.' She smiled, warming to his soft-spoken voice and kind brown eyes.

'If you will excuse me for a while?' the contessa said before gliding away.

Pinsky leaned forward slightly. 'How quickly are you falling for the charms of Venice, Lady Swift?'

She laughed. 'Too quickly. I'm completely smitten already. To the point that I'm developing a passion to learn her fascinating history. Though I confess, normally, studying history sounds too much like needing to sit still for days on end. And that is definitely not my forte.'

'But here, every step you take reveals more history, and wisdom, and more perhaps, for the taking. If you wish to, of course.'

She took the seat he indicated. 'Are you a doctor of history, then? A professor, to those of us from England?'

He tapped his temple. 'Only in here. By birthright. My formal training is in medicine.'

Now thoroughly intrigued, she shuffled forward. 'Birthright? Or am I being too inquisitive?'

'Not at all. I couldn't be happier to speak of my origins. I am Jewish.'

Ah, Ellie! That's why he wouldn't shake hands.

'My people have a long history in Venice. Not always the easiest, but challenge breeds ingenuity and endurance.'

She nodded. 'I'm fascinated. Do start at the beginning.'

'And then I must find out more about yourself. Well, to start, perhaps you and I shall skip back in time only as far as the thirteenth century. Though, Jewish people had been marginalised for centuries prior to that...'

Some time later, she was pulled from his mesmerising tale by a waiter offering her a drink. She shook her head and turned her attention back to the doctor.

'That is such an amazing tale of perseverance and fortitude. I'm quite speechless for once. It's a shame my butler's not here to see it.'

Pinsky's brow furrowed in puzzlement. 'Your butler?'

'Er, yes. He's always admonishing me for the number of questions I ask.' *And here's another chance to do just that, Ellie.* 'Doctor, you're obviously knowledgeable about this wonderful city's history in general. Do you, by any chance, know much about the contessa's family? And the Vendelinis? Or Seccos?'

Pinsky raised his bushy eyebrows. 'You are a most... unusual woman, Lady Swift.'

Something in his tone made the hairs on the back of her neck stand up.

'Really? I—'

'Good evening.'

She looked up to see an attractive man of around forty in an elegant green linen suit. The man nodded to her companion. 'And good evening to you, Doctor Pinsky.'

The doctor rose quickly and tilted his head to Eleanor.

'Please excuse me, Lady Swift, but I must be leaving.'

She could only assume his sudden need to go had something to do with this new arrival. But why, she couldn't guess. She smiled.

'I'm so sorry, Doctor Pinsky. I'd love to hear more. I do hope we'll meet again soon.'

He nodded slowly. 'Oh, we will, Lady Swift. I'm sure of it. Our acquaintance has been a short one, but it has left an indelible impression on me.'

With a curt nod to the new arrival, he was gone.

10

Left alone with the man in the green linen suit, Eleanor felt strangely uneasy, the doctor's reaction to the new arrival having caught her off guard. She hesitated, wondering if she should excuse herself and find the contessa. Before she could, the man spoke to her.

'Forgive me.' Her self-appointed companion stepped back. 'Italian ways can be too forward for a delicate English lady. I must apologise and I should take my leave also.'

Something in his chivalrous manner felt just the tonic for her unsettled feeling. This was a party. She was on holiday. And in Venice, one of the most wondrous cities in the world.

She laughed. 'Delicate? I wish my butler could hear you say that. He has a habit of respectfully comparing my sensibilities to a rhinoceros.'

His brows rose with amusement.

'How refreshing.'

Her linen-suited companion seemed charming without a hint of impropriety. His sun-tanned olive complexion was flaw-less, and the rest of his bewitching dark Italian features too attractive not to enjoy, even as she shot a guilty glance at her engagement ring.

Together, they made their way through several exquisitely appointed rooms, each full of chic guests conversing vivaciously in groups large and small. Eleanor marvelled over how the decor gradually intensified from jasmine white and golden sand, through to almond cream and rich honey, on into corn silk and saffron, then silver pearl and deep amber. Finally, they reached a vast expanse of cashmere and gold, where her breath caught at the burning orange sunset filling the view as if the sun itself was actually the ceiling.

'The contessa has a wonderful gift for interior decoration,' she said as her companion led her on to the terrace.

He nodded. 'She has. And please forgive me for not introducing myself earlier. I am Vincenzo Vendelini. I am a member of the Venetian Council.'

She blanched. His surname instantly bringing back the haunting memory of trying to haul the motionless Benetto aboard the gondola, praying she might save him.

'Signor Ven... Vendelini!' she stuttered. 'But that's—'

'Too hard to remember? Please call me Vincenzo. I do not stand on formality.'

'Thank you, Vincenzo. Me neither, so please call me Eleanor. But I did not mean your name was hard to remember. Exactly the opposite, in fact. My sincere condolences,' she said earnestly. 'Assuming you are related to the poor man who died in the Grand Canal earlier today, that is?'

He looked surprised. 'Yes. Poor Benetto. But we were not so close. Though in Italy all family is woven tight as a tapestry, in reality. Which can be difficult sometimes.'

She shrugged. 'Having no family of my own, you've no idea how much I would relish that problem.'

He winced. 'I am so sorry. To be alone without family in the world is not a happy place.'

'Oh, I'm not really alone. My staff is a sort of surrogate family. They are here on holiday with me.' At his confused look, she hurried on. 'But gracious, I would have thought your family would do anything for harmony after all the troubles over the years with...'

His eyebrows rose so high, her words faltered. He took her arm and gently led her through the plushly padded settees and marble tables, nodding to the other guests until they reached the far corner of the terrace. There, he let go of her arm.

'Please accept my apologies, Lady Swift.' He lowered his voice. 'But it is best we are not overheard.' He glanced around and then shook his head. 'You surprise me. Knowing this about our two families. But it is true. And the reason why almost all the contessa's guests tonight are of Marcello descent. I am the sole Vendelini invited. And we are both large families.'

She cursed her runaway tongue, thinking she must have sounded insensitive. 'I see. I'm sorry too. But what is the problem? I mean, I was told the feud was over years ago.'

Although the man I saw murdered only this morning might contradict that theory, Ellie.

He gave a deep sigh. 'Yes. It is. But to save you more awkward conversations, I will tell you this. It has, for some time, been an uneasy truce. Which is why I was invited tonight.'

'Well, that's very positive.'

He spread his hands. 'In small part. Because I am an important city official, often I receive invitations to dinners and parties. People want favours, Lady Swift. Venice was built on commerce, as a certain gentleman is fond of saying!'

She laughed. 'Nonno, I know. I've already met him.'

'Ah! Then you understand. But what he didn't add, I presume, is that it was also built on favours. And not always the honest kind.' He shrugged. 'One thousand years later, it is no different.' He seemed to study her for a moment. 'May I ask how you know the story of our families?'

'Actually, I was at the scene of your poor relative's death.'

His dark brows met. 'You were there?'

'Yes.'

He nodded sombrely. 'It was important I came tonight. To show I consider this incident an isolated event. And nothing to do with our families.'

'So very commendable of you.'

He shook his head. 'It is a duty I could not avoid. If the feud restarts, it would not just be bad for our families, it would be bad for all of Venice!' He took a deep breath and stared out over the water.

Eleanor hesitated. She didn't want to upset Vincenzo, but her natural inquisitiveness and desire to know the truth wouldn't be denied.

'You said you didn't know Signor Benetto that well? But was he the kind of person to... you know, get into a fight with someone?'

Vincenzo shook his head. 'Not at all. Benetto was very mild-mannered. He was, however, passionate about some things, which, being Italian, goes without saying.'

She remembered what Angelo had told her. 'Passionate about Venice, perhaps? And its future?'

He nodded. 'Yes. He believed Venice needed to modernise. More, and quicker.'

'Which was not always a popular viewpoint? Perhaps it led to him having enemies?'

He shrugged. 'There are always those who stand in the way of progress. We men of action all have enemies.' He laughed softly. 'Whenever Benetto was challenged, he would say, "Time and tide wait for no man. Nor does progress. Not even for a Venetian!"' He shook his head. 'Perhaps a lighter topic might be better now? This is a party, after all.'

She grimaced. 'I am sorry. You're quite right.'

'Ahem!' A familiar cough sounded behind her. She turned

to see her butler, holding a gold tray loaded with two drinks and looking even more distinguished than ever in a tailored white suit jacket and black bow tie. An outfit which he certainly hadn't accompanied her there wearing. That most of Venice's female elite on the terrace were eyeing him without pretending otherwise didn't surprise her, however.

'Honestly, how do you do it, Clifford?'

'Merely a matter of balance, my lady.' He turned the tray towards her. 'And coordination.'

She tutted. 'You know I don't mean managing not to hurl drinks over all the guests! I meant seamlessly appearing as if you're one of the staff.'

'Simple, my lady. For tonight I am.' He gestured for her to select a glass of cool-looking amber fizz. 'And, sir?'

He offered Vincenzo the other glass on his tray. Eleanor's companion seemed too caught up looking between them in confusion to notice.

'Oh, this is Clifford. My butler.' Eleanor was about to do introductions the other way, but caught Clifford's discreet shake of his head.

Vincenzo took his drink with a nod to her. 'How fortunate to have one's *maggiordomo* to hand. And chaperone, perhaps?'

Clifford bowed from the shoulders. 'Prudence, my lady,' he murmured as he slid away.

Vincenzo's lips twitched as he watched her butler leave.

'Tell me, are you enjoying Venice, Lady Swift?'

'Enormously. I could gush all evening, yet I've hardly seen anything this unique city has to offer.'

'Then perhaps you might permit me to show you a few parts which mere tourists in our city rarely see?'

'I'd absolutely love that!'

'Tomorrow at ten o'clock, then? At the base of the Torre dell'Orologio.'

'I'll be there. Now—'

At the far end of the terrace, a flash of amethyst-blue eyes in a heart-shaped face caught her attention.

The young woman I bumped into in St Mark's Square, Ellie!

'Vincenzo, please excuse me. There's someone I simply must catch.'

He took her glass as she swept up the train of her gown and darted along the terrace, ignoring that polite ladies weren't supposed to charge about at parties.

'Dash it! Where did she go?' she muttered. Unable to see her on the terrace, she zigzagged between the huddles of guests as she hurried back through the house. Arriving in the grand entrance hall, she spun around, but the young woman was nowhere to be seen.

Perhaps she's leaving altogether, Ellie?

Hurrying down the path to the landing jetty, she caught the burble of a motor starting.

'I say!' she called out, sprinting as fast as she could. In the light of the huge lanterns now burning along the length of the jetty, she saw the young woman hesitantly step into a launch. Almost before she had sat down, the capped man at the wheel jammed the throttle forward.

'I've got something of yours I wanted to return!' Eleanor's words were lost in the engine's roar.

As the boat surged out of the channel into the open water, she threw her arms out. 'What a shame!'

'Is everything alright, Lady Swift?' Vincenzo joined her in a few elegant strides.

'Yes. Well, no. I missed her.' Her face lit up. 'But maybe you know who she is?'

He shrugged. 'Who?'

'The woman who just left in that boat. She's got the most mesmerising blue-lilac eyes. Long dark lashes. Slender. Young. And very pretty.'

He looked thoughtful for a moment, but then shook his

head. 'There are lots of pretty women here tonight. That covers a great many of them. I'm sorry.'

She accepted his elbow to be escorted back inside. As she went, she glanced over her shoulder. The boat had been swallowed up in the night, only the pinprick of its navigation lights still visible.

Who is she, Ellie? And why was she looking so troubled again?

11

The rest of the evening passed in a blur of too many names for Eleanor to even think of remembering. Signor Vendelini had been scooped up on their return to be courted by a succession of smart-suited and sharp-eyed men, and a few women too. All of whom had the look of somebody who wanted a favour, just as he'd mentioned to her. Venetian stamina for socialising seemed tireless. She, on the other hand, was finding being the stranger, in an admittedly very welcoming midst, exhausting.

Somewhere in the house, a clock struck midnight.

Miraculously Clifford appeared, her beaded wrap over his arm. 'Before the lady actually falls over,' he muttered, holding it up for her to slide into.

The inevitable round of farewells meant it was another twenty minutes before she reached the entrance hall. The contessa was waiting, surrounded by the gaggle of children who had lost none of their energy.

'Please forgive me leaving,' Eleanor said. 'It's been the most wonderful evening. But I'm ashamed to say, weariness has got the better of me.'

'Run along, dear. The launch is waiting for you.' Her

hostess smiled, but Eleanor hadn't missed the slight strain in her voice. 'If you think you are tired now, wait until the children have you for a whole day shopping and at the Lido!'

'And covered in gelato, sand and all manner else, no doubt,' she heard her butler mutter.

Clifford's barometer hadn't let them down. The night air was deliciously warm and dry, the sky entirely cloudless, and to her delight, lit by a full moon. In the launch, she breathed in the salty breeze, letting the lulling swish of passing water soothe her frazzled thoughts as they motored back far slower than they'd arrived.

'Goodness, what a night to be crossing the lagoon,' she said to the pilot. 'It's so peaceful and serene.'

He nodded. 'Mr Clifford asked me to go more slowly on the return that you might enjoy it more.'

Caught up in the beauty all around her, the island of Murano hove into view again. And then the small, almost square island she'd noticed before. She pointed at it.

'What's on that?'

'Nothing of interest, as I said before, my lady,' Clifford called.

The pilot shook his head. 'It is of great interest, Lady Swift. It is Cemetery Island. Where we have buried our dead for many centuries.'

'Thank you,' she murmured, throwing Clifford a grateful look, knowing he'd been trying to stop memories of that morning's death intrude on the evening. As she settled back in her seat, however, she cast the island another glance.

Perhaps it will soon have a new inhabitant, Ellie? Benetto Vendelini, God rest his soul.

As the launch slipped alongside the jetty outside her hotel, she peeped at the pilot, but he was busy making sure the craft's immaculate varnish stayed that way.

She turned to her butler and whispered, 'Clifford. After seeing that young girl again, I remembered something Vincenzo told me earlier.'

'Which is, my lady?' he whispered back.

'That he was the only Vendelini at the contessa's tonight. Which means the young girl must be part of the Marcello family. Or possibly the Seccos.'

'If Signor Vendelini is correct, then it would seem so. The significance of which, however, is?'

She shrugged. 'I don't know, but everything seems to keep coming back to those three families. Coincidence?'

'I really couldn't say at this juncture, my lady, but possibly not.'

He offered his elbow to help her alight from the motor launch onto the jetty. After thanking their pilot, he gestured up the steps. 'A small restorative to soothe the lady's mood after the unfortunate last words of your moonlit tour?'

She nodded gratefully. 'If my butler will join me... hang on! What's that rumpus going on in the lobby?'

With Clifford on her heels, she hurried inside. The sight of three policemen all gesticulating at the harassed-looking hotel manager made her groan.

'Hello, Lady Swift!' a cheery voice called from somewhere behind the policemen.

'Kip? Is that you... Oh my!' She failed to hide her amusement as he pushed his way forward. Dressed only in what seemed to be sky-blue long john underwear which finished at his calves, his blond hair was plastered to his head. Not surprising, she mused, as he was soaked, a large puddle already forming at his feet.

Clifford tutted sharply.

'Kip, what on earth is going on?' she called over the noise of the telephone ringing and the policemen arguing with the manager.

'I've only been swimming,' he called back with a shrug. 'Re-enacting Lord Byron's famous race across the Lagoon in 1818. He challenged some Venetian chaps. Started on the Lido, then past the Doge's Palace and along to the far end of the Grand Canal. Not that I can boast a hint of his swimming prowess. He did the whole thing in around four hours and won easily. But these uniformed chumps ruined the entire affair. I didn't know it's illegal to swim in the canals these days!'

She caught the manager waving at her and holding out the receiver. She hurried over.

'It is Signor Seldon on the telephone, Lady Swift.'

'Hugh!' She took the receiver with joy. 'Hugh? It's Eleanor. Sorry to have kept you... what? No, I can't hear you properly either.'

Her fiancé's agitated voice rumbled out of the earpiece. 'What the deuce is going on? Sounds like a pub brawl. Isn't it the early hours of the morning over there like here?'

'Yes. But don't worry, Hugh. It's just the police.'

'Police!'

The tallest policeman held up a commanding hand, silencing everyone else. 'Unless someone vouch for this man' – he pointed at Kip – 'he will go to jail. Now.'

'What man, Eleanor?' Seldon's voice came down the line again.

She laughed. 'Oh, it's only Kip, Hugh. Nice young chap staying here.' She waved her free hand. 'I will vouch for him, gentlemen!' She turned back to the receiver. 'Oh, sorry, Hugh, I was talking to the police.'

'I say, too good of you and all that,' Kip shouted, waving at her. 'But are you sure? I mean, I can't promise I won't get into a bit of a bind again.'

She laughed. 'It's alright, Kip, I don't expect you to behave.'

'Eleanor!' Seldon's gruff voice came forcibly out of the receiver. 'Tell me I didn't hear what I think you said, please?'

She frowned. 'Why? I can't let Kip be dragged off to jail in what is basically just his underwear, can I?' The only sound was a sharp click on the other end. 'Hugh... Hugh?'

12

The sun caressed Eleanor where she sat waiting on an azure cushioned seat on her private hotel terrace. In her lap, Gladstone and Tomkins shuffled expectantly, eyes fixed on the empty breakfast table. Her stomach gurgled.

'I know, chaps. We're ravenous, aren't we?'

Clifford's silhouetted form appeared behind the ivory silk curtains inside.

'I'm beyond decent,' she called.

He didn't appear.

'Dash it, Clifford. I can't have to get fully dressed before you'll pour me a cup of coffee out here. I'm swaddled in my house pyjamas, with my hotel robe over the top. Both of which I'm sweltering in, purely for your benefit, by the way.'

There was still no movement.

'Point taken.' She scraped the feet of her chair back. 'As these togs aren't decorous enough for you, I shall peel them both off out here and then step inside past you to change. How's that?'

'Deviously iniquitous,' he muttered, stepping out. 'As are all of a certain lady's wily contrivances.'

'Then you shouldn't teach her by example.' She caught his lips quirk. 'That's better. Good morning. Isn't it a beautiful one to be in Venice?'

'Indubitably, my lady.' He wheeled out a trolley, draped in immaculate silver-threaded linen, a domed salver above a glowing brazier presiding on top. 'Though it might be afternoon by the time your so-called "breakfast" is over, given the proportions ordered.'

'Actually, no. I shall have to devour it all quicker than I wish. I am meeting Vincenzo this morning, remember?'

He sniffed. 'A butler never forgets an appointment.'

'Speaking of which, I haven't told you what I learned from him.'

'Apart from the young lady you seek possibly being from the Marcello or Secco family.'

'Yes. Apart from that.' She recounted the little she'd gleaned about the murdered man.

Clifford picked up a silver coffee pot from the trolley, the smell of the finest rich Italian roast tantalising her nostrils. 'Signor Vendelini's information seems to concur with Angelo's.' He poured her a cup.

She nodded. 'I know. Nothing we've learned seems to suggest the police have arrested the wrong man by hauling Gaspo, the gondolier, away. But I can't shake the thought that we need to locate the man on the motorboat. Maybe Angelo knows him. Or could ask around for us? Maybe one of his gondola colleagues might remember him?'

He placed the coffee pot down. 'Actually, I foresaw such a request, and asked him this morning before you rose. He did not recognise the gentleman, but will ask his fellow gondoliers.'

'Splendid!'

'Now, my lady. Comestibles, or package first, with your coffee?'

'Package? Not more flowers, is it? Because I think poor

Hugh would be rather miffed if it was. Dash it, I tried four times to get through to him on the telephone before I fell asleep last night.'

Clifford produced a brown paper-wrapped parcel from the bottom of the trolley. 'Thankfully then, not more flowers. I believe it is the sketch you commissioned. It seems the artist wanted to hand it over personally but had to leave it with the manager on being told you were otherwise indisposed. Evidently, the rest of his customers rise at a far more seemly hour.'

She rolled her eyes good-naturedly. 'Let's have a look while you pour some more coffee.'

Reaching over her pets' heads, she took the package. 'It's heavier than I imagined. It must be quite a frame.' Tomkins pounced on the string ties, hooking both sets with his claws.

She tapped him gently between the ears. 'Hopeless! You've made the knot impossible to undo now, you rascal!'

Clifford passed her his pocket knife, the miniature fold-out scissors ready. As she removed the wrapping, Gladstone threw his head back to stare up at her in disappointment.

'Nothing edible inside. I know, old friend.' She lifted out the framed sketch. 'I say, it's wonderful, Clifford! He's captured the Grand Canal perfectly with this hotel's palatial façade in the centre as I asked. Viewed as if one were standing on the opposite side, looking across the water. It will be a lovely memento of our time here.'

'Remarkably detailed too.' He scrutinised the sketch through his pince-nez. 'Right down to the Roman Doric columns of the very balustrades where you are sitting.' With a white-gloved finger, he pointed to a dormer window in the roof. 'He has even included the carved stone monkey who stands guard above my quarters.' He peered admonishingly over the top of his spectacles at her. 'My quarters, which for a mere butler are far too—'

'Far less than I would like you to stay in while we're here,' she said firmly. 'But I'm delighted you can see the view. Now, breakfast time!'

'Not interested in your other sketch first, my lady?'

She frowned. 'What other? I only ordered one.' She moved her bulldog's head out of the way. 'Gracious, our artist must have made a mistake. Or misunderstood me. Not surprising, with me not speaking any Italian and the poor fellow being deaf. It was entirely a conversation in charades.'

Clifford held up the other sketch to show her. 'The precise opposite view to the one you commissioned. Looking across there, as we are now. Although, I feel this second one was completed with a little less care.'

She shrugged. 'They still make a captivating pair to hang side by side back at Henley Hall. We shall have to find him on the way to meet Signor Vendelini, though, and insist he take payment for both. I'm sure he's only charged me for one.'

'Most gracious, my lady.'

As Clifford enticed Gladstone and Tomkins off to a safe distance with a bowl each of their favourite titbits, Eleanor settled in for an hour of blissful breakfasting. A rainbow of fresh fruits drizzled in honey was followed by a delectable platter of cured meats and seasoned cheeses. Served with savoury, herbed biscotti, she declared them all too sublime not to finish.

'This spicy sweet chutney fellow accompaniment is equally divine.'

'It is *mostardo*, my lady. The principal ingredients being Venetian quince, candied fruits and mustard oil, I understand. From the salver, you have baked eggs, crisp-coated sardines and, as a particular concession for the English palate, grilled *prosciutto* in lieu of bacon.' He added a selection of olives, dried figs and toasted almonds to the table. 'Plus a basket of speciality breads and crisp *ciriola* rolls, in their traditional shape of a dancing flame. Will that suffice, or shall I ring for more?'

She laughed. 'No. It will suffice, I'm sure.'

With breakfast finished and much chivvying on Clifford's part, Eleanor appeared from her bedroom in her mint and jade striped tea dress. The soft scoop of the neckline nestled demurely against her collarbones, the loose-flowing elbow-length sleeves promising to keep her cool, as did the fulsomely pleated skirt swishing low at her calves. She'd chosen her larger green leather shoulder bag to accommodate the supply of local lace handkerchiefs and exquisite hand fan her ever-thoughtful butler had surprised her with.

He nodded approvingly as he held out her matching broad-brimmed hat.

'Let's go.' She paused and frowned. 'What is that peculiar rustling sound, though?'

'Guess,' he said drily, pointing at the bottom tassels of the nearest settee, which were swinging wildly.

She peered underneath and laughed at the sight of Tomkins who had rolled the brown paper wrapping from the package she'd received into a tube which he was now in the middle of, tail twitching furiously.

'Silly boy!' Her brow wrinkled. 'Hang on, if he's being that naughty on his own, where is...'

'Master Gladstone?'

The hesitant clack of doggie nails on marble flooring rang through to them.

'Not my new shoes!' she cried as Gladstone appeared, one of her Venetian slippers hanging from his jowls.

'I believe I am to blame, my lady,' Clifford said, shaking his head. 'To save space in our trunks, I omitted Master Gladstone's own beloved leather slipper collection from home.'

'Oh, boy.' She beckoned her bulldog forward to ruffle one ear and gently extract her shoe. 'I will buy you your own slippers, how's that? Now, the concierge is waiting to spoil you both for the day.'

Gladstone woofed loudly and gave her an enthusiastic lick, which necessitated her returning to the bathroom. As she washed her face, she called out.

'Clifford, please slide those sketches into a safe place in case the terrible two take umbrage at them later for delaying their breakfast.'

Outside her hotel, Clifford gestured left along the narrow concourse.

'I say, is it our artist chap?' She squinted into the shade.

But the figure faded into the dark of the arches under the building opposite.

Clifford looked at her quizzically. 'No, my lady. It is a merry band of mischief-makers who seem to think you will be pleased to see them.' He pointed past the arches.

'Ladies!' she cried, hurrying towards her staff, who all curt-seyed on seeing her.

As she drew level with the building, she furtively scoured the gloomy recesses of the arches, but they seemed devoid of life. Sensing her staff were staring at her, she tore her gaze away.

Ellie, you're becoming paranoid!

'Goodness, how smart you look in your beautiful blouses!'

'The young 'uns wanted to show you 'em, m'lady,' Mrs Butters said.

Eleanor clapped as the four of them gave a delighted twirl, which showed off their modest balloon sleeves and blouson hems. Polly failed to recover from her pirouette and almost spun into the canal, only being saved by Clifford's quick hands.

'Butters borrowed a sewing machine from the nice lady who runs our boarding house.' Mrs Trotman patted her friend on the shoulder. 'We was all too hot with this unexpectedly warm weather in what we brought. Even though we've hats, none of us is ever normally out in the sun for more than a minute or two.'

'Aye, and I learned how to cut out the pattern on the fabric we all chose,' Lizzie chirped. 'And Polly sorted the buttons.'

Eleanor beamed. It warmed her heart how the older ladies tried so hard to include her younger maids in everything. A thought struck. She threw her butler an imploring look. He nodded.

'And where are you off to now, ladies?'

'To a museum we can't say the name of.' Lizzie giggled, starting the other three off.

Mrs Trotman nudged Eleanor's housekeeper in the ribs. 'Via as many washing lines as we can. For our challenge of finding the most—'

'Ahem!' Clifford arched a brow. 'Counting Venice's bridges, or her palaces, is a more traditional pastime for tourists, ladies.'

'Maybe we've invented summat new, Mr Clifford,' Mrs Trotman replied innocently.

Looking unconvinced, he walked around each of them as if conducting a regimental uniform inspection. 'Beyond passable, troops. Remember to watch your bags vigilantly. Dismissed.'

Linking arms with more giggles, the four women wished Eleanor a wonderful day with another curtsey, before turning in awkward formation and marching away with Mrs Trotman marking time.

Eleanor shook her head. 'Oh but, Clifford, I thought you realised I meant—'

'To furnish the ladies with a top-up of spending money?' He nodded. 'Hence the inspection, my lady.'

Her jaw fell. 'You mean, with your dubious sleight of hand, you slipped an envelope into each of their bags without any of us noticing?'

'I really couldn't say. But having anticipated my mistress' ever-gracious propensity to spoil her staff, perhaps. Shall we?' He gestured in the opposite direction to the one the ladies had gone in.

'I thought St Mark's Square was the other way?'

'It is. However, you have twenty-five minutes before your rendezvous. Ample time to take an alternative route there and discover more wonders in this fascinating city. All the more so as we are on the correct side of the Grand Canal already.'

She nodded in agreement and set off into the crowds. Soon she was deep in Venice's less populated maze of narrow streets, canals and even narrower footbridges. Pausing for a moment, she looked up at the washing strung above their heads like bunting, laughing as she remembered her ladies' saucy challenge. Obviously reading her thoughts, Clifford rolled his eyes, then tapped his pocket watch.

She shook her head. 'Surely we can't have been that long already? We must have time for a little more exploring?'

'Indeed, my lady, we have not been twenty-five minutes yet. However, we have no idea where this alley will lead any more than where that canal' – he pointed to the one running alongside them – 'will end up. This network of streets is as confusing as the canals that dissect them. One can't simply go where one wants like a normal city. Here, one is at the mercy of water and bridges!'

'I do see what you mean, Clifford. I suppose we'd better try and get back to the Grand Canal. Or at least, one of the main streets.'

Several unfathomable twists and turns later, she threw her hands out.

'Alright, Clifford, you were right. It's taking us a lot longer to find our way out of this maze of backstreets than I thought it would.' She jerked to a halt. 'I say! Just look at that incredible display of masks!'

He joined her at the shop window. 'Indeed, my lady. They must be the sort of thing we'll see at the Carnival. More like headdresses, given how enormous most are.'

She nodded. 'Gracious, there are hundreds! Jesters and

emperors mingling with giant rabbit faces and lion heads. And Harlequins and unicorns and... sprites of some kind, I think?'

'Plus a multitude of cats, my lady. Quite bewildering.'

'We could just step inside...' She tailed off at his admonishing look.

'We could just return when you do not have a gentleman waiting.'

She turned contritely to start back, reaching for the shoulder strap of her...

'Clifford! The strap of my bag has been cut! It's gone!'

13

Clifford rapped his forehead with his knuckles. 'Fool, man! How could you let that happen?'

They both stared up and down the narrow street. Apart from them it appeared deserted. They hurried to the end where it met another, slightly wider street. A hundred yards or so away on the left, a slim man with closely cropped hair in a smart blue suit was strolling along. He looked to be about her age. Eleanor frowned.

Where have you seen him before?

As he turned to glance over his shoulder, Eleanor caught the flash of familiar green leather.

'That's my bag! Grab him!'

Even before the words left her lips, the thief broke into a run.

Cursing her choice of footwear, she grabbed her skirt as she sprinted after him with her butler alongside. For once, Clifford's longer stride failed to outrun hers, fuelled as she was with indignant rage. She dodged the few other people in the street with a hurried, 'Scusi, scusi!'

'There! He's ducked down this alley,' she panted, hurling herself around the corner.

Clifford halted her with a tap to her elbow. 'No, he's there, up on the bridge over the next canal.'

'But I definitely saw him turn right here!'

Clifford shook his head. 'Possibly, but there's no way across on this side. The walkway ends at that dead-end wall.'

Unbelievably, the thief paused on the bridge and half-bowed to Eleanor.

It is, Ellie! It's the man who was staring at you in the crowd at Benetto's murder and in the window of the tea house.

Even more incensed, she charged down the alley, relying on little more than luck to find the way to the bridge.

'Right or left?' She caught Clifford questioning himself as they neared a choice of alleyways.

'What's blunted your infallible sense of direction when we need it most?' she cried.

'Venice!' he cried back.

Purely by good fortune they both knew, the bridge appeared, but minus a thief.

'Well, he must have gone long ago, I guess,' she groaned. 'And there's a junction of three routes the other side. We'll never—'

'There!' Clifford pointed. 'Blue suit, and not that far down. He's taken the middle street.'

The reason for the thief's choice was immediately obvious. The street was deserted except for a small group of lace-bonneted women. The women were stringing glass beads from the wooden crate on their laps, much like the one they were each perched on.

'The women are *impiraresse*,' Clifford panted as they ran on. 'They often string the beads before they are exported so in the event of the crates being upset, the beads don't—'

'Spill everywhere!' Eleanor cried as the thief tipped one of the crates off a woman's lap as he shot past.

This caused an instant riot of waving arms and shouting from the women, while Eleanor and Clifford skidded on the marble-like beads before regaining their balance enough to sprint on.

'STOP!' Clifford shouted as the street ended in yet another canal.

Instead, the thief hunched down and, adding an extra turn of speed from nowhere, leapt over the water with the grace of an acrobat.

'What the—?' She could only gape as the man landed squarely on the other side, turned around and doffed an imaginary hat to them before strolling on, patting her bag.

Shaking herself, she stared up and down. 'Where's the nearest bridge!'

Clifford shook his head. 'I have no idea. And the wretch has just shown it to be irrelevant! Bridge or no bridge, I fear we could pursue the cur fruitlessly all day.'

'Well, we have to try. The audacity of that man!' Despite herself, she couldn't help feeling a hint of admiration at the man's nonchalance and athleticism.

Even the thieves are extraordinary in Venice, Ellie.

Shaking herself again, she chose a direction at random. But before she could run more than a few paces, the heel of her left shoe snapped off, leaving her tottering into a wall.

'An admirable effort, my lady,' Clifford said, holding his hand out for the other shoe. 'But I feel even his lordship would have admitted defeat at this juncture.'

She nodded and winced as he snapped the other heel off by placing it in a narrow gap between two stones and twisting.

He gave it back. 'Apologies, but they are ruined anyway and at least you can now reach the hotel. On the plus side, since you have also lost your hat, more shopping is now required. Much like an urgent change of clothes for both of us.'

She had no idea how they ended up back at her hotel. Her brain was too full of the blur of alleys, winding canals and annoyance with herself for being so careless.

'They key to her ladyship's suite please,' Clifford said to the thin-moustached manager, trying to shield her dishevelled view from him.

'The lady did not leave it this morning. But I will send the passkey to be waiting when you reach the door, Signor Clifford.'

True to his word, a liveried porter was waiting for them outside her suite.

'*Grazie*,' she said as Clifford gave him a coin.

But on unlocking the door, she gasped. 'We've been burgled! All the bureau doors and drawers are open!'

Clifford was instantly beside her, his expression uncharacteristically thunderous.

'Alert the manager, at once. Tell him to come up with the police. Quickly!' he instructed the porter.

She stepped inside, surveying the scene.

'Today of all days,' she murmured, suddenly feeling the effects of trying to chase down the man who stole her bag.

Clifford pursed his lips. 'Perhaps you might be persuaded to retire to the terrace while I make a thorough list of what is missing.'

She managed a wan smile. 'A gallant thought. But the drawers in my bedroom are filled with a mix of all manner of lady's—'

'Ah! Perhaps you should tackle that when you feel up to it and I will do the rest.'

She nodded. 'I'd best just ring Signor Vendelini first to rearrange our sightseeing trip for this afternoon.'

They both arrived back in the sitting room as a policeman entered with a flustered-looking manager.

'Lady Swift, I cannot begin to apologise enough—'

'I should think not!' Clifford said sternly. 'A gross lax in security.'

The manager muttered a raft more apologies and slid towards the door.

The policeman pulled out a notebook and a pen, looking between the two of them.

'What has been stolen?'

'Nothing,' Eleanor heard Clifford chorus with her.

They stared at each other. 'Nothing from your quarters, my lady? No jewellery missing?'

'Not a single thing. Same in here?'

He nodded, clearly as mystified as she was.

The hotel manager reappeared in the doorway with another policeman.

'One piece of good news, Lady Swift. Your bag has been found.'

He held it out. She took it, noticing the cut strap. Her brow creased even further.

'But... but how did you get it?'

The uniformed officer beside him stepped forward.

'A child handed it to me and told me it is yours, and that you stay here.'

'Which child?' Clifford said.

The policeman threw his arms out theatrically, with a snort. 'How do I know who he is! He says a man gave him a coin to hand it in.'

Eleanor looked up from rummaging in her bag. 'Everything is here as well. Even the hotel key I forgot to hand in to reception.'

She held up the key with an enquiring look to Clifford. He shrugged.

'I must confess I am at a loss, my lady.'

The first policeman looked from Eleanor to Clifford and back in exasperation.

'Lady Swift. Has anything been stolen or not?'

She shook her head. 'No, officer.'

The policeman scratched a couple of lines before stuffing his notebook and pen away. 'If you should find later anything is missing, please report it to the manager who will pass it on.'

He strode out of the door, bundling his colleague out with him. The manager cleared his throat.

'I'll get housekeeping to put your room to rights straight away, Lady Swift. You can stay in room 163 until they have finished. Here is the key.' Having handed it to Clifford, he edged towards the door. 'And dinner is on the hotel tonight, of course.'

He slid out of the room again, his footsteps hurrying down the corridor.

Two hours later, Eleanor made a point of bounding out of her hotel and down the steps.

'Really, I'm fine, Clifford,' she insisted.

'My lady, you were the victim of two unsettling incidents in one short morning.'

'Perhaps. But all your solicitous efforts have worked their inimitable magic. From the delectable box of chocolates which magically appeared, to persuading the concierge to part with the terrible two for an hour so they could smother me with bulldog and tomcat cuddles.' She smiled. 'And those soothing bath salts were just the thing to help scrub away that feeling of having been sullied by someone rifling through my things. Now, I'm one hundred per cent back in holiday mode.'

The concern etching his face fell away as they set off along the canalside. 'Heartening news, my lady. And my barometer suggests the good weather intends to continue.'

'Marvellous! Because tomorrow I shall be out of your hair all day shopping and swimming with the contessa and her delightful family.' *And asking some pertinent questions about Benetto and this supposed on–off feud, Ellie.* 'Although I imagine the sea might still be a tad chilly at this time of year. So, while I'm doing that, I expect you to do exactly as you please and only return to the hotel in time for a late evening chess tournament, if you can bear it. But only so I can enjoy you waffling endlessly on about all the dreary scientific, architectural and engineering wonders you will no doubt have spent your day ogling.'

He sniffed. 'I do not ogle, my lady. Now, shall we stick to the larger, more populated streets? Just for ease, as it were?'

She nodded, mostly to appease the ferocious terrier in him where her safety was concerned.

'I'm sure we'll be fine, though. I first noticed the thief in the crowd around Benetto's body before the police arrived. I assume he'd been tailing me ever since, waiting for an opportunity to snatch my bag. Now he has, I'm sure I'm of no more interest to him.' Her butler's silence spoke volumes. 'Come on, then, Clifford. Permit yourself to disagree politely before it eats you up.'

He pursed his lips. 'If the thief's only interest was in stealing your bag, why would he take the trouble to return it, and with the key inside?'

She sighed. 'I know. I was just waiting for one of us to say it. The same man who stole my bag must have ransacked my room.'

The larger thoroughfares were ten to twelve people wide and lined with the grandest of shops. Venetian luxury glistened and glittered back from every window in the form of jewellery, ladieswear and exquisitely crafted leather accessories. Peppered at right angles to the main thoroughfare were smaller boutique-lined alleyways which led on to even more tantalising shops.

Her butler, however, seemed to have other matters on his mind. She tugged his jacket sleeve, the lack of his usual tutting confirming her suspicion. 'Clifford, what's wrong?'

His brow flinched. 'My lady, at the risk of testing your fortitude for bad news, we are being followed, three shops behind. And by the very man we were recently discussing!'

She pretended to peruse the gown shop they'd stopped by.

'Why would he follow us now? He must have taken everything he wanted. Which, weirdly, seems to have been nothing!'

Clifford frowned. 'Unless he failed to find what he wanted? And he assumes you still have it upon your person? But what that could be, and why he should think you would have whatever it is, eludes me completely.'

A mad thought flashed into her head. 'You don't think he could be the mysterious man on the motorboat, do you? The one who might be responsible for Benetto's murder, if the police do have the wrong man in Gaspo? After all, I first saw him at the scene of the murder.'

Clifford frowned. 'As you did Signor Gaspo Secco.'

She grimaced. 'I know. It was just a wild thought.'

'Unfortunately, Angelo is not back on his gondola until tomorrow, so we shall have to wait to find out what, if anything, he has discovered. In the meantime...' His frown deepened. 'More immediate, and potentially worrying, is why our thief is not trying to conceal that he is dogging our trail?'

'I don't know. But I intend to find out,' she murmured through gritted teeth.

'My lady,' Clifford's tone had a hint of pleading. 'If you approach him, I am convinced he will run.'

'And we know chasing him is a waste of time... but I have an idea!' She turned and jabbed at the glass.

'Wait for me here,' she said loudly. 'I simply must have that turquoise velvet affair at the back.'

Immediately catching her drift, Clifford bowed from the shoulders and stood waiting as she went inside.

A smartly dressed assistant approached her. Eleanor explained loudly that she was English and did not speak Italian. Leading the woman to the back of the shop, she pointed to the velvet gown. Then, with the speed of a greyhound, she shot out the rear door into the street behind. Darting back in the direction she and Clifford had come, she turned into the first alleyway and sprinted up it.

At the top, she risked a quick peep into the street. The thief was still leaning with one shoulder against the wall, his back to her.

Clifford took a step closer to the gown shop doorway, nodding slightly as he called, 'Most definitely, my lady, the green gown also needs be tried on before you could possibly decide.' He nodded as if agreeing with someone in the shop.

Clifford's seen me, Ellie. Time to catch this cocky thief!

She walked stealthily forward as Clifford ambled back along the shop windows towards her, as if waiting for his mistress to reappear. But with only one shop between them, the thief seemed to have second sight. He half-turned and, on seeing her, shot across the street to the alleyway opposite.

Sprinting after him, she reached the alleyway only to run smack into someone striding out from a doorway. The impact sent her reeling to the ground. Scrambling back up, she shook herself. But before she could set off in pursuit again, Clifford's leather-gloved hand lightly touched her arm.

'Too late, my lady. He has gone.'

14

'Eleanor. Are you alright?'

She brushed her ruffled red curls from her eyes, realising the voice had come from the person she had collided with.

'Gracious! Vincenzo. It was you I bumped into. I'm so sorry.'

He looked penitent. 'It is for me to apologise. For knocking into you. And so hard your butler has needed to march after your hat. And mine also.' He gestured to Clifford a few yards away, flicking a pristine handkerchief over a fedora of rich apricot which she noted matched Vincenzo's exquisitely tailored suit perfectly. 'So clumsy of me. I stopped in this *tabacchi* for some cigarettes on my way to meet you in St Mark's Square.'

'Well, we've rendezvoused alright. Just not quite where, or how, we expected.'

He smiled, but it faded quickly. 'You are not hurt? Truly?'

'Not at all, thank you. I bounce well.' She crouched to retrieve the contents of her handbag, still scattered around her feet and beyond.

'Please allow me to assist.' He pinched the tops of his

trousers as he bobbed down.

'In that beautiful suit?' She glanced at him, thinking there was probably no colour the man couldn't pull off with consummate panache.

He let out a soft chuckle. 'It is just a spring suit.'

She sighed. 'You know, I've been simply captivated by the bolder tones Venetian gentlemen wear. Walking anywhere, one passes a positive rainbow of colours. Men's suits in England are so conservative.'

He held her gaze. She swore she could see a fire smouldering deep in his eyes. 'To be Venetian is to lead a life of passion. Never to play safe!' For a moment, she felt like a rabbit hypnotised by a snake. Then the spell was broken as he collected the remaining items and held them out to her as they both rose. 'You were not rushing to meet me, I hope? A lady is always permitted to take her time.'

She shrugged. 'No. But I wasn't engaged in a very lady-like pursuit. I was chasing the man who made me miss my original appointment with you. The one who stole my bag.'

Vincenzo's brows rose. 'You are sure it was the same man?'

'Yes. Oh, tell me, did you recognise him?'

'Recognise... him?' He turned his gaze down the alleyway. 'No. No, I did not. I am sorry.'

She fought her brow furrowing. Had that been hesitation before he'd answered? Or had he simply been trying to make sure?

His easy smile made her feel bad for doubting him.

Pull yourself together, Ellie. All the previous unsavoury business you've been mixed up in has made you jaded and over suspicious.

'Allow me to call the police for you, Lady Swift. Wealthy visitors such as yourself can be a prime target for thieves, unfortunately.'

Clifford cleared his throat quietly, having materialised

unnoticed, much like her hat, which was somehow now in her hand. 'A most generous offer, sir, if you feel it would be of use? However, on informing the policemen who attended her ladyship's suite after the break-in that nothing had been taken, it was abundantly clear it was no longer of concern to them.'

She nodded. 'And only a perfunctory note of both incidents was recorded before leaving. But you know the Venice police better than us.'

Vincenzo held up his hands. 'I do. And I know they have very limited resources, so I think to call them would achieve nothing. Now, it seems you have not had many good experiences in my city yet, Lady Swift. To correct this, may I take you to Caffè Florian for a little refreshment before we visit the Torre dell'Orologio? They are both in St Mark's Square.'

Never one to turn down the merest hint of coffee and a nibble, she nodded animatedly. 'Lovely, thank you.'

'Your Borsalino, sir,' Clifford said, holding out Vendelini's hat.

Caffè Florian was set behind billowing ivory canopies under the ornate columned arches on the right side of St Mark's Square as they approached. In front of its long run of ornately framed windows, a throng of tables were dressed in immaculate vanilla linen, gleaming glasses awaiting. Clifford glided away as a waiter welcomed Eleanor's host by name.

'If we might save the delights inside until we have time to do them full justice?' Vincenzo said to Eleanor. 'The six Florian halls are each a masterpiece in themselves.'

'Absolutely. Let's not squander that treat. I already feel as though I've woken up in a centuries-old fairy tale just sitting out here.'

'That is because Florian's has been open since 1720.'

'Remarkable.'

He waited for her to get settled, then sat himself. It didn't take long for her drink to arrive.

Served in a tall glass with a delicate frosted etching of juniper sprigs, the light ruby-red liquid danced with sparkling soda bubbles, the taste of mellow citrusy-pear wine perfectly complemented by spiced bitters. She took a second sip, her shoulders instantly relaxing.

'That is quite simply heavenly. I don't think I've tasted such a divine cocktail.'

Vendelini laughed. 'You have been in Venice for more than one afternoon without tasting our spritz? A crime! We have much to do together to ensure Venice is always calling for you to return, Eleanor.'

She felt her cheeks flush, even though there wasn't a hint of salaciousness in his demeanour. She busied herself with the sublime selection of flavoursome round toasts, or *bruschetta*, that arrived. Each was generously layered with sweet tomatoes, basil and piquant, nutty cheese, with the addition of either succulent shrimps, sumptuous grilled aubergines or heavenly smoked salmon. Coupled with the bite-sized quiches of seasoned beef or anchovy and olive, she was beginning to wish this was all Vincenzo had planned for her for that afternoon. Especially as she found him a wonderful listener as she explained how she'd fallen into her new, more settled life after one of restless adventuring. In return, he explained his love of Venice, but, she noted, very little else about himself.

After a cup of rich roast coffee accompanied by a dainty slice of what Vincenzo insisted was tiramisu, but tiramisu like she'd never tasted, she felt completely refreshed.

He stood up. 'Ready for a little climbing?'

As they crossed the ever-bustling St Mark's Square, Clifford appeared and fell into step a few paces behind her.

'Always the chaperone, it seems,' Vendelini said with a touch of amusement.

Or was it frustration, Ellie?

At the base of the Torre dell'Orologio, she glanced up at the magnificent clock tower. On her first visit to St Mark's Square, she had been too preoccupied with all the other wonders to appreciate there was so much more to it than just a clock.

Above the cobalt clock face itself, which oddly had no hands and was set between two ornate white pilasters, was a stone statue of the Virgin Mary and the baby Jesus. Standing under a columned half dome, encircled by a balcony, they were flanked on either side by a tall panel of Roman numerals, which told the actual time. A strange way around to do it, she mused. Above the Virgin Mary, a winged lion, the symbol of Venice and its patron saint, looked out on the square. And finally, on the roof were two bronze figures with hammers who struck the clock's bell.

Vincenzo broke her reverie. 'I hate to hurry you...'

She laughed. 'Not at all. I'm dying to see inside.'

The wiry man who opened the ancient wooden door under the arch doffed his hat to Vendelini and then her. He wore a buff-brown wool waistcoat over a grey shirt, sleeves rolled up to his elbows. He seemed surprisingly cool, given his trousers looked as if they had been made from the wool of a particularly long-in-the-tooth sheep. The man's face was as lined as a creased roadmap, but his pale grey-blue eyes were lively and welcoming.

'Signore, signora, as the keeper of this magnificent clock, I am delighted to open her up for you especially.'

'You mean it's never open for visits?' she said in surprise.

Vincenzo smiled. 'This is my gift to you, Lady Swift. To enjoy the best view of Venice few, except government officials and their guests, ever have the chance to see.'

'Are we permitted to go all the way to the top, then?' she said enthusiastically.

At the clock keeper's proud nodding, she noticed that her ever-respectful butler had assumed his patient stance in the corner. A plan up her sleeve, she set off up the flight of stone steps emerging into a much smaller room than she imagined. Looking around, she marvelled at the series of weighted pulleys which ran up out of sight, rising and falling without a sound.

'How amazing!' she said to the clock keeper. 'Whatever you do to keep these running so smoothly must take all day.'

He laughed. 'It is the beating heart of this masterpiece of engineering. Please climb up to see.'

She nodded eagerly, but didn't move. 'Do you know, I fear I shall have so many questions for you but be too much the blunt brick where engineering and mechanics are concerned to understand the answers.'

Vincenzo's brow furrowed momentarily. 'I had not anticipated you would find the workings of the clock so interesting, Lady Swift?'

'Neither did I until I came to Venice. But suddenly, I've developed a fascination for everything.' *Except murder, Ellie. That seems to have a fascination with you.* She smiled at the clock keeper. 'I wonder if you might be kind enough to explain the technical parts and the history of the clock to my butler, Clifford. The more detailed the better, as he's a complete egghead about such things. Then he can relay it to me in simple terms later?'

'Of course, signora. The pleasure is mine. Signor Clifford?' he called down the stone steps. Her butler appeared, his expression impassive as always, but she could see the eager animation in his eyes and that his leather pocketbook was already in his hand. The only snippet of his life he'd ever imparted to her was that he had been taken in as an orphan by a clockmaker until he was twelve. But that had cemented a lifelong infatuation in him for anything to do with timekeeping.

'I will do my best, my lady,' he said with a coded nod of gratitude.

Vincenzo pointed to the stairs. 'Then, Eleanor, let us ascend to the heavens!'

15

Rather than stone, the spiral staircase was metal. It reminded
Eleanor of the one in the library back at Henley Hall, which led
up to the galleried landing where her uncle had kept his most
precious books. This one, however, led to the clock's main mechanism, which stood over twenty feet high. To her, it was a confusing
tangle of chains, rods, wires and cogged wheels of every diameter
from a few inches to almost as tall as she was. The pulleys she'd
seen below ran down through a hole in the floor, while the staircase continued on up through another hole in the ceiling.

On the next landing, she worked out they had to be level
with the statue of the Virgin Mary on the outside. However, she
was greeted by life-sized, and extremely lifelike, statues of the
Three Wise Men and a beatific angel.

'These figures turn in procession around the balcony of the
Virgin Mary outside, above the clock face,' Vincenzo explained.
'But only on two special days; the feasts of Epiphany and
Ascension.'

'And those must be what actually tell the time?'

He nodded as she pointed to the Roman numerals she'd

noticed above the clock face, which she could now see were several feet high and set on rotating barrels.

The next landing seemed to be a museum-cum-graveyard of spare or worn-out parts and mechanisms. He waved her past them and on out of a door at the far end. As she stepped out, her eyes widened.

'Gracious, I never realised there would be such a view.'

He laughed. 'We are not finished yet.'

He nodded to a narrow staircase that spiralled up even more tightly than the first.

Having reached the top, the first thing she saw were the two muscular figures she'd noticed from below who struck the bell with their twin hammers.

'Come, see St Mark's Square as the birds do,' he called from the stone balustrade.

The view was stunning, with a panoramic vista of the rooftops of Venice on one side and the wide expanse of the lagoon in the near distance on the other. Strain as she might, she couldn't make out the contessa's island. Or, she realised gratefully, Cemetery Island. She peered down into St Mark's Square itself.

'Goodness, the crowds look like swarms of clockwork toys. And the basilica is beyond breathtaking from this angle. I hadn't appreciated how many exquisite frescos and carvings there are. Look at the realism of those enormous brass horses. And that's the Doge's Palace next along, yes?'

'Yes. From here you can not only appreciate the beauty of architecture,' his features darkened, as did his voice, 'but also the beauty of power. You see, the most powerful man of the church presides below in the square. And next to him, the most powerful man of the aristocracy. And the most powerful men in politics occupy the rest of the square in the *procuratie*.' He pointed to the myriad arches running around three sides.

'Between them all, they decide the fate of the inhabitants of Venice. And of Venice itself!'

Thrown by her host's sudden intensity, she tried to lighten the mood.

'Then the square itself must positively fizz with all that power and wealth!'

He laughed, his features and voice returning to normal. 'And commerce, as the Marcellos' Nonno would doubtless remind us if he were here. It was, and is, an important place for men of commerce to do business. Every night when I leave my office, I imagine all those who have plotted and planned for a successful venture.'

She smiled. 'I imagine some succeeded, and some didn't. Not everyone can be a winner.'

'Only if they accept defeat,' he said firmly. He shrugged. 'I am sorry. I am perhaps, again, a little too passionate, but it is how we Venetians are made. Come, let us admire the rest of the city.'

The vast ocean of terracotta roof tiles and ribbons of green water were split by the occasional squares and churches, some even bigger than the squares themselves. Looking at them, she thought even the smallest would probably qualify as a cathedral back in England.

She shook her head. 'Think of all those people down there, just getting on with their normal, everyday lives.'

He shrugged, a hard edge in his voice. 'Powerful men need someone to do their bidding, Eleanor.'

She looked up at him in surprise.

He spread his hands. 'Ah! The Italian straight way of speaking will see me in trouble with you one day before you leave, I think. Can I apologise in advance?'

She nodded with a smile, just pleased that he'd hinted he'd like to meet her again. Despite his occasional sudden mood swings, she enjoyed his company.

'But you don't need to apologise. I haven't had such a wonderful time in Venice since I first saw the Grand Canal.'

His voice turned wistful. 'I wish we had wings, Eleanor. Because I would fly you over the rooftops to the Rialto Bridge which is just over there' – he pointed in the distance – 'and on to my own personal gondola. It is the best in Venice.'

She felt her breath catch.

'Perhaps I need to apologise again?' he said, her face clearly having given her away.

She shook her head. 'No. It's just that... well...' She bit her lip. 'It felt horribly like a funeral procession when we ferried Benetto's body to the quayside in a gondola, you see. Especially as it was painted black, like hearses are in England.'

Vincenzo seemed momentarily lost for words. After a beat, he said. 'In *your* gondola? Eleanor, I thought you had seen it from a distance only? At the party, I did not want to ask because it was not the place to do so. But here we are alone. Would you mind telling me what you saw, if it will not upset you?'

She nodded. 'Of course. He was a relative of yours, if not a close one, as you said.'

She took a deep breath and recounted the tale from the point of hearing the gondolier and his passenger arguing.

Vincenzo listened intently without interruption. Once she'd finished, he was silent for a moment, tapping his finger on the top of the rail.

'Could you hear what they were arguing about?' he finally asked quietly.

She shook her head. 'We were too far away and there was too much other noise, even when we got closer.'

'I see.'

'I'm sorry I couldn't be of more help, but...' She hesitated, then made up her mind. 'I wondered if it might be to do with your two families feuding?'

He shot her such a sharp glance, she almost recoiled. 'Why do you say that?'

'Well, I know at the party you told me that you were there to show Benetto's death was just an isolated incident and nothing to do with any past hostility or rivalry. I just wondered if you might have changed your mind at all since then?'

For a moment he said nothing, then he shook his head. 'No. I'm still sure it was just that. The police have told me that the gondolier was known for his quick temper.'

'I heard that too. But you told me Benetto was a mild-mannered individual and it takes two to argue?'

'Yes. But perhaps the gondolier did not like Benetto's politics. We Italians can become very passionate about such things.'

And passion is often at the root of murder, Ellie.

He looked at his watch. She cocked her head enquiringly.

'Have I kept you too long?'

He smiled. 'Not at all. But business calls. The appointment I rearranged this morning I could only put off until late this afternoon. But I do not wish to leave you with the mood sad.'

'I'm fine. Thank you. This has been a most pleasant, and eye-opening experience.'

As they made their way back down, they found the clock keeper deep in conversation with Clifford concerning the clock's mechanism. Vincenzo waved at them to continue and turned to Eleanor.

'I really need to leave. Please don't think me rude.'

She smiled. 'Not at all. It was I, after all, who rearranged the meeting.'

'Thank you.' He set off down the stairs.

Clifford closed his pocketbook and offered his hand to the clock keeper. 'You are truly the eminence in your field, sir. And nothing less than this remarkable timepiece deserves.'

The clock keeper tutted. 'Not a bit of it. But there is nothing more I could wish for than caring for this treasure.' He sighed.

'But I do miss the old life sometimes. I used to run the clock department in Signor Friedman's antiquities shop. Such an honour. I tell you, he is the greatest expert in his field in all of Italy!'

Back in the square itself, Clifford bowed, a rare smile breaking out of him. 'My lady. Thank you, that was—'

'Nothing,' she said gently, 'compared to the treat for me to see my butler so captivated, surrounded by precisely what makes him tick. No pun intended, of course.'

A flash of closely cropped hair above a blue suit caught her eye among the milling crowd. 'Clifford! Look, it's the thief—'

He shook his head, gesturing for her to follow his leather-gloved finger. 'No, my lady, it is not. Any more than it is that gentleman admiring the basilica. Nor that one staring at... ahem.'

'At the pretty woman with the ample upstairs?' She laughed. 'You're right, if too respectful to say it out loud. I'm getting paranoid. Well, there's only one cure for that. Shopping!'

'Though you are meeting the contessa for precisely that, only tomorrow?'

'I know, silly. That's why I need a new dress to meet her in. So I can go shopping regaled in the latest Venetian *exquisita*.'

'Pyjamas, my lady,' he said enigmatically.

She stared at him in confusion. 'I can't wear pyjamas! We're going to the Lido to swim afterwards. Have you lost your senses?'

But all the way back to the hotel, he simply mimed buttoning his lips and would say nothing more.

16

How the contessa could look just as elegant in her cream silk tailored dress suit as she had in her evening gown two nights before, Eleanor found mystifying. And rather daunting. She was confident about most things, her own figure, however, wasn't one of them. After all, she'd even once been compared to a pencil!

The contessa greeted her with arms outstretched as she floated over to their arranged meeting point.

'Just look at you, Lady Swift. My dear, you have the most divine outline for Venice's finest designs this season.' Her silken tone tripped along, her irresistible Italian overtones sounding like warm honey.

'I do?' Eleanor said disbelievingly, running a hand down her slender form.

The contessa nodded. 'Absolutely! Now, here comes everybody, so let's get going. Where shopping is concerned, there is no time like the present!'

Scooped up by an eager gaggle of childish faces, Eleanor put an arm around the two nearest, ecstatic she was spending the day with them all.

'Gracious! I know I'm going to have just the best fun ever.'

'I shall alert the appropriate authorities then,' Clifford murmured as the children let out a whoop of agreement.

She laughed. 'Be off with you, you terrible man!'

He bowed respectfully before gliding away.

The tiny doll of a girl Eleanor remembered was Bella had evidently named herself spokesperson for the group. She tugged on Eleanor's hand.

'Lady Swift. We're going to teach you how to be Venetian!'

'Thank goodness.' Eleanor bent down and beckoned the ring of young faces closer. 'Because I have no idea where to even start,' she whispered. 'And do call me Eleanor, all of you.'

The contessa looked over the children's heads as if she'd misplaced something.

'I'm here, Mother,' another smooth female voice called. From inside a ladies' tailor, an equally striking but younger version of the contessa emerged. 'I was ordering a *tela aurea* gown.'

'Good for you, darling.' The contessa cupped the young woman's chin. 'You'll look even more irresistible.'

'I know, Mother.' The new arrival turned to Eleanor. 'Lady Swift, good morning. I'm Regina.'

Eleanor was surprised by her worldly confidence. She couldn't be more than twenty years old.

'Lovely to meet you, Regina. And I'm Eleanor.'

'Delighted, of course.'

'And what, by the way, is *tela aurea*?'

'Cloth made of spun gold,' Regina purred.

'Come everyone.' The contessa slid her arm into Eleanor's. 'Shopping awaits us!'

A minute later, Eleanor could barely resist clapping her hands with delight. After yesterday's events, she needed a pick-me-up. Angelo had drawn a blank. They'd met him that morning, but none of his fellow gondoliers who were at the scene of

Benetto's murder could identify the pilot of the small motor-boat. It was generally agreed that they'd all been too busy dealing with the wash from the barge. Angelo had made it clear that there was little doubt among the gondoliering community that their colleague was guilty. Even the pilot motoring away from the scene didn't strike Angelo as odd, he probably had no idea anyone had been killed. If he had then it would have been a natural response to leave as quickly as possible rather than get caught up with the police and a murder enquiry. Gondoliers were different, Angelo had explained. The canals had been their streets for hundreds of years and one of their own had been involved.

Judging by the luxuriously canopied awnings stretching ahead, all bearing a gold emblem, this had to be the most exclusive avenue of boutiques in Venice. Which accounted for the fine, tailored clothing of those who were passing by. In true keeping with the city's unique layout, however, the street was still pedestrian and little wider than their party, should they have linked arms.

Eleanor did a quick headcount, worried some of the younger children might have become separated. The fear of being lost and alone, after her parents had disappeared one terrifying night when she and they were abroad, still occasionally surprised her. Evidently this was quite a routine excursion for the children, she realised with relief, spotting that leading their party was Bella, skipping happily in front.

'Here we are.' The contessa steered Eleanor into a marble frontage, past two doormen wearing enough gold braid to pass as ships' captains.

Inside, the refined blend of cobalt and silver decor, boldly geometric-patterned wall reliefs and gleaming marble floor proclaimed that only the wealthy need enter. Plush, deep, buttoned lounge chairs peppered the scene, while crisp, cream-suited assistants tweaked the exquisite garments displayed on the elegantly posed mannequins.

To Eleanor's amazement, even the boys seemed keen on shopping.

No wonder Venetian men pull off such impeccable style, Ellie. They learn to shop as soon as they can walk!

But what delighted her most was, despite the rarefied surroundings, the contessa and the children lost none of their Venetian vivacity that she found so captivating. Evidently, one could be titled and still emphatic, expressive, even emotional. No stiff upper lip here! She wondered if she stayed in the city long enough, that her butler's unwavering aim that one day she would fit the expected mould of an English lady of the manor might fade. She sighed.

That's never going to happen, Ellie. Besides, you'd have no reason to squabble with him then.

The contessa and her eldest daughter had immediately been swamped by assistants. They obviously know them well, she thought. And know just how much they will spend. She politely waved away the one assistant who approached her, preferring to quietly peruse the garments on offer. The price tags alone would be enough to send her financially prudent butler into paroxysms of horror. The girls, however, despite their young age, had other ideas and were keen to assist their new friend, showing an uncanny knack for helping her select what suited her. Delicate weaves in fern green, summer clover, pear, and shimmering peacock were soon hanging in soft folds from her slender frame. And, she noted with approval, fluttering at her shoulders in fine feathery fronds and swishing against her calves or ankles. She felt feminine, a princess and a star of the silver screen all in one.

A blur of sumptuous silk, cashmere, velvet trims and embroidered exquisiteness later, she found herself at the counter beside the contessa.

'Excellent, my dear.' Her hostess nodded at the daunting array of boxes and packages deftly being ribbon-wrapped in Eleanor's name. 'You will be the belle of every ball!'

She nodded back, biting her lip. *Clifford will have a fit, Ellie. But those young girls were so persuasive.*

'Now,' the contessa said, having had her and her daughter's far more numerous purchases wrapped. 'We must remember beachwear for all of us.'

Before Eleanor could recover from the shock of needing to buy more outfits, the contessa waved a hand at the three counter assistants.

'Those to be charged to Lady Swift at her hotel. The rest to my account, as usual.' Two more sales assistants appeared, bearing more clothes. The contessa smiled indulgently. 'Well done, children. You've been busy choosing too, I see.'

Eleanor's resolve to look, but not buy this time, was elbowed out on entering the next boutique she was led into. Mesmerising arrays of sinfully beautiful silk scarves, leather bags and shoes beckoned her. With great fortitude, she resisted. However, there was then the matter of gloves. As they'd left the first shop, having rummaged in her handbag to check she hadn't misplaced her sunglasses for the beach later, she'd realised one of hers was missing. She must have dropped it when she'd collided with Vincenzo.

Her mind flipped back to St Mark's Square where she'd had a similar collision.

'Contessa, at your delightful party, there was a beautiful young woman. With sapphire-lilac-blue eyes. A little shorter than me. I think she was about the same sort of age as Regina?'

'Hmm.' The contessa waved an assistant away. 'Let me think. Oh, yes. That could have been Catarina, one of my second cousins. Her parents are dead. She is therefore the ward of my grandfather, Nonno.'

Eleanor's heart constricted for the young girl. She knew all too well how it felt to be orphaned and taken in as a ward.

The contessa rolled her eyes. 'You remember my Nonno?'

'Everyone's Nonno!' Regina added as she passed with a handful of scarves. 'But we don't see much of Catarina, anyway. She's not like us.'

'No, darling, she isn't,' the contessa agreed with a dismissive shrug. 'Let Nonno be her sole guide if he so wishes.'

Eleanor's lips parted. She wanted to ask more, but something inexplicable stopped her.

Could it be that after the children's innocent guileless company, these two women's comments feel a tad heartless? A tad uncharitable, Ellie? Or was it something more?

Chiding herself for growing cynical and distrustful, she opened her mouth again, the question of the young woman's name and address burning on her lips. But again, she hesitated. She'd only seen her twice, the second time as she hurried uneasily onto the launch to leave the party. And both times, she had seemed... afraid, was it? But afraid of what? Eleanor pondered. Surely not the contessa or someone in the family? That would be too awful. And surely it had nothing to do with Benetto's murder? But that didn't make sense, she'd bumped into her before that terrible business.

Her thoughts were interrupted as more wrapped purchases were ordered to be dispatched to her hotel. She briefly thought of fleeing back to England rather than face her butler. She was saved from such an extreme course of action by the beachwear she'd purchased being needed that afternoon and the contessa admitting she was shopped out for the day and lunch at the Lido was next on the agenda.

They arrived at Venice's famous Lido by the contessa's private launch, which seated all sixteen of them. Bella won the clamorous vote to sit on Eleanor's lap. The oldest three boys had taken turns standing between the pilot's arms and steering as they'd crossed the turquoise lagoon, a request Eleanor had whispered to him as they set off.

Eating al fresco was something Eleanor hadn't realised how much she had missed since her travelling years. It was, of course, possible in England, and she often did so on the terrace at Henley Hall. But you could rarely be sure, with the uncertain English weather, whether you would finish your meal where you started it. And whether your lobster thermidor might not end up in a sudden summer squall as lobster consommé.

Admittedly, much of her al fresco dining while cycling abroad had been impromptu. And far less glamorous than the near-tropical garden terrace of the Hotel des Bains, where she now sat at a table dressed fit for a royal wedding. The memory of having only desert ants for company and little, if any, food on the wilder sections of her travels struck her as at odds with the luxury she was now enjoying. The children caught her amusement and broke into giggles without knowing why. Eleanor glanced at thirteen-year-old Justina who seemed the only introspective one among them.

'What do you recommend?'

'The same as me.' Justina giggled and held up two fingers to the waiter, ordering something in such musical Italian, the words themselves sounded good enough to eat.

When the food arrived, she was amazed to see the children's portions were the same size as the adults, except for the very youngest, who still received a hearty bowlful. Her own looked wonderful, a delectable-smelling bowl of wide, coarse-ground ribbon pasta with a rich tomato and beef sauce, topped with shavings of pecorino cheese. However, she wasn't sure how to eat it without her dress also enjoying a fair amount. Bella came to her rescue, tucking her napkin into Eleanor's collar with a giggle.

'Do like us when you eat pappardelle!'

The pasta carefully consumed and her dress thankfully unblemished, Eleanor sat back, thinking a fine coffee would follow. Instead, another bowl appeared before her and everyone else; small round pasta-type balls which smelled deliciously sweet and reminiscent of Christmas, she thought.

'It is gnocchi. Made from potato and...' Justina tailed off with a frown.

'Semolina,' Regina said.

'Yes! That. With cinnamon and butter,' Justina continued. 'It's only made around the time of the Carnival.'

'And it's beyond delicious,' Eleanor said, eyes closed as she savoured the first taste. Coming to, she realised the contessa was looking at her over her gnocchi.

'You are beginning to see how life works here,' she said with a contented smile. 'It is for living and enjoying!'

Fearing life might work by her needing a quiet nap in the shade if she ate any more, Eleanor merely nodded in reply.

There was another treat to come, however, before they all descended on the beach. Changing into her beachwear, she admired how it skimmed the top of her slim thighs and hugged her trim waist. A further reminder that Italian ideas of decorum were refreshingly lenient compared to English ones. She donned her pièce de résistance purchase, a two-piece sleeveless trouser suit in swirling emerald and fern patterned silk with a matching short wraparound jacket and tie belt. The children had all insisted that she couldn't go to Pyjama Beach, as it was called, without one. *Which finally explains Clifford's oblique reference to pyjamas yesterday, Ellie.*

Feeling chic for possibly the first time in her life, Eleanor stepped out, breaking into a smile as she lunged to untangle the youngest's swimsuit ties before they strangled her.

17

The beach itself was gloriously warm under Eleanor's bare feet, the sand tickling her toes. Unexpectedly it also brought a stabbing pang for her missing parents. Her all too short life with them had been spent aboard their yacht, sailing the seas for her father's work as an advisor to developing countries striving to implement educational reforms.

The contessa, with Regina next to her, had settled into one of the luxurious loungers under the shade of a tasselled silk parasol, so Eleanor stepped over to her.

'Do you mind if I spend some time with the children?'

The contessa shrugged. 'Anything you like, my dear. They simply adore you. The Lido is for each doing just as they please. For me and Regina, that is reclining here until we leave.'

Her daughter nodded emphatically. 'I am too old to play in the sand and sea!'

But I'm not.

In a flash, she hurried back to the rather grandiose-domed kiosk beyond the steps and returned.

'Buckets?' the children chorused.

'And spades! My new young friends, will you help me make something very special?'

They all nodded eagerly. Handing a bucket and spade to each of them, she led the charge down the beach to a vacant spot where the sand was still damp.

After a brief explanation, work started in earnest. Each child filled their bucket and then upended it, Eleanor showing them how to tap the bottom to make sure the contents came out intact. A busy, fun-filled hour later, they stepped back as a group, hand in hand, to admire their sand kingdom. Replete with an almost intact fourteen-turreted castle, moat, and village, it was declared worthy of a name by Petro, the oldest of the boys.

Eleanor suddenly felt the need to wipe the corner of her eye, being careful not to get sand in it. The castle looked remarkably like the one she had made with her father on a remote island beach too many sad years ago. 'What... what shall we call it?'

'Wobbly City,' Luca, the second oldest boy giggled. 'It's not built properly, like Venice. It won't last an afternoon, let alone a thousand years!'

'Sand-izetti Land then!' Bella said.

'Ducato Marcello-Swiftali,' Petro said with a courtier's bow. 'The Duchy, I think you say in English, of Marcellos and Lady Swift.'

After a vote, it was unanimously agreed to go with Petro's suggestion.

A vast tray of gelato cones of every imaginable flavour arrived at just the right moment for them all to raise a toast to Italy's new sandy principality. Eleanor's ice cream turned out to be a sublime pistachio with salted caramel pieces.

Once she'd finished hers, she clapped her hands, smiling at the ring of expectant faces. 'Now, we've done what I chose, it's your turn. What's next?'

What was next was daring Eleanor to join them in the sea. She received a shock, however, after stepping out of her beach pyjamas and into the water with the children.

'Oh my! That is icy,' she stuttered.

'Ah!' one boy called. 'Not if we have a water fight! That will warm you up.'

The children converged on her, but she dived first, swimming between them and emerging behind them. As they turned around, she sent an arc of water over them. The next twenty minutes were passed in attack and counter-attack. Eleanor kept an eye on the smallest as everyone splashed about, trying to out-do each other with the amount of water they could drench the others in.

The children's energy was far from waning as they staggered out, soaked but gleeful.

'Next game!' Eleanor collapsed on the sand. 'Each of you needs to think what creature you'd be if you lived in the sea?'

'Is it a riddle game?' Justina asked.

'No. It's a game of sand sculptures,' she whispered, as if letting her in on the world's best kept secret.

Needing only to tame a few of their wilder fantasies, she had each of them scoop out a trough of sand, long enough to lie in, save for their head.

'Arms out to the side. Now, I need a volunteer.'

Every hand shot up, warming her heart.

Somehow, forty minutes later, she found herself also lying up to her neck in a cocoon of sand in the middle of their line of mermaids, dolphins, octopuses and crabs. The spectacle drew a small crowd of spectators, young and old alike.

'Children, we need to leave in half an hour,' the contessa called. 'And surely poor Lady Swift deserves a drink and a sit down?'

Eleanor prised herself out of the sand, thinking a long cool anything sounded delightful. As she rose, a pretty woman of about eighteen wafted past and Eleanor was reminded of the young woman from St Mark's Square. Her keepsake glass heart was still nestled safely in Eleanor's jacket pocket.

She joined her hostess and Regina on a lounger, filled with questions.

'Telephone for Contessa Contarini.' A smart hotel porter bowed to her hostess. 'It is the count, your husband, calling from Switzerland.'

The contessa turned to her daughter. 'You see. Papa never neglects me while he's away, Regina darling. Just as your husband will not, once we've seen you married. And to someone who deserves you!'

'I want to speak to Papa too,' Regina said, following her mother.

Eleanor watched them go, somehow feeling the contessa's remarks had been directed at her as much as at her daughter.

Justina, the quietest of the children, slipped away from the others who were writing their names in the sand and perched on the lounger next to her. For a moment, she said nothing. Eleanor waited, giving her time to gather courage for whatever she wanted to say.

'I heard you asking about Catarina when we were in the store,' she said finally.

She smiled at the young girl. 'It's a lovely name, isn't it? Like yours.'

Justina looked down, scuffing her foot in the sand. 'She is very pretty, isn't she?'

Eleanor nodded. 'Why yes, she is. But you are too.'

The girl looked up, her eyes shining. 'She has a sweetheart, you know. Do you have a sweetheart?'

So Catarina has a beau, Ellie? Maybe I could give the heart to him to pass on?

She nodded. 'Yes. I have a sweetheart. We're engaged to be married. His name is Hugh. He's a policeman. And a very good one, too.' She remembered the mix-up last time he'd called and winced. All her repeated efforts to telephone him back had failed, and she felt even worse that his ever-burgeoning work-load rarely allowed him to make it home.

Justina giggled. 'I bet he's handsome. Like Catarina's.' Suddenly wide-eyed, she held her finger to her lips. 'But he's a secret.'

Eleanor leaned in conspiratorially. 'That's alright. I won't spoil her fun by telling. But how do you know if he's a secret?'

'Because I got left behind playing hide and seek. In a cupboard at the villa. And I saw them holding hands and kissing through the gap in the door. Catarina heard me after she'd said goodbye to him and asked me not to say.'

Treading carefully because she didn't want to encourage Justina to break any promises, Eleanor said, 'Are you allowed to tell me his name?'

'Only you, I will. Because you're different from the other grown-ups. He's called Leonardo.'

Like half of the men in Venice, no doubt, Ellie.

'Well, it's nice he is a friend of the family. Even if Catarina wants to keep him a secret for some reason.'

Justina shook her head. 'But he isn't. I've never seen him before and we're always at Villa Isola. I don't know where he lives.'

The other children scampered over, cutting dead their conversation. But not the idea that flashed through Eleanor's mind.

Several hours later, the contessa's launch deposited her on the Grand Canal's right-hand bank, a way down from her hotel. It was still light, and she fancied the walk. She accepted her butler's waiting elbow to alight.

'Thank you all! That was too wonderful to ever forget,' she called to the children.

Clifford picked up Gladstone and waved his paw, Eleanor doing the same with Tomkins as the children squealed in delight.

As the launch disappeared out of sight and they started walking back to the hotel, she turned to him.

'What have you been up to then, Clifford?'

He shot her a sideways glance. 'Ahem! Dealing with the raft of packages which arrived a short while ago, my lady.'

She grimaced. 'Ah, yes! The thing is, I might have got a teensy bit carried away. Much to your chagrin for the household accounts, I'm sure.'

'On the contrary. Your new trunk is also waiting in your suite.'

She frowned. 'Trunk? We didn't visit any luggage shops.'

'Perhaps not. The trunk I refer to, however, I ordered after you accepted the contessa's invitation to go shopping.'

'You mean, you're not secretly fuming?'

He shook his head. 'Butlers do not fume.'

'And I wasn't just shopping.'

'Clearly, my lady,' he said drily, running a scrutinising eye over her. 'I believe, however, the penalty for pilfering the greater part of the Lido's beach by secreting it in one's hair, clothes and likely everywhere else will dent the household budget even further.'

'Good point. Then you'd best pop back there with me in your bathing whatnots and we'll return every grain. No, don't fancy that?' she added at his horrified sniff. 'Then instead, listen. There's something I really do want your help with.'

At her earnest tone, he instantly became serious. Having got his full attention, she recounted her conversation with Justina on the sunloungers.

'So we need to get the keepsake glass heart back to this Catarina girl without arousing suspicion.'

He raised an eyebrow. 'My lady, I am immediately minded of a needle and a field's worth of haystacks!'

'Don't be. We can trace Catarina's secret sweetheart and give it to him to give to her.'

He raised the other eyebrow. 'A young man named Leonardo in Venice? One of a hundred, probably, if I may be so bold.'

'A thousand, I thought. We may not know his last name or where to find him but I had a flash of inspiration earlier, and I think I might just know a person who does!'

18

Back in her hotel suite, Eleanor was itching to make a telephone call. But there was one thing she needed to do first. Seated on a settee, Gladstone cuddled into her on one side and Tomkins on the other, she addressed the terrible twosome.

'Since you can't always come everywhere with me while we're in Venice, you both deserve a...' she waved a wrapped parcel in each hand, 'a present! What do you say?'

'"Please,"' Clifford said in an amused tone. 'However, as neither menace has learned the concept of etiquette, I fear disappointment awaits, my lady.'

'Speaking of that.' She eyed him sideways. 'I've had quite the eye-opening day observing first-hand just how easy-going the Venetians can be about decorum in certain situations. So, you and I have a date with your precious rule book governing titled ladies. And you'd better bring a big red fountain pen with a strong nib for crossing things out!'

Gladstone came to Clifford's rescue by woofing impatiently as he scrambled up her front to press his wet nose eagerly against hers. It was only then she realised Tomkins had already sunk his sharp catty teeth into the corner of one parcel.

She shook her head affectionately. 'That's probably as close to "please" as I could ever ask from you two. Here you are then. One for each of you.'

Gladstone's gift of a pair of soft leather slippers clearly made everything perfect in his doggy world. Disappearing with them into Eleanor's bedroom, he cosied up in his quilted bed with his head nestled on both, eyes already fluttering into sleep by the time Eleanor peeked in. Conversely, Tomkins was in a frenzy of excitement over his present. After meeting Clifford off the contessa's launch and starting back for the hotel via a detour or two, she'd been amazed to find a shop catering purely for the indulgence of cats. The thick hessian-covered hollow roll, lined inside with fake fur, she'd chosen, was the perfect size for her tomcat to slink into. What she hadn't appreciated was the speed he could then spin around the room, still hidden inside, making the three attached tin bells ring out frenetically.

'The good thing is,' Clifford said drily, 'the discordant jangle won't become irritating at all.'

She grimaced. 'Because it already is, I know. But it's his treat. Though, I will have to make that telephone call in my bedroom now or I'll never be heard.'

It wasn't long before she returned to the sitting room, having to leap over Tomkins in his new roll as it spun towards her feet. Clifford gently halted the cat's progress for a moment.

'My lady. Having consulted the barometer, the weather looks to be changing. So you may wish to change if we are going out?'

'I will, and we are. Because I believe I've just been given our mysterious young man's full name. And where we can find him!'

He arched an appreciative brow. 'Bravo, my lady. Might one enquire how?'

'Yes, only' – she waved at Tomkins, who had started another

circuit of the room – 'let's talk in the butler's pantry so we can hear each other.'

Clifford closed the door behind him as she leaned her hip against the edge of the countertop.

'If I might confess, I am beyond intrigued, my lady. You have only been in Venice a few days, so how you found out... ah! Feminine guile was no doubt involved, I imagine?'

She tutted. 'No. Logic and reasoning, actually.' She gave a mock huff at his incredulous expression. 'Listen, Mr Sniffy, it's not only you who can whip those two out. It seems I can too on rare occasions. Clearly I've subconsciously absorbed the ability from you.'

He shuddered. 'Then before we digress into the unwelcome knowledge of what might have subconsciously been absorbed the other way...' He pointed from her forehead to his.

She laughed. 'Quite right. Let's get back to the matter in hand. Well, I worked it out after I'd been racking my brain over why Catarina, as we now know her, would hide her relationship with Leonardo from her family? I first thought maybe because he was from a humble background. But then I thought, maybe it's because he was from an equally elite one! Maybe from the very family the Marcellos have feuded with for centuries!'

'Mmm. Very Romeo and Juliet. Which, incidentally, was set not that far from here in Verona. Although, it is believed Shakespeare based the play on a work by the Italian writer, Luigi Da Porto, who lived in Vicenza, at one time part of Venice's own dominion.'

She folded her arms. 'Very interesting, Clifford. But this is real life. Not a play.'

'Indeed, my lady. And as far as we have been informed, the Vendelinis and Marcellos are not feuding, unlike the Montagues and Capulets in Shakespeare's famed play.'

'Though there seemed a lot of tension at the party.' She

flapped both hands. 'But let's not get distracted for the moment. We've no idea if Catarina has anything to do with all this. There's obviously some history between the contessa and Catarina though. Or possibly Regina. But as that's all within the same family, I can't see what it's got to do with any apparent feud between families. And certainly not Benetto's murder. All I do know is that I want to give Catarina back her keepsake. It's probably a token of Leonardo's feelings towards her, something she could carry unobtrusively in her handbag. Things like that are precious to us women. I've kept the unusual pink pebble Hugh gave me on our hideously awkward walk on Brighton cliff when we barely knew each other.'

'Heartening news, my lady,' he said gently. 'Then your telephone call was to?'

'Vincenzo. My charming and ever dapper guide to Venice. From what I was able to tell him about the elusive Leonardo, which was little more than his forename and approximate age, he suggested it might be a second cousin of his. Not that he has seen the young man in a long while, apparently.'

'Was the gentleman not curious as to why you were asking, my lady?'

'Yes. But don't worry, I didn't give away any of our two lovers' secrets.' She rolled her eyes as she stepped towards the door. 'Instead, I played along with Vincenzo's "polite observation" that Leonardo might be a little young for me.' As Clifford's lips quirked, she added, 'Although, I'm not at all sure Vincenzo was joking!'

Twenty minutes later, she looked up at her butler in confusion. Then back at the tall watchtowers on either side of the canal they were standing beside. Fluted turrets topped off an impressive arched door flanked by statues of warriors and goddesses, she guessed. And two lions, surely three times her height.

'It seems Vincenzo was having a joke at my expense. This can't be right?'

Her butler eyed her like a small child. 'Might one ask what you expected to find at somewhere named the "Venice Arsenal"?'

'Well, not King Neptune, Clifford!' She pointed at the muscular statue, sporting only a beard and a minute loincloth which she was itching to remark upon, just to make him squirm. Instead, she shrugged. 'I thought an arsenal was where governments store their munitions and... thingywhatsits.'

He bowed. 'Welcome to Venice, my lady. For this has been vastly more than that for centuries. From 1100, evidently.' His tone softened. 'A fact I happened to read in one of the engrossing new books which were delivered anonymously to my room. It was beyond gracious of a certain person.'

She smiled, delighted she'd been able to arrange the surprise for him through the hotel manager.

She stared back at the building. 'So what did they do here?'

'It was a centre of industry from the 1300s, with the ability to produce a hundred galley ships at the same time.'

Her jaw dropped. 'But they were enormous!'

'As is the arsenal.' His brow furrowed. '"That have cried shame to every ear in Venice? Ay, doubtless they have echoed o'er the arsenal. Keeping due time with every hammer's clink."'

She groaned. 'This is no time for going all poetic, Clifford.'

'Merely a few lines from Lord Byron's historical tragedy, *Marino Faliero*, to help me think, my lady. I'm sure your young Mr Kip would approve. Now, what exactly did Signor Vendelini say regarding the other young gentleman's likely whereabouts?'

She tapped her forehead, willing the conversation to replay itself. 'That Leonardo works as a junior order clerk in the... the coupling office. I just assumed it would be obvious from the way he said it. But what on earth is that?'

He gestured forward. 'Not to worry, my lady, a-hunting we shall go.'

19

Only five minutes later, Clifford stopped. 'From the significant fortifications, I would hazard this is the Venice naval base itself and thus out of bounds to civilians. The coupling office must be somewhere else.'

She bowed down to his superior sense of direction and let him lead her on. As they went, she half-listened to the long list of unfathomable items he explained were being made in the buildings they passed along the quayside of the canal. Finally, he paused.

'A particularly fine piece of engineering, isn't she?'

'That giant wooden ring on the opposite side of the water? With the... cogs or whatever on the inside?'

'Indeed. It is an old propeller shaft coupling. I believe we have arrived at the department where, I assume, they make its modern counterpart.'

'Well done, Clifford!' She wrinkled her nose. 'Only thing is, I don't want to simply march in and ask around for him because his colleagues are bound to ask what it's about. And neither of us is going to be very plausible, posing as customers for whatever do-dah coupling they're making today. I mean, it's not likely to be a common tourist souvenir, is it?'

Clifford closed his pocket watch case with a snap. 'Time may be on our side, my lady. I imagine the office clerks will finish soon, though the works themselves will continue tirelessly throughout the night. Patience is all that is required.'

Just as her limited amount of self-restraint threatened to give out altogether, a flurry of six white-shirted men in various coloured waistcoats exited a small door on one side of the factory.

'In the, ahem, no doubt, absence of a plan to identify the gentleman, my lady,' Clifford said. 'May I suggest we—'

She discreetly pointed to one man, slightly apart from the group. 'The one in the heather-coloured waistcoat.'

He raised a brow. 'On what basis have you chosen this particular gentleman to be the one we are seeking?'

'Because even here in Venice where the men dress in the most vibrant colours without censure, I haven't seen anyone wearing a waistcoat that colour. It's so specific. I think he's chosen it because it reminds him of Catarina's eyes. And with those flowing dark walnut curls, he's just the man I would have chosen if I were her.'

'Similarity to a certain chief inspector back in England notwithstanding. Please duck the other side of this stone pillar, my lady,' Clifford whispered as the group of men headed in their direction. A moment later, she frowned as they walked around Clifford, who stood in their way as if brooding over something.

What's he up to, Ellie? The one I think might be Leonardo is dawdling behind the others, seemingly lost in thought, but we'll lose him in a minute.

'Oh, signore!' Clifford called out, making her jump back out of sight. He waved a leather wallet in the air.

'You total scallywag,' she muttered, delighted he'd come up with a better ruse than simply accosting the man cold.

She heard the clerk hurrying back. 'Grazie. Così gentile.' He held his hand out. 'You are English, I am guessing? So, thank you. Too kind.'

'No problem, Leonardo,' she said, stepping out.

He nodded with a warm smile, which lit up his soft-brown eyes. But then it faltered as he seemed to take in her fiery red curls and register she'd used his name.

'Excuse me, but we have not met, I believe?'

'They are quite magical, though, aren't they?' Her words halted his polite about turn. 'Her eyes, I mean.' She pointed to his waist-coat. 'Even late in the evening... on a jetty? Perhaps at Villa Isola?'

Clifford caught her eye questioningly.

She held up a hand. 'Leonardo, we may not have met, but we both know a beautiful young woman, named—'

'Don't say it, please,' he begged, glancing around furtively. 'However much you want, I can find a way to pay you.'

She was flummoxed. 'Pay me? I'm not asking for money, Leonardo. Why would you imagine that?'

'Er... It is not important,' he said hurriedly.

She took in his deeply troubled expression. 'Oh, but it is. Because whatever made you think that, it has to do with the woman you love.' She dropped her voice to a barely audible whisper. 'Catarina Marcello.'

After a long, suspicious scrutiny of her face he nodded, closing his eyes briefly. 'I only live to be with her. But someone is trying to stop us.'

'From marrying?'

He nodded again. 'But we have told nobody and have always been very careful. Still, somebody has found out. Or maybe guessed, or you would not be here perhaps?'

She shook her head. 'Why would anyone be so opposed to

you marrying? Surely, that would be perfect given the two families have stopped their feud?' His silence made her add. 'Or
perhaps it really is only a rather fragile truce?'

He threw his hands out. 'Some of my family do not agree
with even that! Nor Catarina's either. They do not want peace.
They want war!'

Clifford cleared his throat. 'Is that why the young lady
seemed so nervous on both occasions her ladyship saw her,
signore?'

'Yes.' He turned back to Eleanor. 'You were right. I was
driving the boat away from Villa Isola the night of the party. My
love has known the pilot since she was a child. She trusts him.
He was happy to let me take his place for a little money.'

She grimaced. 'Only I nearly blew your wonderful plan of a
romantic moonlight ride by charging after her, calling and
waving. I'm so sorry.'

He smiled. 'It is for me to say sorry for speeding away,
signora. Not good manners.'

'Nor very dignified of me,' she said, warming to this demonstrative young man.

'Ever the mistress of the understatement,' Clifford
murmured before turning to Leonardo. 'Signore, who do you
believe is so against you marrying the lady?'

He shrugged. 'I wish this was easy to answer. When the
truce between our families was made, anyone against it was
straight away... disfavoured, maybe you say in English?'

'Ostracised? No longer considered part of the family?'

'Ah, yes, that is the word then. After the truce, no one dared
disagree in public with the head of the families. But in private!
That was a different matter!' He held out his hands. 'Everyone
wears a mask in Venice. Not just at Carnival time.'

*That's exactly what Catarina said the first time you met her,
Ellie.*

'You said the "head of the families"? Surely both families have separate heads?'

He nodded. 'Yes, of course. But on my side, he is no match for Catarina's Nonno. He is the lion with the biggest roar. And the sharpest claws that can reach anywhere in this city and beyond too.'

'Ah!' Her thoughts ran back to the formidable old gent she had met at the party.

Leonardo held his hands out. 'This is why I do not know who is trying to stop me and my love from marrying.'

She shook her head. 'I still don't really understand *why* someone is so intent on stopping your marriage?'

'Because,' his voice lowered further, 'it will be the first time two people from the families have done this. A Marcello marrying a Vendelini! It will be more than a... a union of hearts. It will be a physical union of the families! Afterwards, it would be much harder then for the truce to be broken and the feud to be started again.'

Eleanor frowned. 'You... you don't think Signor Benetto Vendelini's murder is connected in any way with...' At his horrified look, she held up her hand. 'No, of course not.'

He gripped his waistcoat and looked around furtively. 'I would run away with Catarina this very minute, leaving Venice, no, Italy herself, to build a new life! But that would not solve our problem. Whoever this enemy is, they would find us. And besides, however willing I may be, I cannot ask her to sacrifice her family, even though she has said she will.'

Despite feeling jaded and cynical of late, the young man's declaration was so passionate, Eleanor was sure it was genuine. She reached into her pocket.

'Leonardo, please can you give—'

A piercing scream made her freeze. Another instantly followed. She sprinted in the direction it came from, Clifford alongside. About fifty feet ahead, a woman was lying on her back on the ground, two men kneeling over her.

'Is she alright?' Eleanor called, dashing up. Three women standing nearby let loose a torrent of Italian and hand waving. All Eleanor could decipher was the woman was fine, but there was someone who needed help in the canal. Rushing over with Clifford, she stopped dead. In the water was a body, floating face down.

Without his usual protestations, Clifford grabbed the hand she thrust behind her so she could drop to her knees and lean out to reach the collar of the man's striped shirt. Gripping it, she dragged him towards the side. They were joined by three other men, two of whom jumped in the canal and helped haul the man out of the water and onto the bank.

She knelt down and, with Clifford's help, rolled the man onto his back. She gasped. The man's face told her they were too late. He was already dead. But it wasn't that which made her gasp – unfortunately, during the war she'd seen enough death for it to no longer catch her entirely unawares. It was the livid scar on his left cheek that caught her off guard.

'Clifford, it's Gaspo Secco, the gondolier who was arrested for killing Benetto!'

He nodded sombrely. 'It is indeed, my lady. One dead and one gone,' he muttered.

She looked up. 'Who's gone?'

'Our young man.'

She jumped up and scanned the area, but there was no sign of Catarina's sweetheart.

20

Visions of bodies floating face down in murky canals gave Eleanor a fitful night's sleep. She lay awake for hours, her thoughts full of fruitless fretting over the two young lovers' future and the two dead men's lack of one. At three in the morning, she declared sleep a hopeless cause and dragged herself out of bed. Throwing her woollen robe on over her pyjamas, she stumbled to the door. There she found her butler, back turned, bearing a flask of warmed milk and a plate of chocolate biscuits, his travelling chess set tucked under one arm.

By the time she slid into her seat in the small restaurant for lunch, her mind was clearer, if no less sombre. The weather seemed to mirror her mood: chillier as Clifford's barometer had predicted, with a veil of grey cloud obscuring the sun.

He ordered two of the house specials of *pasticcio di radicchio*. The tender magenta chicory leaves between soft baked pasta sheets with piquant, but not spicy, slices of sausage was exactly what her sleep-deprived stomach needed.

'Angelo's recommendation was spot on, Clifford,' she said. 'I didn't think I could eat anything, but this seems to be going down alright.'

'I am gratified to hear it, my lady. He has been most helpful.'

She wiped her mouth with the napkin as she finished another forkful. 'He was very keen on giving us a guided tour of the Jewish Quarter this afternoon. I should be up for it by then.' She rested her fork against the side of her dish. 'And speaking of Angelo, if he hadn't explained on the way here, we would never have understood why the gondolier we fished out of the canal yesterday wasn't still in jail.' She sighed. 'Poor fellow, if the police hadn't released him because of lack of evidence, he would still be alive.'

Clifford steepled his fingers. 'I agree, it is odd. They seemed quite happy with their evidence when they first incarcerated him. And, if you will forgive a contrary opinion, would he still be alive? Angelo told us that among the gondoliers who, it seems, are Venice's unofficial grapevine for spreading news, the gossip is that the police recorded a verdict of suicide by drowning. Something shored up, we're told, by the attending priest disclosing that the deceased gentleman had attended his confessional the afternoon before.'

She pursed her lips. 'Though, of course, the priest would never have divulged what the gondolier may have actually confessed to, because the seal of confession is sacred.'

'Categorically so. But the picture is clearly complete to the police. A fit of guilt, leading to a confession. But then, overcome by an even greater wave of remorse, taking his own life as the only fitting penance. And sadly, my lady, such matters are far from unheard of in jail. Therefore, the gentleman's release probably had no bearing on his fatal actions.'

She grimaced. 'Although we both feel that his suicide is too coincidental, don't we?'

Clifford peered at her over the tips of his fingers. 'Not an opinion I recall having mentioned, my lady?'

'You didn't need to. You referred to the deceased gondolier

twice as "the gentleman", something you would never have done if you believed he had a murderously guilty conscience.'

He nodded slowly. 'True. Though it pains me to articulate it, I cannot shake off the creeping certainty that his death is related to that of Signor Benetto Vendelini.'

She winced. 'It smacks all too strongly of revenge to me. A tit-for-tat killing? Another deadly step in the feud between the Marcellos and Vendelinis being brought back to life?' A shiver ran down her spine. 'Taking the score—'

'To one all,' Clifford said gravely. 'And this time, *I* will articulate what I believe we are both thinking. That it is unlikely either family will leave it at that.'

They paused in sober silence at the prospect of more murders as their dishes were cleared and coffee served.

Alone once more, he inclined his head as Eleanor sat pondering her napkin.

'What? I haven't said anything.'

He permitted himself the luxury of a quiet sigh. 'No need to, my lady. I believe you were searching for a way to sweeten the truth.'

She bit her lip. 'Which is?'

'That, whether we like it or not, we are caught up in this unsavoury matter. For the sake of seeing justice done and preventing further deaths. Not to mention for the sake of a young couple's uncertain future, which is also clearly concerning you deeply.'

'Ever the mind reader.' She stopped fiddling with her napkin, eyes glistening. 'Oh, Clifford! I lay awake most of last night thinking about them. And all I could see was myself and Hugh standing in their shoes. Feeling all the pain and heartache he and I would be going through if we thought our love could never be because of the meddling actions of another.'

He passed her a fresh handkerchief. For a moment, he

tapped the table quietly without replying. Then he nodded. 'I understand, my lady. But what can we do to help them?'

Her fists clenched. 'We have to work out who is responsible for these murders. And stop them.'

He held her gaze for a long minute. 'Remembering we are but first-time visitors to Venice and hence entirely ignorant of its ways.'

'Yes. And there's no point us going to the police because they're convinced there's nothing further to investigate, leaving us at the wrong end of an already very sticky wicket.'

'Indeed. And if Signor Vendelini and the gondolier were killed in tit-for-tat murders, it suggests by the very nature of these acts that it was not the same killer.'

She let out a long breath. 'I know. Putting both families under suspicion. Although we still have no firm evidence that Gaspo didn't kill Benetto. So maybe we do just have one killer to find. Gaspo's, if he didn't commit suicide like the police think.'

She took a sip of her coffee and bit into one of the accompanying chocolate-drizzled fruit and nut wafers.

Clifford ran a finger around the rim of his cup. 'Ideas, my lady? Thoughts, even? Straws and clutching being appropriate starting points for both from where I am seated, I hate to admit.'

'Then maybe we should change chairs!' she said forcibly. 'Because I know what to do next.' Her eyes widened. 'Clifford! I've just had the most extraordinary moment where words came out of my mouth before I'd even had the thought.'

'Not an everyday occurrence for you, my lady. But almost,' he added with a hint of his familiar teasing tone.

She laughed. 'That's better. We're not going to make any progress letting the other wallow in the doldrums. Which the person at our next port of call would understand perfectly, albeit literally.'

'Are we to play riddles the entire way?' he said, rising from his seat.

'No time. I need your flair for taming the slight rhinoceros in me, so I don't blunder into Gaspo's uncle's yard and unwittingly trample all over his grief.'

He took a moment to process what she had said. 'Ah! Bravo, my lady. Because of the particular implement used to despatch Signor Benetto Vendelini?'

'Exactly.' She slid out of her chair as he held it for her.

'Yet one more fact that convinced the police that the gondolier was guilty of the murder: his ready access to the tool used as a murder weapon through his uncle's business.'

'Exactly. And luckily, we have Angelo waiting for us. He'll know where it is.'

The bill settled, they hurried outside and started towards where Angelo was waiting at the junction with another, wider, canal. On the other side of the canal was a walled courtyard peppered with arches of scrolling grillework. As they passed the footbridge, Eleanor hesitated in calling out a greeting to the man dressed in black facing one of the arches. She caught her butler looking in the same direction.

'I know, Clifford. It's Pinsky, the Jewish doctor I met at the contessa's party. But right now, we're on a mission to...' She faltered as her eyes tuned in to the man on the opposite side of the grillework. The one Doctor Pinsky was surreptitiously handing something to. Or maybe it was the other way around. 'Look! It's the rogue who stole my bag!' she hissed.

Without needing to say a word, they both darted back to the footbridge and sped over it. But on reaching the wall of the courtyard, the doctor seemed to have melted into nowhere.

Clifford scoured each of the scrollwork arches. 'I can see from here, my lady, they have both gone. Vanished!'

An involuntary shiver took hold of her. 'Clifford, you said

almost those exact words last night. And they've just conjured
up a thought too awful to say aloud.'

'Try,' he coaxed gently.

'It didn't strike me yesterday, nor all the waking hours of last
night. But why didn't Leonardo come running with us at the
sound of those fearful screams?'

'Mmm. Perhaps the question should be, why did he run
away?'

'Exactly! When I telephoned his office this morning, they
told me he'd gone on extended leave. When I asked why, they
said it was a personal matter and they couldn't tell me when he
would be back at work.' She thought hard, desperate to hang on
to her belief in the ardent young man. 'Maybe, as a Vendelini,
he feared if he was found at the scene of Gaspo's death he
would automatically be under suspicion?'

Clifford rubbed his chin. 'Possibly. Although we had been
conversing with him for some minutes before the body was
discovered.'

She shook her head. 'Yes. But when I... saw the gondolier—'
She swallowed hard and held up a hand as Clifford opened his
mouth. 'I'm fine. And you know what I'm trying to say. The
gondolier had been dead for some time. Leonardo could have
slipped out of his office and dispatched the poor fellow and then
nipped back to his desk as if nothing had happened. And then,
rather inconveniently for him, met us as he left.'

Clifford thought for a moment. 'A possible conjecture, but
one without any supporting facts, if I might be so bold.'

She smiled weakly. 'Nice try, Clifford. But think about it.
We couldn't see there was a body in the canal until we ran up to
it. And certainly not that it was Gaspo until we pulled him out.
All we knew was that a woman screamed.'

He pursed his lips. 'So why did he run away from, rather
than to, a lady in obvious need of assistance?'

She felt her trust in Leonardo wavering. 'He's a very

passionate young man. But we've both seen how passion can burn as love. Or hate!'

Clifford nodded at a shop window across the street. 'Maybe the gentleman also wears a mask. He seems to have the heart of an ardent young lover. But beneath the mask...'

Her mouth set in a grim line. 'Maybe lies the heart of a murderer!'

21

'We have arrived,' Angelo called to Eleanor, where she was seated in the gondola's grand red velvet armchair. 'This is where you say to bring you. The *squero* of Gaspo's uncle. His building yard for the gondolas.'

'Oh!' was all she could manage. Now she realised why she hadn't been able to spot it for herself. It was far from the impressive building she had expected given the exquisitely created craft made there. Instead, a hotchpotch of five weathered wooden outbuildings bordered three sides of a patched slipway which ran down into the canal. Most of the yard looked as if it was being used for an impromptu spring clean; piles of materials, old canvas, and she had no idea what, littered the area.

Angelo deftly stopped the gondola and secured it. 'I give you this piece of advice. This man is angry. All the time. It runs in his family. I do not think he will be very happy to see you. He is never happy to see anyone!'

Stepping out, she prayed he wouldn't be too bad-tempered or preoccupied to answer the questions eating her up. With Clifford following closely behind and Angelo at her side, she headed towards the main building.

'You want me to translate?' Angelo said.

She hadn't considered that. So far, she'd only been among people with a reasonable command of English. She hesitated, not wanting to drag him into the unpleasantness that had brought her there. But what other option did she have? Clifford's imperceptible nod let her know he thought so, too.

'Actually, yes please, Angelo.'

He pointed straight ahead. 'In the workshop.'

Inside, even with the patchy clouds blotting out half the afternoon sun, the difference was as marked as day and night. She stared around in the semi-gloom, only to reel back at the fiercely flaming ball of fire that swung at her face.

'Tomaso!' Angelo called out. 'Visitatori importanti.'

The fire swished away, leaving her blinking in the aftermath of its super-heated brightness.

As her vision returned, a short, stocky man, bald except for the surprisingly still-dark tufts on either side of his head, swam into view. He held the flaming firebrand further away and peered at her.

'Good afternoon,' she said, shielding her eyes with her hands.

'Pah! English.' He flapped a muscular, chapped hand at her which she noticed was missing part of its thumb, only a scarred cleft arching into the remainder of his digit. 'You cannot order a gondola. It is forbidden.'

She shrugged. 'More's the pity. Because they are masterpieces of art, deserving of hanging in a gallery, to my mind.'

He grunted as if she was trying to teach him the moon lived in the sky. 'Naturally. They are made from my heart.'

'I can see that, Signor Secco, is it?'

'No. Tomaso!' He patted his chest emphatically, which raised a cloud of fine wood dust that floated around his head like a swarm of lace-winged moths. 'I am too busy for "signore" and polite talking.'

She groaned inwardly. *That's all very well, Ellie, but how are you going to come straight out with it and tell him you're here about his dead nephew?*

'I appreciate you're busy, Tomaso, so I'll be direct. But forgive me. You see, I am here about your... nephew. The one who...' She tailed off, not able to bring herself to articulate the unpleasant truth.

'The one who was found in the canal,' Clifford finished for her.

Tomaso's head jerked up. 'Gaspo?' Slapping Angelo hard across the chest with the back of his hand, he growled, 'Why did you bring them here?'

'Because the lady asked to come!' Angelo said equally forcefully. 'And she has only the best reasons, I think?'

He looked at Eleanor, who nodded. She hadn't actually given Angelo any idea why she'd asked to come there, but he'd obviously worked it out for himself.

'I am sorry, Tomaso. I don't want to upset you.'

He said nothing, staring up at the arched ceiling. Planks of all lengths, thicknesses and shades lay on wooden struts placed from wall to wall. Finally, he spoke.

'Little Gaspo grew into the fine gondolier his papa always wanted. But now he is gone. And before his old uncle. That is not right.'

'I don't think so either,' she said with gentle determination. 'Which is why I want to ask you some questions. May I?'

He shook his head vehemently. 'I have to get back to work.'

Angelo reached between them to take the still-burning firebrand from Tomaso's hand. 'The curving of the prow will wait a few minutes, Tomaso. Gaspo first, eh?'

Tomaso eyed her closely, then her butler. 'Come.' He beckoned them stiffly further inside.

'Mind the plethora of tripping hazards,' Clifford whispered

to her. 'To topple the gondola in progress might poke more than a spanner in the works.'

She nodded and carefully stepped around the unfinished gondola's ribbed wooden carcass set on a thirty-foot frame attached to the floor. Avoiding the heaps of cut-out wood patterns, buckets and iron brackets, she wove between the raft of ancient bench frames and a terrifyingly large-bladed saw table.

At the rear of the dimly lit space, Tomaso cranked back a makeshift shutter to let a shaft of dust-filled light in. The smell of freshly sawn timber, paint, varnish, and several other strong odours hung in the air. The walls on two sides were lined with shelves stuffed with tins, sandpaper, cloths, brushes and pails of nails. The last wall was festooned with every bladed tool she could imagine; saws, axes and myriad chisels jostling next to planes. Swinging between them all was a series of long-handled adjustable vices and a multitude of hammers and mallets.

She faltered, not knowing where to start. Before she could gather her thoughts, Tomaso suddenly spat, 'My Gaspo did not kill Benetto Vendelini!'

'Go on,' she coaxed. 'Because the police believe he did.'

The veins in his neck stood out. 'I know this. But they not know Gaspo. I am his uncle. I do! He come straight to me the minute the police open the door of his cell. He say to me he no kill Vendelini. And I believe him. As much as I believe I know how to build the finest gondolas in Venice.' Before she could reply, he continued. 'And I tell you one more thing. He no die by suicide!'

The fine hairs on her arms prickled. 'You seem very sure about that, Tomaso?'

He thumped the bench beside him, causing the tools to jangle. 'Signora, a gondolier never drowns! They spend every day on the water. And the police say he was found floating in a canal. Pah!'

'He was, yes,' she blurted out.

Tomaso's brows disappeared past any hairline he might have had. 'You know because you talk to the police about this? Then, I no talk to you!'

Clifford cleared his throat. 'Sir, Lady Swift helped pull your nephew out of the canal in the hope she could resuscitate him. Alas, it was too late.'

Tomaso's jaw fell. He spun back to her. 'You do this?' At her nod, he hesitated, his face becoming thunderous. 'Okay, signora. I tell you what I believe. Gaspo was murdered.'

She held his burning gaze. 'Why?'

He shrugged angrily. 'Because of Benetto Vendelini. I not know what exactly.' He slapped his hand over his heart. 'But I feel it here.'

'Do you think it could have been revenge by someone from the Vendelini family?'

He swallowed hard. 'A Marcello for a Vendelini? Maybe.'

Angelo threw her a cautionary look. It was time to change tack, evidently.

'Tomaso, the police think the tool that killed Benetto came—'

'From my *squero*!' he said fiercely. 'But it did not! The police think I say this only to protect Gaspo. Not true. Come, look, I show you not one of my tools is missing.'

Feeling sceptical that he would even know, given the lack of appreciable organisation in the workshop, she followed him around the back of the gondola to the far wall.

'See?' He thrust a tool into her hands. It looked like some sort of chisel with a uniquely shaped handle.

'It's incredibly sharp,' she said, noting the razor edge but none the wiser over what she was holding.

Clifford leaned respectfully over her arm. 'I believe it is a specialist wood carving tool akin to a double-bevelled gouge, my lady.'

Tomaso nodded. 'I adapt the handle myself. Like all my tools in my *squero*.' He turned his hand over and demonstrated that the handle was carved precisely to fit his partly missing thumb. Whipping a handful more tools from the wall, he showed how they, too, had been adapted.

'The one which killed Signor Vendelini wasn't like that, I'm sure,' she said, her mind flashing back to trying to haul the man's motionless form onto Angelo's gondola.

Tomaso's eyes narrowed. 'Don't be telling me you see him too! What kind of tourist are you?'

'A confused one at the moment,' she said quickly. 'But is this a common tool for all gondolier builders?'

He nodded. 'We need only three for the different...'

'Gauges?' Clifford said.

Tomaso pointed the tool at him. 'Yes!'

Eleanor swallowed down a shiver. 'But surely you told the police this?'

He threw his arms out, Eleanor shrinking back as the tool flashed by.

'Pah! They say it mean nothing. They say Gaspo stole a new one I buy before I have time to adapt it for my injury.'

'Was the tool that killed Signor Vendelini new, in your opinion?' Clifford said. 'Assuming the police showed it to you?'

Tomaso see-sawed his head. 'Yes. The blade was little used. Maybe three or four times on wood—'

'And once on a person,' Eleanor finished for him, with a shudder. 'So you think the one which killed Signor Vendelini came from another... *squero*?'

'Where else?' Tomaso said.

'What about Signor Vendelini? Was he a regular customer of Gaspo's?'

He clucked his tongue. 'He tell me never before has that man stepped in his gondola!'

She exchanged a glance with Clifford.

'Then why, Tomaso, was he arguing with a total stranger?'

He laid the tool down on the worktop and looked up at her from under his bushy brows. 'Because to a gondolier, all the canals are their streets. This is their city. A city on water. And they are proud to continue the life of their fathers and the grandfathers.' He slapped Angelo on the arm. 'I do not know him well, but I put my money that he would do the same as Gaspo did.'

'What exactly did he do?' Eleanor said.

Tomaso drew himself up. 'He stand up to that Benetto Vendelini for throwing rubbish into the canal. That is why they argue so hard.'

Angelo's jaw tightened. 'If this is the case, he is right, Lady Swift. I too would not have let anybody do this without strong words!'

She looked at him and Tomaso. 'But how strong?'

'Ah!' Tomaso shook his head sadly. 'I confess, Gaspo had a temper!'

She raised her eyebrows. *It's not hard to see where he gets it from, Ellie.*

Tomaso pointed to the other end of his workshop. 'Often I said to him, I could take his angry words and use them as the burning flame I need to bend the wood for the front of my gondolas.'

Having no more questions she could think of, she glanced at Clifford. He looked thoughtful for a moment before speaking. 'What kind of rubbish was it that Signor Vendelini threw into the canal?'

Tomaso glanced at him oddly and shrugged. 'I do not know. Gaspo just tell me rubbish. I no ask him what sort and he no say.'

'Did he say where Signor Vendelini threw this rubbish?'

'On a side canal, a few hundred feet before you turn into the Grand Canal.'

A flicker passed over Angelo's face.

He knows where he means, Ellie.

Figuring she'd ask him later, she turned back to Tomaso, who was now gesticulating at her.

'I have no more to say, I tell you! My business is gondolas. No other thing in all the world.' His face clouded as he picked up the tool again. 'Unless you find the man that kill Gaspo... and then' – he hammered the blade violently into the worktop – 'maybe there is another murder!'

22

'Poor fellow,' Eleanor said as the three of them walked back down the slipway towards Angelo's gondola. 'Even allowing for the passionate Venetian temperament, Tomaso seemed terribly upset about his nephew.'

Angelo shrugged his shoulders. 'Family means the world here. Everything we do, we do for the honour of the family.'

'That's what's worrying me most,' she murmured to Clifford. 'Just how far might the Vendelinis or the Marcellos go after this?'

'Indeed,' he muttered earnestly.

Angelo frowned. 'Why are you whispering? You no trust me?' He waved an affronted hand at Tomaso's workshop, now behind them. 'I help you in the *squero*, no?'

She nodded, but found herself still hesitating. 'You did. Although actually, Tomaso spoke enough English for me to not need a translator.'

'Which perhaps you knew all along?' Clifford said quietly.

'Of course!' Angelo replied readily. 'Many peoples in Venice speak a little English. It is no surprise because Venice was the most important centre for trade and merchants from all over the world. Then the British decided to make much of this world their own, so we speak it here like a second language. And then there are the tourists!'

'Ah.' She nodded. 'That explains it.'

'And anyway, it was not your words I knew Tomaso would not understand, but why he should talk to you at all. You are not from Venice. To him, like many other people, you have no business here but to spend your tourist money.'

Put firmly in her place, she found herself liking her gondolier all the more for his straightforward honesty.

Her butler, however, was eyeing him sternly. 'Angelo, I'll thank you to remember who you are talking to.'

He grinned. 'Oh, I not forget, Signor Clifford. She is the strangest fancy lady I ever meet! I bet you my gondola there is not another like her in all of Venice.'

Clifford nodded, a twinkle in his eye. 'A wager you would undoubtedly win hands down.'

As she and Clifford stepped back into the gondola, Angelo picked up his oar. 'So now I take you for a special tour around the Jewish Quarter as promised, yes?'

She threw Clifford an enquiring glance, receiving a nod in reply.

'Actually, no, Angelo. But I am looking forward to it,' she said genuinely. 'There's just a rather more immediate matter we need to deal with first.' She set her shoulders determinedly. 'We are going to visit every gondola yard in Venice until we find where that murder weapon came from!'

Twenty minutes later, Angelo pointed to a slipway leading to a large wooden building. 'This is the next *squero*. Good luck.'

The stocky builder she accosted more keenly than was probably wise stared back at her like a dragon about to vaporise her with his fiery breath.

'No, you cannot! This is not a museum for tourists. Get out. This is a serious business!'

'Oh, definitely. I'm sorry to have troubled you,' she said, thinking that, like Tomaso, his workshop was too disorganised for her to confirm on first sight if he had any tools missing. Throwing on her most winning smile, she turned around as if to leave, deliberately catching the hem of her skirt on the gondola's carcassing frame attached to the floor.

'Oh, clumsy me!' she cried, bending over to examine it.

Out of the corner of her eye, she caught Clifford spinning Angelo about face, their backs to her. The gondola builder let out an exasperated snort and shuffled around to her side, his footsteps slowing as he did to take in her bent-over rear view. Or so she hoped, to her shame and silent apology to women everywhere.

'Hmm, I better help you with that, signora. Or you might knock my new gondola off.'

Not with it held by foot-long braces on a frame bolted to the floor, Ellie.

'Thank you.' A moment later, she politely waved him away as she straightened up. 'Oh, but you've torn my dress! Still, never mind. I suppose that will be my souvenir from trying to find out how gondolas are made by the best boat builder in Venice.'

'Disgraceful,' Clifford murmured ten minutes later as the three of them returned to Angelo's gondola.

She shrugged. 'But effective. During his rather shamefaced tour, after he'd come to my supposed rescue and ruined my skirt in the process, he did show me he still has all his carving gouges. And vehemently confirmed none of his tools have ever gone missing.'

'I was referring to the gondola builder's behaviour, my lady. Yours, however, was too filled with feminine guile to observe comfortably.'

'Then keep looking the other way, my chivalrous knight. Because there are lives at stake. And a young woman's love, remember?' She bit down her worries over Leonardo. 'And to get to the truth, I'll relinquish a little decorum if I need to.'

He eyed her sideways. 'Assuming any such actually made it into your travelling trunks?'

'Well, I did not think the day would get so interesting!' Angelo chuckled, pushing his gondola off with one foot. She took her seat, hoping a different approach would work in their next port of call.

It didn't. In fact, it didn't at their next three stops. As the day wore on, Clifford's face became redder and redder. And Angelo's more amused. Eleanor just wondered how many more times she could catch her dress before it was beyond even her housekeeper's expert repair skills.

Angelo broke into her thoughts. 'Not far now to the last *squero* on the main island. But for this, we must go via the Grand Canal. I have been avoiding it because there are too many barges now. It is only three days until the Carnival starts and they bring the extra deliveries for the private parties.'

She shrugged. 'Whatever way is quickest.' Remembering his admonishment, the first day she'd met him, about everyone always wanting to go faster, she raised an apologetic hand. 'Or the most scenic. So long as we get there before the place closes, you choose.'

He nodded gratefully. 'Then we will go as quickly as possible, but via some of the wonderful sights you have yet to see, Lady Swift.'

'Goodness, that's a strange bridge,' she said a few moments later as they turned off the Grand Canal and glided down yet one more enchanting waterway. 'None of the others have been enclosed. It's even got windows with bars on them.'

'Unusual, but of no import,' Clifford said quickly.

She sat straighter. 'I'll only ask Angelo when you're not listening, Clifford, so what is it? You clearly know.'

He nodded reluctantly. 'In the inimitable words of Lord Byron's Childe Harold, "I stood in Venice, on the Bridge of Sighs, a palace and a prison on each hand."'

'Bridge of Sighs? What's wrong with that? It sounds very romantic.'

'Indeed. Lord Byron thought so too and immortalised it in verse. However, it was actually named so because those crossing the bridge were being escorted from the interrogation rooms of the Doge's Palace to prison, whence few ever returned. Thus, the view from those barred windows was, for many, their last views of Venice and their freedom.'

She shivered. 'Angelo, tell me we're really nearly there, please?'

He shook his head. 'I cannot, Lady Swift, because we have arrived.'

The last *squero* turned out to be a larger, more sprawling affair than the others. And manned solely by a youth of about sixteen.

His stammering Italian she answered with a smile and a pleading glance to Angelo, who fired a couple of rapid questions off at the boy.

'He say that the *squerariolo* and his other assistants have gone to test the new gondola. Always the builder does this before the customer tries it. This is the youngest apprentice who has stayed behind to clean the tools.'

'Ah,' she said. 'Then please let him know I'd like to watch him at work for a moment out of touristic curiosity.'

Angelo's request, however, was met by fervent headshaking.

'For a suitable tip, of course,' Clifford said.

The clink of coins into the young lad's hands did the trick as he led them inside, chattering away to Angelo.

But it was all in vain.

'Dash it!' she groaned a while later at the bottom of the slip-way, throwing the young lad another thank you wave over her shoulder. 'All tools were present and correct.'

Clifford see-sawed his head. 'Perhaps, my lady. Perhaps not.' He hesitated. 'At the risk of sounding hypocritical and suggesting more feminine guile...'

A moment later, he was explaining to the confused young lad why they'd returned to the yard. 'Naturally, Lady Swift wishes to, er, repair her dress in private. So, would you kindly stand guard with our gondolier' – he pointed at Angelo – 'in front of the wood store until she is finished?'

Angelo translated, then clapped the young lad amicably on the shoulder. 'Signore inglesi! Sempre così timido, eh?'

As they left the yard for a second time, Eleanor turned to Clifford. 'Well, my scallywag butler, what was that indecorous charade you forced me into all about?'

'Apologies, my lady, but on reflection, something about the largest of the last three tools the young man showed us struck me as odd, hence my surreptitious return for a closer look. I am now sure it is not from the same set as the other two. That is evident in the different wood of the handle. Neither has the blade seen an ounce of usage.'

She thought for a moment. 'And it is definitely the same type of tool that killed Benetto?'

'Absolutely.'

She frowned. 'Tomaso swore he believed Gaspo when he said Benetto had never taken his gondola before. Unless he was lying, it seems whoever was in the other boat that collided with Gaspo's took the original tool from here, with the express purpose of murdering Benetto and throwing suspicion on the poor unfortunate gondolier whose passenger he was.'

Both Clifford and Angelo nodded their heads in sombre agreement.

She bit her lip. 'It might have just been a lucky coincidence for the killer that Gaspo was related to the Marcellos. And a terribly unlucky one for Gaspo.' She drummed her fingers on the side of the gondola until she caught another disapproving look. 'Tell me, Angelo. Who owns that yard?'

Angelo frowned. 'Traditionally, all the *squero* are independently owned. But like I say, the people start buying motorboats, so now every year, there are less and less gondolas... and gondoliers! This also means less work for *squeros*. Some have closed altogether. Others have had to sell to other businesses. This one is owned by the Rialto Company, I think.'

'And who owns the Rialto Company?'

'I do not know exactly, but I think it is a member of the Marcello family.'

Eleanor exchanged a look with Clifford. 'Well, there's only one thing to do next. Angelo, we need to go diving!'

23

Daybreak in Venice was undeniably mesmerising. And they had the city to themselves, as Angelo had promised when he'd insisted on such a horribly early start. Lilac, lavender and wisteria bands of cloud streaked the sky, the crisp cool air smelling like freshly salted dew and somehow tinged with the optimism of a new day. Full of life-imbuing coffee, Eleanor sat listening to two lithe and muscular young Venetian men deep in what, to their minds, was probably a whispered discussion with Angelo on the quayside. To her it sounded like a fierce argument. Her decorous English butler obviously felt their navy swimsuits were insufficient, being a form-fitting sleeveless vest sewn to the waistband of a pair of skimpy and equally body-hugging shorts.

'Seeing a man's knees is not going to compromise my virtue, for heaven's sake, Clifford!'

She took the sunglasses he was holding out and shoved them pointedly into her cardigan pocket. 'And I can't sit here in Angelo's gondola being a prim princess who won't lift a finger to help. Those chaps are only up and dressed at this unspeakably early hour at my request.'

His lips pursed. 'If that is "dressed", I shudder to think what constitutes undressed!'

Cuddled in her lap, Gladstone let out a contented woof. Still wrapped in his cosy dog bed comforter he had refused to give up, he looked hilariously incongruous with the sporty pair now slapping their taut thighs awake. Her ginger tomcat stretched leisurely in his open kitty kit bag, twitching his tail cheekily up her butler's nose.

'And that is helpful how, Master Tomkins?' Clifford gently tweaked the cat's ears while calling softly to Angelo. 'Since it appears the tone of this endeavour has reached rock bottom, perhaps the two gentlemen might be ready to follow suit by starting their dive?'

Eleanor dangled her hand over the side, hoping the water wouldn't be too cold for them.

'Gracious, it's positively freezing. How deep is it, Angelo?'

'Maybe a foot or so taller than my friends,' he said nonchalantly. 'But don't worry. This is not the first time for them. It is quite common for people to drop things in the canal. You would be amazed what they have been asked to pull out before! And it is near low tide.'

At her surprised look, Clifford nodded.

'The majority of the Venetian canals are tidal to one degree or another, my lady.'

'Well, maybe that will help, then. And we are sure this is the spot where Benetto threw whatever it was from Gaspo's gondola?'

Angelo shrugged. 'It is the correct side canal. We know this because we all saw Gaspo turn out onto the Grand Canal from here. And a good point to start, I think, because of the loudness of the men's argument when they reached us. Signor Clifford thinks so too.'

'Fingers crossed then.' Despite being a competent swimmer herself, she still blanched as the two men jumped in. She nodded a moment later as they hung their water-beaded arms over the side of the gondola. 'Thank you, gentlemen. I'm very grateful for your assistance.'

'No problem,' one of the pair said with a grin. 'If Angelo say he want to help a pretty lady, we no argue.'

His companion reached over to slap Angelo's leg. 'What is it we look for?'

'I don't know.'

All eyes turned to Eleanor. 'Ah, well, that's the thing.' She held up her hands. 'I have no idea either.'

Thankfully, the swimmers didn't seem fazed. 'Then we bring to you everything we find, I guess?'

Desperately hoping that wasn't another dead body, or worse, part of one, she nodded. 'Is there lots of weed, though? Because that will make it harder.'

'No. The bottom of the canals is clay,' Angelo answered for them. 'With, I think...' He tailed off, scratching his head.

'Sediment?' Clifford said. 'A layer of silt deposits?'

'Like fine mud, yes. But until they start the search, we do not know how much. And, in any case, whatever was thrown in may have floated away by now. Or been swept along by the boats passing over.'

With a signal from Angelo, the two swimmers disappeared below the water.

While they waited, Clifford wrote in his slim leather pocketbook, which slid further up his leg with every swipe Tomkins batted at the silk ribbon page marker. With Gladstone leaning against her legs, Eleanor shuffled into the opposite seat, needing a distraction for her impatience.

'What are you working out, Mr Egghead?'

'Not the dimensions of my cranium,' he said drily, without looking up.

'Shame. Tomkins and I could have helped with that.'

He looked up from his jottings. 'I am actually working out

the possible distance the item might have moved due to the current from the Grand Canal and the disturbance caused by motorboats passing. Of course, not knowing the mass of the object, or where exactly it was dropped, skews the calculations. But I can only work with what I have, my lady.'

One of the swimmers appeared at the stern of the gondola to report the sediment was patchy and not too thick before diving again.

Disappointed his news hadn't been that they'd discovered something already, Eleanor tried to settle in her seat, fighting the urge to jump in herself. Her restless mind turned to Hugh. Was he at a crime scene just like this one right now? Maybe fearing the next thing the police divers *would* dredge up would be a body? Her heart ached that she still hadn't been able to reach him by telephone.

Twenty minutes or so later, the section around the gondola was declared to have been scoured and nothing found. Angelo stepped off and pulled his boat further along to another set of mooring posts with the ease of silk sliding over polished glass. The swimmers dived again.

The same disheartening tale, however, played out for another twenty minutes. And then another.

'Oh dear, Venice is starting to wake up,' she said, as a gondola glided past, just missing one of the swimmers who was bobbing on the surface, taking a quick rest.

Then she caught a gurgled cheer of triumph behind her. The other swimmer had resurfaced and was waving something above his head as he struck out one-armed to reach the side where she was sitting.

'What have you got?'

'Is a small woman's bag,' he panted. 'You think this is it?'

She stared at it for a second. 'I can't imagine what Benetto would be doing with a bag. Can you, Clifford?'

'Not off the cuff, as it were, my lady.'

'Anything inside?' Angelo said, hurrying over.

She twisted the metal clasp, which opened easily. 'Empty. And it hasn't got a loose lining for anything to be hidden in.'

'Stolen by a pickpocket and thrown in after emptying the contents.' Angelo waved at the swimmers. 'Keep going, my friends. Maybe there is something else.'

Twenty minutes later, the increase in passing pedestrians and gondolas was making Eleanor uneasy. A priest in flowing black robes halted to wave his prayer book ceremoniously over the water around them. As he walked away, one of the swimmers bobbed up, an item held in one hand.

'A small rudimentary camera, my lady,' Clifford said on examining it, his interest piqued more this time. 'Of amateur construction, I believe. And with no photographic plate behind the lens.'

Angelo shrugged. 'How is that useful to anything?'

'I'm not sure,' she said, trying to keep the glumness from her tone for the sake of her volunteers. She turned to the swimmers. 'You've done a wonderful job, but we should stop before you catch cold.'

'But we have not found what you want, I think?' one of them said.

The other nodded. 'We warm up quickly. Then we try the last section.'

'Sounds like a job for a hot Thermos flask, Butters,' a familiar voice called cheekily.

Clifford pinched the bridge of his nose as Eleanor's four ladies scurried forward, Polly almost ending up in the gondola as she tripped over her feet.

'Hello,' the swimmers chorused, obviously enjoying the appreciative wide-eyed looks they were being given in their wet, figure-hugging bathing suits.

'Ahem, ladies.' Clifford rose, collected Tomkins, and stepped out of the gondola.

Eleanor helped the scrabbling Gladstone up and out and then followed herself. On the quay, Clifford gestured for them to turn away from the swimmers, which wasn't easy given the exuberant welcome her bulldog and the cat were treating the ladies to.

Eleanor's cook tutted. 'Sorry, Mr Clifford. But you insisted as you wanted to see us all several times a day to make sure we hadn't got lost.'

'I believe I said to ensure you were behaving yourselves,' he said firmly.

'Ach, we are that, Mr Clifford,' Lizzie replied over the other three's stifled giggles, sneaking a quick peek at the swimmers.

Clifford pursed his lips. 'Hmm, perhaps I will be the judge of that. However, later, ladies. As you can see, her ladyship is currently too occupied to be descended upon by her band of mischievous elves.'

'Mischievous, us?' Mrs Trotman protested innocently, giving herself away by bumping hips with her friend. 'Well, how about that, Butters? After all, we only thought to bring her ladyship, and those what are helping, a little breakfast.'

Clearly outnumbered, Clifford gave in with good grace. 'Very well. Gentlemen!' he called to the swimmers. 'Though an encompassingly suitable wrapping of any nature would be appreciated while breakfast is served.'

As ever, her ladies had done their best to produce a marvellous impromptu spread, even if their motive had been an ulterior one. And still was, Eleanor noted, trying to hide her smile at their obvious fussing and cooing over the two swimmers.

'Can't have the gentlemen sinking to the bottom of the canal from lack of sustenance.' She caught Mrs Trotman's gleeful whisper as she topped up their coffee. Angelo laughed into his ham and cheese roll, evidently having heard it too.

Gladstone and Tomkins delighted in the raft of titbits from

everyone, and all too soon, the wicker breakfast basket was emptied.

'Not wishing to play killjoy, my lady' – Clifford shut his pocket watch with a snap – 'but time is moving on at a prohibitive rate.'

He's right, Ellie. Venice is waking up.

She nodded and turned to the swimmers. 'You're sure you want to try the last section?'

In reply, they whirled out of their wrappings, threw them over Clifford's horrified arm, and dived back in. Eleanor gathered her ladies quickly.

'Thank you all. I'm sorry, but it is best you leave now. We're trying to be quiet about what we're doing.'

Polly jiggled on her willowy legs, the sign she was waiting for Clifford's permission to speak up in front of the mistress. Receiving his nod, she leaned forward and whispered, 'Don't worry, your ladyship. We won't tell a soul as you'll be swimming with the undressed gentlemen.'

Back in the gondola, Eleanor could see Clifford was ruminating on Polly's remark.

'Are you going to share or do I have to play twenty questions?' she said, settling Gladstone and Tomkins beside her.

'I was merely thinking this debacle of decorum is actually something of an improvement, my lady. The determined nine-year-old who came to Henley Hall as his lordship's niece and ward, and who grew into a fiercely independent young lady, would have indeed been the first to dive in not long ago.'

She groaned. 'That makes me sound old. And sensible!'

'I said "an improvement", not a miracle, my lady.'

They both jerked straighter at a whistle which came from a few yards further along the canal.

'They've found something else. Quick!' She leaped out and ran down the quayside, with Clifford in more dignified pursuit.

She bent down as the swimmers reached the quay. 'What have you found this time?'

'You tell us. When you undo this.'

She looked down as they dropped a soaking wet parcel into her hands. She shook her head.

'Well, whatever it is, we've run out of time. Let's hope we haven't just dredged up a load of rubbish, but the answer to Benetto's murder too!'

24

The entire population of Venice seemed to be charging out of every door and leaping in gondolas as if the last one in line would get stuck with the collective bill. Everyday life had begun in earnest in a mere blink, albeit with that inherent vibrancy and kaleidoscope of colour that Eleanor was convinced made this city unique.

Right now, however, standing beside Angelo's gondola with a baffling puzzle on her hands, that energetic hurly-burly felt like a conspiracy to hinder her next move. Not that she was at all clear on what that should be, save for finding a discreet spot to examine the items recovered from the canal.

'I've no idea how we can be sure which, if any, of them is the one Benetto dumped,' she groaned quietly to Tomkins and Gladstone.

Further along the quayside, Clifford was furnishing Angelo and the delighted swimmers with a thank you from his wallet on her behalf. That done, he turned to her, the black soft cloth bag he'd optimistically brought along blending inconspicuously with his suit jacket.

'And now, my lady?'

'And now' was another recommendation from Angelo. A discreet café on the fringe of the Jewish Quarter, with a quaint galleried upstairs. They were the only people there except for the waiter, who supplied them with some very welcome coffee and then disappeared back down the dog-leg stairs. Gladstone and Tomkins shared the cushioned bench seat beside her.

After a sip of coffee, Clifford undid the drawstring closure on the cloth bag and held it open for her. They shared a look.

She winced, reaching inside. 'I know. This is one of the most perplexing puzzles we've been caught up in.' Her hand fell on the woman's handbag first. They both examined the two interior compartments under the light of Clifford's pocket torch. 'An empty dress purse, as we knew. Hang on, though!' She delved to the bottom and peeled a soggy scrap of paper from the lining. 'A... museum entrance ticket?'

Clifford peered at it through his pince-nez. 'Hmm. It is dated yesterday, which suggests it has not been in the canal long enough to be the item we are looking for. And as it is free from ladies' paraphernalia—'

She rolled her eyes. 'Paraphernalia, indeed! Says the man, the contents of whose pockets would astound a world-class magician!' She reached into the black cloth bag again. This time, she pulled out the camera.

'No film plate,' she remembered as Clifford bent over the open casing, his torch inching over the minimal workings.

'And no chance a photograph of any useful nature has been taken with it either, my lady. An early amateur project, I would venture, as I remarked before.' He gestured with his pince-nez as he continued. 'However, this small gnarled wheel should release this copper flap so it can act as the shutter, but due to heavy corrosion, the flap is immovably stuck. Given that Venice's canals are only part saltwater and part freshwater, this level of corrosion would have taken months to form.'

'Well then, that leaves option three,' she said, trying to

sound more positive than she felt as she reached into the bag for the final item.

Let it be what we're looking for, Ellie, although I have no idea how it could relate to Benetto's murder, whatever it is. Her mind flashed back to finding something very different in the water not long ago. She grimaced. Leonardo's inexplicable disappearance when they had found Gaspo's body floating in the canal still had to be explained. She rolled her shoulders back and reached for the miniature fold-out scissors on Clifford's pocketknife, which he was holding out of her reach.

He bobbed an apologetic head. 'On second thoughts, perhaps the contents might not be the stuff of restful dreams, my lady?'

'Oh, goodness. Something grisly, you mean?' She shivered. 'I don't want you exposed to that either, then.'

But he was already snipping at the parcel's strings, his back turned just enough to obscure her view.

'Hmm,' he muttered a moment later.

'Hmm? Body part or... or not?'

'Not. A glass figurine.' He placed the clear statue threaded with two contrasting colours still lying on its bed of wrappings on the table between them.

Her breath caught. 'Clifford, that first layer of whatever this packing material is, is the same stuff I picked off Benetto's body! I thought it was just rubbish from the canal.'

He frowned. 'Indeed. One can assume, therefore, that this is the object we were seeking.'

He lifted the figurine up carefully and turned it slowly back and forth for her to see. It was of a man who was clearly of importance, given his commanding features and the determined line of his jaw. One arm was held out as if about to shake hands.

She stared at it in silence for a moment, then sighed. 'Clifford, why am I not as elated as I want to be at finding what Benetto dumped?'

'Because we do not know if it had anything to do with his death?'

She nodded. 'Is it very old, perhaps? Or made of special glass, maybe? Or valuable?'

'I am unable to say.' He drummed his fingers silently on the tabletop. 'If we were at home in Henley Hall, I would have the perfect contact for us to visit. But, regrettably, here...' He shook his head.

She slapped the table. 'But here you do, too! The greatest expert in all of Italy. Thank heavens you truly are an egghead.' Jumping up from the table, she headed for the door.

With Gladstone gambolling on ahead, they made their way to St Mark's Square and the Torre dell'Orologio. Having secured the address from the clock keeper, they set off, ironically back towards the Jewish Quarter.

After some searching, they arrived outside a high arched oak door, a detailed galleon carved in deep relief in the centre. Surrounding it were other intricate carvings. She pointed at it.

'This door should be in a museum, Clifford.'

As she reached for the lion-head iron knocker, she froze. It felt as if a spider were crawling up her back, its hairy legs tickling her skin.

Get a grip, Ellie. This paranoia has to stop. There's no one behind y—

'What fate then for what rests inside?' a tremulous voice said.

Eleanor spun around. An exceptionally tall man with a square-cut grey beard and a pronounced stoop held her gaze intently. Dressed in a dark-brown suit, shoes, shirt and almost brimless hat, he folded his long pale fingers across his jacket front and blinked slowly behind his polished brass-framed spectacles.

She gulped, forcing a smile. 'A good question, I'm sure. Err, Signor Friedman, are you, by any chance?'

He shook his head. 'Not by any chance, young lady, no.'

About to reach for the door knocker again, she caught Clifford's brow flinch.

'In that case, sir,' he said, 'perhaps you might offer an expert opinion on an artefact?'

'No. There is no question of that.'

Eleanor's brows threatened to become one. 'The gentleman in St Mark's clock tower said—'

'As I suspected.' The man's face broke into a warm smile. 'My excellent friend sent you.' He laughed, his eyes dancing with animation. 'Forgive my terrible sense of humour. It is the intricacy of the English language which still fascinates and amuses me. I was fortunate enough to study in London for two years, many moons ago, as a curious and eager young man, you see. So, yes, I am indeed Signor Friedman, but by descent, not chance. And there is no question of my offering an expert opinion. I will. Come, please.'

From his trouser pocket, he pulled out a long black key that Eleanor thought looked formidable enough to be the one to unlock Venice's city gates, if it had any. Pausing to cup Tomkins' face at his kitty kit bag window, Friedman slipped the strap from Clifford's shoulder and added, 'Let me bring this fine velvet feline in for you.'

Gladstone's indignant woof followed him over the threshold.

'Goodness,' Eleanor breathed, glancing around at the hexagonal expanse of marquetry floor and deep, walnut-panelled walls and ceiling. Ancient ceramics, richly decorated caskets, pewter jewellery, sections of primitive stone carvings, clay amphoras and an impressive array of medieval-looking helmets lined the shelves. A series of six archways led off towards more tantalising realms of antiquarian wonder. A large circular table with golden, eagle-clawed feet presided over the centre of the main room. Above, a vast glass globe containing a ring of flaming oil wicks lit the windowless space with a flickering glow.

'In here,' their host called from off to their right.

Following the wafts of centuries-old leather, wood polish and varnish, she stepped into the next chamber, which was filled with foot-thick reference tomes and framed parchment manuscripts, scrolled in rust-brown inked script. Through the next archway she could see a restoration workspace, peppered with jars of yellowy liquids, brushes, large-handled tin cans and several small paint-speckled tables. An enormous painting of what she recognised as Venice's Grand Arsenal, with a galleon's masts billowing in the wind, overhung a three-legged easel in front of a hessian-seated stool. Beside it, Friedman was bending over a book-covered desk, rubbing noses with Tomkins.

He straightened up at the sound of her footsteps on the wood flooring and selected a second pair of spectacles from a basket overflowing with others. 'Now, what is it you wish to show me, my dear young lady?'

Clifford held the black cloth bag open for her.

'Honestly, I don't know. Except that it is a figurine. A glass one.'

She reached inside for the parcel Clifford's meticulous hand had rewrapped, just as it had been found, and laid it gently on his desk.

'Venice is renowned for glass artefacts of the finest quality,' Friedman said. 'Our glassmakers' guild is almost one thousand years old!'

She felt a frisson of anticipation as she deferred to her butler's respectful cough that he untie the strings. 'Then maybe this is very old too? Or valuable?'

Friedman arranged his extra spectacles over the first pair with the precision of a surgeon setting out his life-saving scalpels. Clifford stepped back, holding Tomkins clear of any chance they might soon be standing among shattered glass.

As Friedman shuffled forward, Eleanor couldn't help craning her neck so she could see his expression on seeing the figurine for the first time. She hoped for a look of awe, or at least interest. And for a moment, she thought she saw something in his gaze as his eyes widened. But just as quickly, the light in them faded. He picked the item up and turned it around a few times before replacing it on the table, while shaking his head.

'I am sorry to offer disappointment. But this is neither aged nor of monetary value. It is nothing more than a piece of rather mundane Murano glass.'

'You're absolutely sure?'

His face loomed into hers. 'After forty years in my profession, I believe you can trust my assessment.'

'Of course,' she murmured. 'I didn't mean to seem rude.'

As Clifford rewrapped the figurine, Professor Freidman tutted. 'My dear young woman, I would never have suspected anything of the kind.' He led the way back out through the library-like chamber. 'Venice's greatest marvels line every side of every canal; her architecture. Perhaps they might offer you a less disappointing focus of interest.' He gestured up the steps with the slow farewell nod of a scholarly tortoise.

Outside in the street once more, she turned to Clifford.

'Where do we go from here?'

He rubbed his chin. 'I must confess, my lady. I have no idea.'

25

Clifford's efforts to distract Eleanor from her disappointment had left him profusely apologetic. He followed her up the short flight of steps to her hotel. 'A poor suggestion, my lady. Forgive me.'

She paused to turn and flap a hand at him. 'Don't be daft, Clifford. Looking for our sketcher again en route was a very kind-hearted idea of yours. If I'd managed to pay him the extra money for that second sketch he included, the morning wouldn't feel such a disheartening washout.' She cursed her runaway tongue. 'What I meant was—'

'Precisely what you said, my lady. I know. However, your four disreputable ladies will be gathering shortly, as arranged. Their company seems to lift your spirits, for some unaccountable reason.'

She laughed. 'It does. And along with my butler's tireless razor wit, tales of their mischievous antics will definitely restore my spirits.'

As she entered the hotel and thanked the doorman, the sight of the manager bustling behind the reception desk gave her an idea.

'Good day, Lady Swift,' he said cautiously. 'More complaints today?'

Thinking that was a bit rich after she hadn't blamed him for lax security when her room was broken into, she spotted Clifford's stern gaze.

Ah! He has clearly done a thorough job of it on your behalf, Ellie.

She shook her head in reply. 'Signor, I want to ask about the street artist who left a wrapped package for me. At the time, did he perhaps say...' She winced, remembering the poor chap was a deaf mute. 'Did he, perhaps, leave a message for me?'

The manager's bottom lip pouted. 'Messages are always taken very carefully,' he said in a defensive tone. 'There was none.'

'I see. Do you know if he moves around Venice?'

'When most of the tourists visit only the same few things? No, Lady Swift, always he sits in the usual three places; the Rialto Bridge, St Mark's Square, and along here to paint the Grand Canal joining the lagoon.'

'Which are the places where I've looked. Gracious, I hope he isn't unwell.' She pictured the many obviously unsold pictures she'd seen him pack up one evening. 'It seems a rather hit and miss livelihood.'

The manager shook his head. 'He did not seem ill. More... how do you say in English? Ah! Agitated, I think.'

'Ahem.' Clifford gave her a pointed look. 'Perhaps a restorative before luncheon?'

She nodded. 'Alright, you read my mind again.' She sighed. 'I think I'm becoming a worrywart, you know.'

She was soon ensconced in a winged-back chair in her suite with Tomkins curled around her neck, Gladstone sprawled across her lap and a delectable glass of amber grappa shimmering in her hand. As soon as Clifford had left to store the cloth bag with their seemingly uselessly retrieved items, she pulled out the two sketches and examined them carefully.

A minute later, she jumped. 'Agh! You frightened the wits out of me, Clifford. I didn't hear you return.'

'Sincere apologies.' He eyed her sideways. 'Scouring these secretly, however, is unlikely to soothe the lady's nerves.'

She tutted. 'Which is why I was trying to do it without you seeing me.' She shrugged. 'Alright, I confess, I hoped they might help me work out where I could find our sketcher.'

'"We",' he said in a kindly tone. 'If you feel so strongly over the gentleman's welfare, our collective thoughts might better succeed. If you will forgive my overstepping?'

She smiled gratefully. 'Please do. You can start by being my voice of reason. Staring at this second sketch, I've had the strangest feeling now that he didn't give me this by accident. Nor in the hope I'd order more from him, given that it is rather poorly done compared to the other.'

His brows knitted. 'Go on...'

'You'll think it ridiculous, I know. But I've been pondering if it might also give us a clue as to *why* he's disappeared?'

'For which there are many simple possibilities. However, let us see.'

They lapsed into thoughtful silence as they studied the second sketch, Clifford repeatedly removing his pince-nez with a blink and returning them to his long, distinguished nose.

'It really does appear to be simply the view across from here, my lady. Showing the small, modest hotel centrally opposite. Nothing, however, seems out of the ordinary in any of the picture's composition.'

She thought for a moment. 'What about showing the ladies the sketches? I'd love their suggestions as to where we hang them back at Henley Hall anyway.'

That agreed, fifteen minutes later, she stepped out of her bedroom in a sage cashmere dress with a pleated drop-waisted skirt. She'd bought it, among many other delights, while shopping with the contessa and her children. With the matching cardigan jacket, her ensemble felt right, given the cooler air the midday clouds had heralded.

Opposite the appointed café, the sight of her ladies dancing and kicking their heels up to the wheezy strains of a concertina being played by a good-looking street musician made her smile. And Clifford sigh in despair.

'Oh please, pretend you haven't seen them,' she pleaded, trying to quiet her excited bulldog, who'd started barking on spotting them. 'Other people are dancing too. They're only joining in.'

He turned his back hurriedly. 'With far greater gusto and ahem, anatomical revelations I, or anyone else, should ever have to observe.'

She laughed. 'Let's hope he doesn't know "Knees Up Mother Brown" then. Now, let's sneak into the café so they don't realise we saw them.'

Inside, Eleanor smiled as her staff trooped in a short while later and curtseyed behind their seats, Gladstone's excited woofing setting Tomkins off with equally exuberant meows.

'You all look very rosy-cheeked, ladies,' she said.

'Very,' Clifford added pointedly.

'Oh, it must be this Venice air,' Mrs Butters flustered.

'Best taken in lusty lungfuls, I agree,' Eleanor said impishly. 'Now, please, take a seat. Clifford has ordered all sorts for us to try. I hope you have lots to tell me. How about starting with this morning's fun and working backwards?'

'The repeatable elements only,' Clifford said quickly.

'That's all there is, Mr Clifford,' Mrs Trotman said innocently.

'Really?' He smiled equally innocently at Polly. 'How about you enlighten us, then?'

The young maid nodded enthusiastically, much to the other ladies' evident dismay.

'Well, Mr Clifford, after wanderin' around and playin' the washin' line game, we were all breathless from laughin' so hard. So we went to the museum with all the statues.'

'An admirable choice,' he said encouragingly. 'And which can you remember particularly?'

'None, sir. Because...' Polly broke off on being flapped down by the other ladies who were stifling a round of giggles.

'Come on, share the joke,' Eleanor said, already caught up in their infectious mood.

'We might have been shown out quicker than we planned, m'lady,' Mrs Butters said. 'On account of Trotters taking too long to study a few of the statues.'

'Up very close.' Polly giggled.

The cook's eyes glinted cheekily. 'It's not my fault, Mr Clifford, that they've made so many as wearing not so much as under—'

He quickly raised a hand. 'Thank you, Mrs Trotman. I think we get the picture!'

To spare his further blushes, Eleanor pulled the two sketches out.

'Talking of pictures, I'd like your suggestions for where to hang these back at Henley Hall.'

She laid them side by side on the table, facing the ladies.

'That man is so clever!' Mrs Trotman said. 'I could never even start to hold a brush with any hope it wouldn't just daub splodges on the canvas.'

'Or the walls, my dress and probably Gladstone too, in my case,' Eleanor said, ruffling her bulldog's ears.

'Indubitably,' Clifford muttered mischievously.

She hid a smile. 'Look, ladies, there's Clifford's room. He's got a statue of a stone monkey outside for less ear-battering company than I am.'

They all laughed at him, nodding.

Mrs Butters, however, was rubbing her eyes.

'You dozy mare.' Mrs Trotman opened her friend's handbag. 'You've got that magnifying glass her ladyship bought you to help when you're embroidering. It must be in here amongst everything.'

Clifford glanced at Eleanor. 'Too much feminine paraphernalia to find it, perhaps, Mrs Butters?'

Eleanor laughed. 'Don't answer that!'

'Oh, that's better,' the housekeeper said a moment later, scanning the first picture again through the magnifying glass. 'I see Mr Clifford's monkey now. And his window open a few inches, just like he always insists at Henley Hall.'

Clifford's brow flinched as he rose, pince-nez in place. 'A detail I had not noticed had been captured, Mrs Butters. May I?' He leaned over to peer at the sketch, then shook his head.

He sat back down, his usually implacable composure slightly dented, to Eleanor's mind.

'There's nothing wrong with needing an eye test once in a blue moon, Clifford,' she whispered.

'If you say so, my lady.'

The ladies' giggles made them both look up.

'Aye, it's too funny,' Lizzie said to Mrs Trotman, who was now holding the magnifying glass up to make her eye appear enormous to the others.

'I wonder what was going on behind the curtains in this second picture, mind,' Mrs Trotman murmured to Eleanor's cook as Polly took her turn shyly.

'Just a man looking,' the young maid said, having missed the mischief in the remark. She leaned closer. 'With funny large spectacles. Must be because it's so dark in there.'

'In where exactly, Polly?' Clifford said, a slightly taut tone in his voice.

'This top room here, sir. In the mid... middle.' Her bottom

lip trembled as he quickly took the magnifying glass from her. She sniffed. 'I didn't mean to speak out of turn, Mr Clifford.'

'You haven't. No waterworks are required, thank you.' He looked up from studying the sketch, avoiding Eleanor's eye.

'Clifford?' she said, hurrying around to see for herself. 'They're very thick spectacles, aren't they? But gracious! That's looking directly into—'

'The sun. Quite, my lady,' he said nonchalantly. 'A very damaging activity for the eyes. Ladies.' He shook his head as they all jumped up like obedient rabbits, a flick of one finger sitting them back down. 'Please accept her ladyship's apologies. Enjoy your luncheon. Including our share. Something has come up. I shall settle the bill on our way out.'

'And please look after Gladstone and Tomkins for the moment,' she called as they hastened out of the café.

'Probably just a Peeping Tom, caught staring across at my room,' she said, as Clifford hurried her the short distance towards her hotel.

He pursed his lips. 'Hopefully, my lady. I shall see you to your suite first, nevertheless.'

'A wonderfully gallant thought. Rather pointless, though, Clifford. Because I'll only follow you straight back out.'

'My lady, I really must insist.'

'So must I.' She wrinkled her nose. 'Stalemates aren't very effective, are they?'

'Neither are butlers, it appears,' Clifford said ruefully, changing direction and heading for the nearest gondola to take them across to the other hotel.

The reception was even more modest than the exterior. A nondescript picture adorned the greyish walls, doing nothing to brighten the apathetic atmosphere. A young man languished behind the faded counter, barely acknowledging they had entered.

'Her ladyship's parrot has escaped from her apartment.' Clifford flapped his arms with a realistic squawk. 'It is on the window ledge of the corridor on the next floor.' He swept her onwards to a dusty set of stairs. 'We'll be fine, thank you. No need to show us the way,' he called over his shoulder.

'It's the top floor,' she whispered.

'I know, my lady,' he whispered back. 'But in the unlikely event the clerk, whose attire was shockingly crumpled, by the way, should heave his idle carcass out of his chair, I don't want him to interrupt me.'

'Us,' she countered firmly.

'Us,' he echoed resignedly.

On the third-floor landing, he paused and pointed at the door two along from where they'd stopped. 'That one. The building is nine rooms wide. And it is the central one where the man is depicted in the sketch. Please wait a moment.'

He stole to the door and bent to peer through the keyhole. Then, straightening up, knocked half-heartedly enough for it to seem as if it were the apathetic clerk downstairs. There was no reply. He checked the keyhole again and then tried the handle very slowly.

'Not locked?' she hissed, hurrying up. He nodded. 'Good job,' she said. 'As you haven't brought your picklocks to Venice...' His hand sliding something back inside his jacket pocket made her shake her head. 'You have! Is there no end to your scallywaggery?'

'Not until my mistress ceases needing such.' He held his finger to his lips, gesturing to stand behind him, and then quickly pushed the door open. 'Empty,' he whispered.

They hurried inside and over to the window in the middle with the partly closed curtain, as drawn in the sketch.

She gasped. 'Dash it! It does look straight into my suite.' She tried to quell the icicle forming in her stomach. 'But even with strong spectacles, you couldn't see anything of much detail. Mind you, if I was on the balcony, I'd be easily visible, I suppose.'

Clifford held something up. 'Not strong spectacles, my lady. Binoculars. The bottom cover of one lens clearly having fallen off unnoticed.'

'Hmm.' She stared around the room; two made-up single beds, two worn upholstered chairs, a battered coffee table and an open-fronted wardrobe. She waved at the wardrobe.

'He must have left. There are no personal effects of any kind in here.'

'That does not mean he will not return. Since he probably never brought any in the first place,' Clifford said gravely. 'I have the feeling a more thought out plan than just direct confrontation is needed.'

She nodded, then knelt down and picked up a scrap of paper visible under the curtains. As she straightened up, she swallowed hard. 'You may be right. Recognise this?' She held up a black and white sweet wrapper inscribed with 'Golia'.

Unusually, he raised both his eyebrows. 'Regrettably, yes.' Respectfully taking her arm, he propelled her towards the door. 'It is the same as the wrapper you removed from Signor Vendelini's body!'

26

As they hastened out of the hotel, Eleanor let out a long breath.

'Clifford,' she said quietly, 'are you thinking what I am? That our sketcher may have witnessed Benetto's murder?'

'Disconcertingly, it seems a possibility, my lady,' he said gravely, searching the canal for a gondola, the mooring posts next to them being empty.

She shook her head. 'Goodness, that was a risk, drawing that second picture. I suppose he must have been too scared to sketch what he'd actually seen of the murder in case the killer found him with it. So he did what he could.' Her brow furrowed even further. 'It was a long shot on his part, though. How could he have known I'd realise what it meant?'

'I assume, my lady, that having watched your response to Signor Vendelini's murder, he was struck by your determination and fortitude. And having talked, well, communicated with you, your keen intelligence.'

'Thank you, Clifford. Unfortunately, we can't check if that is the case as he's totally disappeared. Which is very worrying.'

'Merely gone to ground, I am certain. The fact he left a

coded message in that sketch, rather than going to the police, tells me he is extremely cautious.'

She stopped mid-nod. 'Wait a minute? We—'

A gondola glided between the mooring posts.

'Just straight across,' Clifford said to the gondolier.

The man shot him a filthy look as he helped Eleanor in. As they set off, she leaned closer to Clifford, who was sitting opposite, looking at her quizzically.

'What I was trying to say was it just struck me that if Gaspo did murder Benetto, and the sketcher witnessed it, why now Gaspo is dead is he still hiding?'

Clifford nodded. 'An excellent point, my lady. Only one answer springs readily to mind.'

'That Gaspo didn't kill Benetto, and the murderer is still at large?'

'Unfortunately, yes. And from extrapolation, that—'

'The same man may have murdered Gaspo and was watching me from the other hotel?'

His silence said it all. As the gondola cleared the midpoint of the crowded canal, he leaned forward.

'It is too coincidental that the man checked in on the very day of Signor Vendelini's murder.'

She grimaced. 'True. However, the desk clerk also told us that he has since checked out.'

Clifford's lips pursed. 'And disgracefully, the only description the clerk was able to give was entirely commensurate with his slovenly attitude. Vague and unhelpful.'

'Hmm. Square-built, shorter than you, with a hat he always wore pulled low.' She frowned. 'Does that ring a bell? Or not?' She shook her head.

'It could be almost anybody, my lady. Hopeless. As is the clerk!' Clifford muttered as they reached the mooring poles of her hotel's smart jetty.

In her suite, she immediately fell to pacing the sitting room. 'Right. We need to work out what to do next.'

He raised a brow. 'If the lady might at least deign to let me relieve her of her hat and gloves first?'

She shrugged and whizzed her hat through the air to him, followed by her gloves.

Ignoring his tutting, she continued pacing. 'Now, let's start with the facts we have about Benetto's murder.' She counted off on her fingers. 'He was a member of the Vendelini family, and a government official on the Venice Council.'

'And, my lady, I believe Angelo told us his push for progress was not popular with everyone, including Angelo himself.'

She nodded. 'Apparently he was largely responsible for the increase in motorised traffic on the canals, among other things, I imagine. And given that Venice seems to be one of the most fundamentally traditional cities on earth, I'm sure he put a lot of other people's noses out of joint! I mean, we haven't been anywhere at all without a Venetian proudly furnishing us with the ancient history of whatever we're looking at or doing. And the canals, as we know, are the absolute lifeblood of the city.'

'And the lifeline of the gondoliers.' Clifford turned back away from the window after checking the hotel opposite again.

She jerked to a stop. 'Hmm, so his unpopular policies could be relevant. Benetto argued with Gaspo just before he was killed. Perhaps that was why Gaspo really killed him. If, indeed, he did?'

Clifford shook his head. 'Facts only, my lady. No conjectures at this point, you said.'

She held out her hands apologetically. 'I did. Thank you for the reminder.'

He sniffed as she continued to wear a groove in the silk rug. 'To continue with the facts at hand then, my lady. Another boat hit that of Gaspo's. Just before Signor Vendelini fell into the canal. And in your recollection, you noted the pilot was standing up. Unlike the rest of us on the canal.'

'Yes, I'm ninety-nine per cent sure, so let's allow it as a fact for the moment.'

'Agreed. Now, Signor Vendelini was stabbed in the back with a tool specifically used to build gondolas.'

'One of which seems to have gone missing from a yard owned by one of the Marcello family. Suspicious, indeed.' She threw her hands out. 'Oh, dash it, that's almost a fact.'

He ignored her outburst. 'And Signor Secco was arrested. In front of us. Fact,' he said pointedly.

'We've no time for point scoring, Clifford.'

'What a shame.'

She laughed, knowing he was just trying to lighten the mood.

'Now, Gaspo was released rather suddenly after his arrest and discovered that evening drowned in the canal.'

'And the police verdict was that he drowned himself out of guilt.'

'Yes.' She hesitated. 'I think that's it. Unless you've remembered any more facts about Benetto's murder?'

'Only that Signor Secco's uncle told us Signor Vendelini threw an item of rubbish into the canal, which we believe we now have in our possession.'

She perched on the edge of the coffee table, trying to arrange the many pieces of the confusing puzzle in her mind. She shook her head in frustration.

'It's no good, Clifford. Let's move on to Gaspo's murder before we try and make any sense of Benetto's. We assume they are linked?'

'Agreed for the moment, although we have no direct evidence. We do know he was related to the Marcello family, and had easy access to the murder weapon.'

'He was known for having a bad, no, a "quick" temper. And

he told his uncle, Tomaso, that Benetto had never taken his gondola before.' Her nose wrinkled. 'We could consider the common, or uncommon, denominators that link the two deaths?'

Her butler's brow flinched. 'Are you referring to the apparently defunct feud between the Vendelinis and Marcellos?'

'Yes. And according to Vincenzo, it may not be that defunct! Well, he said the truce was "uneasy".'

Clifford pondered this. 'Young Leonardo also stated that some person, or persons, are against his marriage.'

Her heart constricted for Catarina. 'Because it will be harder to get the families to feud again afterwards, and someone wants war, not peace, it seems!' She sighed. 'Does that bring us to a helpful conclusion at all?'

'Y-e-s. A deduction at best. That someone is trying to relight the feud for reasons at present unknown. And that person may have murdered Signori Vendelini and Secco to give the impression of a revenge killing.' He rubbed his chin. 'The other deduction is that the feud has already started again, and they were, in reality, tit-for-tat murders.'

She paused in her pacing. 'Gaspo kills Benetto, then an unknown member of the Vendelini family kills Gaspo in revenge?'

'Exactly.'

She paused again, watching him pinch the corners of the cushions so they stood straighter along the settee.

'Tell me, Clifford, does all that twiddling and fiddling really help you think?'

He nodded. 'Clear thoughts cannot flourish in chaos, my lady.'

She sighed. 'I think mine do. So could you bear to abandon logic for a moment and look at another possibility? That Benetto, and possibly Gaspo, were not killed over any family feud, present or past, but rather, were killed for the figurine we dredged up?'

He finished setting the soft furnishings to rights. 'Willingly. However, the only motive we could fathom was that the figurine was valuable. Yet Venice's foremost expert assured us it is worthless. So, unless we can come up with another reason why someone might see red and kill for it—'

'That's it!' She gaped at him. 'And not just red, but deep crimson red. Blood red! Clifford, you clever bean. I can't believe I missed that.'

'Missed what?'

'Catarina's heart that she dropped, and which I still have, is threaded through with the same crimson red as the figurine we recovered in the canal.' She ran to her wardrobe and returned, holding the heart up to the light.

'Ah!'

'Oh, whatever it is, just say it, Clifford?'

'I believe you will find that it is actually Venetian red, my lady. A not uncommon pigment used in Murano glass objets d'art. Although, as you say, it is definitely threaded through with the same crimson and turquoise entwined swirls that give the figurine its distinctive look.'

'Exactly! Now' – she closed her palm around the glass heart – 'let's put our two theories together!'

He folded his hands. 'I am all ears.'

'Good. It strikes me as too coincidental that Catarina had this heart, and Benetto had a figurine which seems to be of the same design. Also, that she's a Marcello, and he's a Vendelini...'

He nodded slowly. 'So the figurine may somehow be linked to the two families?'

'Yes.' She swallowed. 'But here's the rub. The only person we definitely know was in contact with Benetto just before, and after, he died was Gaspo.'

'Save for the murderer, if it wasn't Signor Secco.' He looked up sharply. 'Worryingly, however, I believe my thoughts are now right on the coat-tails of yours, my lady. The thief who stole your bag was also the one who searched this suite, we believe. Nothing, however, was taken from either your suite or your subsequently returned bag.'

'And then we know he shadowed me because we caught him at it on my way to meet Vincenzo at St Mark's clock tower. That can only mean he didn't find what he was looking for before.'

'Surely the figurine! If our conjecture is correct, my lady, the murderer may have killed both Signor Vendelini and Signor Secco for it. Signor Secco was the next most likely person to have the figurine—'

'Having been on the boat with Benetto.' She groaned. 'And the next most likely person to have the figurine after Gaspo, would be—'

He nodded grimly. 'You, my lady. As we were the ones to pull Signor Vendelini's body onto our gondola. And then Angelo, perhaps.'

She buried her face in her hands. 'Dash it! I had no intention of us getting mixed up in this murder, Clifford. Though we seem to be now. And up to our necks!' She took a deep breath.

He shook his head. 'I cannot think why anyone would kill twice for a worthless, everyday piece of what, to Venetians, is local glass.'

'That might be the case.' She pursed her lips. 'However, someone may have done just that. And what's more, they may be willing to kill again to get it!'

27

The next morning Venice was enveloped in a pearl-grey haze, the fog deadening every sound except a single church bell tolling sombrely across the rooftops. The folds of Eleanor's velvet-collared moss-green cape quickly beaded with a fine veil of moisture as she waited.

Soon, a figure materialised out of the fog. Shadowy, in a long dark coat, with a hat pulled low. Behind her, she sensed Clifford stiffen. The figure raised a hand as it approached. Recognition dawned, the hairs that had pricked up on her arms lying back down.

'I did not want to make you jump, Eleanor.' Vincenzo's attractive features were set in the easy smile she'd come to recognise. 'But I could not have picked more unfortunate weather for us to meet.'

'Oh, I don't know,' she said, appreciating his thoughtfulness. 'I thought I'd seen Venice in all her masks.'

'Ah! But you have yet to see her shrouded in a mask of pure white. Let us ascend!' He pointed to the long flight of stone steps leading up to the church. The high portico of decorated columns ran back further than the grand entrance was wide. Vincenzo glanced over his shoulder. 'Your chaperone will be joining us, I suppose? But whether it is because he always does, or he does not trust my intentions, I am not clear.'

'Oh goodness, no!'

Her butler stepped forward. 'Purely duty and habit, signore.' Catching Eleanor's eye, he arched an imperceptible brow of query, despite his assertion.

'Do enjoy the time to sketch the architectural marvels, Clifford, won't you?' she said breezily, her coded reply that she felt at ease in Vincenzo's company. He nodded, having also agreed with her on the way there that Vincenzo was their best option to turn to for insider help. Something she was increasingly realising was essential in a city as unique as Venice.

Having climbed the steps, Vincenzo bowed his head at the church's double studded oak doors before he turned the enormous iron ring handles and pushed them open.

'Oh, my!' she breathed, too captivated to stride on in at her usual brisk pace. 'It's entirely circular inside. I didn't see that incredible dome through all the fog. And it's such an eclectic mix of styles.'

He nodded. 'One of the last religious buildings to be built in Venice. And a celebration of all the architectural styles from the city's very first beginnings. It is living history. And a sanctuary when needed.'

Inside, her gaze roved over the raised altar flanked by saintly sculptures, the deep inset iconographic carvings, and the unusually curved rows of backless pews, in which several people were scattered, heads bent, praying.

'Thank you for showing me this,' she whispered.

'I actually had a secret motive to bring you here, Eleanor.' His words drew her up short. He held up a hand. 'Purely, that our last conversation in the clock tower finished on the sad note of Benetto's death. And you have had upsetting troubles in my city, so I was hoping that the serenity of my favourite church might offer you some comfort.'

'Oh, definitely,' she murmured.

'Then come. Let this visit help you forget all the unfortunate things you have witnessed.' He stepped forward, looking confused as she stayed put.

'Honestly, I can't. Forget it all, I mean. I'm rather tangled in it, you see?'

His eyes searched her face. 'No. Not yet. Perhaps it would help you to talk about it?'

She nodded. 'But it feels disrespectful to talk here. This is a place of worship.'

'And support. What better place to bring troubled thoughts to for guidance?' He smiled. 'But I understand you feel uncomfortable because others are praying.' He looked thoughtful for a moment, then led her around the pews to a cleric. At Vincenzo's enquiry, the man nodded and opened a plain wooden door.

She expected to step into an anteroom of some sort, but instead there was a dimly lit rough-hewn staircase.

Vincenzo noticed her hesitation. 'It leads to the crypt. Before I showed you one of the highest spots in Venice. Now, one of the lowest. The lighting is better at the bottom, I promise. And we will not disturb those concentrating on their devotions. Or, perhaps as importantly' – he shot her an enquiring glance – 'be overheard ourselves.'

The musty air tickling her nostrils at the top was creeping down her throat by the time she reached the bottom. The crypt was lit by flickering oil sconces running along the walls. Myriad pillars rose to the vaulted ceiling, their pale hand-hewn blocks holding together without a hint of mortar.

Vincenzo spread his coat over a block of roughly chiselled stone set in front of a table lit by six double candleholders. For a brief moment, it reminded her of the impromptu sacrificial altar in a penny dreadful novel she'd recently read.

Get a grip, Ellie.

Vincenzo looked at her quizzically. 'Please sit.'

'Gracious, not on your beautiful coat?'

'Why not? Crypts are cold for reasons we do not wish to consider, Eleanor. Because I think you have seen enough bodies in Venice,' he said soberly. 'But perhaps it is the appropriate place for what you wish to talk with me about?'

'Honestly, I'm hoping not.' She sank down onto the makeshift seat, hands held gratefully to the warmth of the candles. Gathering her thoughts, she relayed her story, leaving out only dredging the canal in deference to it being one of his relatives that had littered it in the first place. 'But there has been talk of a figurine being involved somehow,' she ended. There was no missing his jaw flinching. 'Does that mean something to you, Vincenzo?'

'A glass figurine?' he replied slowly, turning one of the candleholders. 'Venice is full of these because of Murano, of course.'

'What if it was of an important-looking man, clear glass, but shot through with Venetian crimson and turquoise swirls? Maybe, if he was holding his hand out—'

His features darkened. 'As if shaking another's?

She nodded. 'And a heart made from similar glass.' His eyes bored into her. She held his gaze until he shook himself. 'Eleanor, I apologise, but you took me by surprise.' He looked at her quizzically. 'But then again, I think you are full of surprises.' He hesitated, then waved around the crypt. 'Apart from you and me, there are only the dead down here. And the dead tell no secrets. So let me tell you one...'

28

Vincenzo slowly paced the crypt, raising flurries of centuries-old dust, which fizzled in the candle flames.

'The importance of the figurine of which I believe you speak cannot be exaggerated! The feud between my family and the Marcellos started many, many years ago because of their two different interests. Vendelinis have always been industrialists. Forever looking ahead to be ready to rise to whatever challenge the city's growing success cried out for. Equally, the Marcellos have always had the same fierce attitude to be the best. But, being merchants, they concentrated on sourcing and trading the materials needed for the city's needs.' He held his hands out. 'Unfortunately, the desire to be the richest, most successful family in the city, and not to share this title, led to fiercer and fiercer competition between them. In the end, it became a battle to ruin the other, no matter the cost.'

She grimaced. 'When, in reality, it sounds as if they were equally dependent on each other?'

He let out a long breath. 'Exactly. If either family fell, let alone both, it would impact almost every industry and trade in the city.'

'Then how does the figurine have any bearing on that?'

'It was made to mark the end of the feud many, many years ago. The head of each family at the time finally came to their senses and realised they were destroying everything their forefathers had striven to build.' He sighed. 'Men can be their own enemy too often! But that is why the two figurines are shaking hands.'

'So there are two halves,' she muttered.

'Yes. And the heart binds them together in trust. The head of each family keeps the figurines for a year at a time. Then, the two families meet for them to be handed over to the other to keep for the next year.'

'I see.'

'It is also the time when the friendship of the two families is renewed. And it is done in something of public view, in Florian's restaurant in the Room of Illustrious Men. This last year has been the turn of the Vendelinis to guard the figurines.' He hesitated. 'But they were stolen recently.' He hesitated again, then shrugged. 'Naturally, my family kept this quiet. But after Benetto was killed, and then the gondolier, the head of the Marcellos demanded to see the figurines early. He is very sharp, their Nonno. Old age has not sliced one hair from his head! Neither from his stubborn temper. When they were not found, he declared that if they are not handed over by midnight on the agreed date, he would take it as a personal insult. And the sign that my family wants to fight again with his. Nothing will sway him any other way. The feud will start again for certain. That is why the Marcellos' Nonno has offered a reward for the return of the figurines, intact.'

'But hasn't the head of your family offered the same?' she blurted out, too late to retract what might have sounded like an accusation.

'Of course! But it does not impress the Marcellos' Nonno.'

'Then why not go to the police? Surely they can help you recover the figurines?'

Vincenzo sighed. 'The police cannot be trusted to be... unbiased. I am ashamed to say this, but it is true. One of my own family and several of the Marcellos hold high-up positions in the force. But this is not the only reason. Venice families sort out their own affairs, rather than go to the authorities. Now, just as they have always. But this?' He perched one hip disconsolately on the edge of the slab table, shaking his head.

Her thoughts flew to Catarina and, with a frisson of hesitation, to Leonardo too. 'Vincenzo, just out of hypothetical curiosity, if the figurines weren't returned on time, what would happen to, for example, two people from opposite families who wanted to, say... marry?'

His brows shot up. 'It would be totally forbidden! And never could they marry until the feud stopped again. If it ever did,' he added.

She hesitated, desperate to tell him at least one figurine was safe. But she imagined Clifford's cautioning cough, despite their agreement Vincenzo may be her only hope.

Vincenzo spread his hands. 'I am so sorry to have rolled my burden out to you, Eleanor. We came down here for you to roll yours out to me.'

'It must be awful for you,' she said, cursing that cynical, jaded whisper that seemed to have become part of her since her first unpleasant experience in Venice.

'And you must be cold, Eleanor. Shall we leave?'

'Vincenzo, you can take comfort that one figurine and the heart is safe,' she blurted out.

What are you doing, Ellie?

He spun around. 'Really? Because that is like song to my troubled ears. But how can you be sure?'

She hesitated. The damage was done. And even Clifford had agreed that they had to trust someone.

'Because I have them.' His jaw fell. She held up her hands. 'Don't worry, it's fine. I've got them in—'

'Stop!' he barked. 'Forgive me for speaking so harshly, but it is better I do not know. Then I cannot let the place slip from my tongue. Or be tricked into telling. It is possible the person trying to reignite the feud is from my family, as much as from the Marcellos'. Please, Eleanor, just guard them well. And I will think how else to find the other half. I have been looking, and asking, and calling in many favours, but nothing has come of it yet.'

'Well, we'd both better think hard, because someone else is looking for the other figurine too.'

He frowned. 'Who?'

'The man who stole my bag. And ransacked my hotel suite.'

He clicked his fingers. 'Now I understand! This is why you have had these troubles. Because you were the one to help pull Benetto's body from the canal. This thief is definitely looking to steal the figurine and heart you have.' He ran his hand through his hair. 'Is this rogue working for himself, I wonder? Or for someone else?' He slapped the table. 'I wish I could answer this.'

'And me, because if he is working for someone else and he's found the other figurine, he may already have passed it on to them.'

He nodded grimly. 'This too, is possible.' He held her gently by the shoulders for a second. 'I wish you were not at all involved.'

'But I am,' she said resolutely. 'So when is the ultimatum to hand over the figurines?'

'The deadline is midnight on the first day of the Venice Carnival. This is traditionally when the two families get together to swear friendship for the coming year and pass on the figurines, symbolising unity.'

She gasped. 'The first day of the Carnival? But that's tomorrow!'

He nodded sombrely. 'Now you understand the timing of the figurines being stolen. Please, you must take extreme care of the one you have. But more of yourself.'

While trying to find the other half, Ellie, that's not going to be easy.

'I will contact you with more information as soon as I have it,' he said.

'One last question.' She paused to stare at him. 'Do you know how it was stolen from your family?'

'It was not!' Vincenzo swept up his coat so hard it blew the ring of candles out in a cloud of spiralling white smoke. 'It had been sent for cleaning and any necessary restoration, as is tradition, before the handover each year. It was stolen from there.'

'I see. And where was it sent for restoration and cleaning?'

'To the best restorer in Venice. His shop is not far from here, in the Jewish Quarter. His name is Signor Friedman.'

29

'I could kick myself. Just listen to what I've learned!'

Vincenzo had gone and Eleanor was filling Clifford in as he led them towards the Jewish Quarter. Between irritation at herself and the damp fog cloying at the inside of her throat, she was uncharacteristically breathless as they crossed endless bridges and turned down endless ill-lit alleyways.

'As enlightening as it is perplexing, my lady,' he said after she'd finished relaying everything, 'I am struggling to believe the antiquarian with a pronounced stoop who introduced himself as Signor Friedman is limber enough to have dealt Signor Benetto Vendelini such a fatal blow. And while standing on a swaying boat?'

She shook her head in exasperation. 'I'm not suggesting Friedman is our killer. Just that he lied to us. And there's another name that keeps popping into my mind, but he's even older and less nimble!'

'The head of the Marcello family, perchance?'

She nodded. 'Nonno! You too, then?'

'To my shame, yes. Since I have formed that conjecture

mostly on the disgraceful carpings of the contessa's staff in the kitchens on the night of the party.'

'Not very complimentary, then?' She grimaced as they paused for Clifford to get his bearings in Venice's confusing labyrinth and for her to catch her breath.

'Not at all, my lady. But the staff have not one ounce of loyalty to the family, so one might take their remarks with a large dose of salts.'

She shrugged. 'Possibly, but even the contessa doesn't stand up to Nonno. And I'm guessing he visits her villa regularly enough to make life difficult for her staff. He definitely doesn't like being challenged. When I put forward a contrary view to his on a relatively trivial matter, I thought he was going to explode!'

Clifford tutted. 'It is generally considered impolite to challenge one's elders in public. Especially—'

She held up a hand. 'Stop right there! It was you who hid a handwritten card in my stoutest Oxford heels the day after I inherited Henley Hall. "Be yourself. Everyone else is already taken." Remember?'

He nodded ruefully. 'Oscar Wilde. But had I realised you would take the advice so much to heart, I might have thought twice.' She shot him a look, and then noticed the twinkle in his eye. But when he spoke again, his tone was earnest. 'My real concern, my lady, is that Nonno Marcello might have let pass your social faux pas, but he will never excuse you meddling if he is the one orchestrating all this. The consequences of his temper and his influential reach—'

'It won't help to dwell on that for the moment! And speaking of Nonno orchestrating all this. That ultimatum about the figurine being returned by the stroke of midnight smacks just a little too much as being a convenient way to start the feud again. Especially if he was the one who "orchestrated" its theft in the first place.'

'My thoughts entirely, my lady. But why would he, exactly?'

'Perhaps he is not satisfied with the Marcellos being one of the two most influential families in Venice. Maybe he wants them to be *the* most influential before he passes away? Vincenzo said that's how the feud started all that time ago.'

'I see.' He paused. 'Left here at this crossroads of passage-ways, I believe. Though it might turn out to be right. Apologies.'

She hurried alongside him, annoyed her lungs weren't taking kindly to the damp again. 'Anyway, there's one thing of which I'm certain.'

He looked at her enquiringly.

'Find the second figurine, and we find the murderer!'

'Indeed,' he said as they emerged from one more gloomy passageway to find themselves at a footbridge crossing yet one more canal.

'And,' she continued, 'when we get back to his antiques' shop, Signor Friedman is going to tell us what he knows. Whether he likes it or not!'

She paused on the other side of the footbridge and stared at a run of scrolling grillework set in a high wall. 'Isn't this where we saw Doctor Pinsky handing something to the thief? Or the other way around?'

'No, it is not, Lady Swift,' came the cocksure reply. The close-cropped head of dark hair framing the thief's grinning face stepped into view on the other side of the grillework.

'You!' she cried, scrabbling to reach through to grab his collar. 'You blackguard!'

But he simply stepped backwards, out of reach, shaking his head. 'It takes one to know one, Lady Swift!' Offering the same mocking salute as he had on their last encounter, he half-turned. 'You should know better than to attempt to win a game of cat and mouse in someone else's city. Because in Venice, I am the cat, and you are the mouse!'

Stay calm, Ellie. Don't let him get to you.

She glanced up and down the wall. In both directions, about thirty or so feet from where she was standing, was a gate.

Clifford shook his head in reply to her unspoken question. 'We agreed not to split up, my lady,' he whispered urgently.

'I know,' she whispered back fiercely. 'But do you have another idea? We have to catch this monster before he kills again.' She gestured at the thief, who was bent over nonchalantly flicking lint from the bottoms of his blue suit trousers as if he had forgotten all about them.

With a shared look of understanding, she turned and sprinted left while Clifford went right.

Reaching the gate on her side, she hurled herself through it and sprinted back down the other side. But when she reached the grillework, the thief had vanished.

More confusingly, and worryingly, there was also no sign of Clifford.

She scanned the area, but it was a small, deserted square with no means of concealing a child, let alone two adults.

'Dash it! Venice really is a thousand-year-old puzzle!' she groaned aloud, a trickle of ice slithering down her spine. In desperation, she sped back the way she'd come in the hope her butler would appear on the original side of the scrollwork. He didn't. But the thief did, waving casually as he crossed the footbridge to be swallowed up in the gloom of the alleyway they'd originally arrived from.

Having no other option, she shot after him. At the end of the alleyway, she saw him turn right, the opposite way she and Clifford had come. A moment later, the narrow passageway she found herself in turned so sharply at a dog-leg that she grazed her hand against the stone wall. She ran on, catching the merest glimpse of her quarry as he kept infuriatingly in sight, but not reach.

She emerged into another alleyway, this one marginally wider than the last. Too late she spotted the man now leaning nonchalantly on the wall, blocking the way she'd come. The thief gave her a cool smile.

'Lady Swift, what a pleasant surprise. Do you by any chance know what the street sign above your head means?'

'*Calle della Morte,*' she read disinterestedly, trying to hide her frustration that she was panting, and he wasn't. 'What of it?'

'In English it means "Death Alley". People who angered the Venice Council of Ten were tricked into coming here. It was the sign they had been condemned to death. And that it was too late for prayers.'

She froze. *The whole thing's a set-up, Ellie!*

She strained to hear Clifford's footsteps hurrying towards her.

'Oh, your *maggiordomo* isn't coming,' the thief said coolly. 'Signor Clifford is... indisposed. This is just for you and me to finish, Lady Swift.'

She had no time to consider his words. Throwing herself into a defensive Bartitsu pose, she cast around for a pole or stick.

Never mind, Ellie. You can do a lot of damage without!

At that moment, an image of her butler's face etched with concern swam into her head. 'Caution, my lady! What would Prudence do?' he murmured. She hesitated, then nodded to herself.

'Alright, Clifford,' she said aloud.

For a second, the thief glanced around. It was all she needed.

As she darted down the only avenue open to her, she could hear footsteps starting after her. Her features were grim. She'd never outrun him, which meant it was probably only a matter of time before he outran her.

With no clue where she was going and only prayers that it wasn't to a dead end, literally, she sped on, flinging herself over every bridge that appeared.

Why is Venice usually so crowded, and yet when you need

help it's so deserted, Ellie? She knew the answer. *Because he's trapped you in the least populated part of the city at the quietest time of day. And the fog makes everyone, and everything, almost invisible.*

Eventually she stumbled to a stop, her breathing ragged, heart hammering in her chest. Even if she faced him now, she was too exhausted to fight. Before she could formulate a plan, she caught the low throb of a motor. As the thief appeared only yards away, she drew on her last ounce of stamina and sprinted along the side of an enormous church, the lagoon on her right.

She knew she was likely just delaying the inevitable, and as she swung out of the last alley, it seemed it had arrived. All around her was water.

Out of the corner of her eye, she saw him gaining on her. She desperately tugged on the church door.

Locked, Ellie!

With a burst of speed she didn't know she had left, she sprinted to the quayside. Only a few feet in front of her, a loaded barge was passing the spit. With a rush of pure adrenaline, she launched herself off the quay.

For a moment, she thought she would land short, but then she hit the barge's deck on her hands and knees with a jarring jolt. Expecting the athletic thief to land next to her, she scrambled up. It wouldn't matter. Even with him aboard, she would have the barge driver on her side. But no one landed beside her.

She turned to give the thief some of his own medicine. But, to her confusion, her mocking salute was met with a smug nod of his head. Spinning around, she stared in horror.

Oh, Ellie!

30

Eleanor awoke with a gasp, heart racing, blood pounding in her ears. A flickering oil lamp was her only companion in the steel compartment that had been her prison for more hours than she wanted to think about, judging by her painfully dry throat.

Strapped in a chair, hands bound behind her back, she groped ineffectually for the hundredth time at the infuriatingly well-tied knots. She frowned again at her legs tied to the chair with more silk bindings. But their softness was no comfort. Her every thwarted attempt to loosen them had exhausted her so much she must have slipped into a fitful sleep.

She shook herself. How long had she been there? How many hours were left until Nonno Marcello's ultimatum expired? Was it still the same day? Her growling empty stomach was sure it wasn't. Her last memory had been the thief smiling smugly down at her from the deck with his accomplice standing next to him, face obscured by a wide scarf and a hat pulled low.

The mystery man who was watching me in my suite, Ellie?

Then the clang of the hatch cover above her had been followed by the sound of three heavy bolts being shot home.

'Dash it!' she cried out. Constantly running back over her frustration at having fallen into the thief's trap had occupied her troubled thoughts for too many hours. But not as much as her fears for what ultimate fate her captors had in mind for her. Or her butler, if he'd also been captured. With her last scrap of energy and determination she willed her aching fingers to try one more time to loosen her bonds.

After what seemed like twenty or more infuriatingly ineffectual minutes, the only result was shooting pains up both arms. Her shoulders slumped.

'Hopeless!' she shouted out aloud. 'He was right. Why did I ever think I could win a game of cat and mouse in this impossible puzzle of a city?'

But more honestly, Ellie, against an opponent who has outsmarted you at every turn.

'Outsmarted both of us,' she muttered, her thoughts turning again to Clifford, who she'd last seen sprinting away from her along the grillework wall in the square, all those innumerable hours ago. She closed her eyes and sent a silent plea heavenward for his safety.

Her heart fluttered. They were a team. And Clifford had risked his life to save hers on more than one occasion. She *had* to escape. For both their sakes.

With her resolve reignited, she dredged her mind for another way to free herself. Clearly, straining at her bonds again would achieve nothing except to ensure she was still trapped there when the thief finally returned.

Assuming he does, Ellie. Her breath caught. *Assuming his plan isn't to just leave you here to die through lack of food and water?*

The thought of Clifford suffering the same fate sharpened her inventiveness. She cast around even more urgently for any kind of improvised cutting tool.

Think, Ellie, think!

But only a few stacks of upturned wooden crates, some metal shelving lashed to a bulkhead, and a pile of hessian sacks stared back at her.

She groaned, willing her mind to find an answer. But for hour after hour, as she watched the oil lamp flicker and fade along with her hope, nothing came to her.

Then the flame sparked back to life, sputtered, and faded, as if mocking her. But in that brief moment of illumination, she'd seen it.

Shaking herself out of her stupor, she mentally slapped herself for not thinking of it before. With all the strength she could muster, she jerked her body sideways. Using her feet as leverage, she hopped the chair awkwardly across to the metal shelving, where one upright was corroded, leaving a slightly jagged edge.

How long she rubbed the rope binding her feet backwards and forwards, using the edge as a makeshift knife blade, she had no idea. Her screaming muscles forced her to stop countless times. Maybe dawn had come and gone, she thought, trying not to feel too despondent as she took another rest. Maybe, somehow, she might make it out before the sun rose a second day in her floating prison?

One foot hit the floor. It had worked! Her legs were still bound to the chair, but her feet were now free. Repeating the process to fray the bindings around her knees was more difficult. She had to shuffle her chair right up to the shelving and wedge one foot at a horrible angle between two crates, the other braced against the hull's side. As the circle of light dimmed even further, it left more and more of the room in darkness. The critical question was not whether she'd get free, but whether the lamp flame would die completely before she was.

She ploughed on regardless until, miraculously, she could see only a shred of rope held her legs captive. With a grunt, she rubbed as hard as she could, crying out as the corroded section of shelving cut through her bindings and the skin on the inside of both knees.

She paused for far longer than she wanted, but she needed to regain her breath. Then, free of the chair, she counted, 'One... Two... Three!' and slid her arms under her legs and over her feet. Now it was up to her teeth to yank on the silk knots tying her hands together. Her jaw ached as she spat the rope out and then slapped and rubbed the excruciating pins and needles from her arms. Scooping up the silken cord, she hurled it angrily into the corner, wishing it was into the thief's face.

Then she saw it; a lidded bucket with a small water-filled bowl on top tucked behind a stack of crates, the soap and neatly folded hand towel mocking her. She groaned. The thief had obviously expected her to free herself all along!

With waning hope, she tried everything to shift the hatch cover with her stiff and aching fingers. Discouraged, she picked up the now almost lightless oil lamp and made an inch by inch search of the riveted walls. She hoped if even one was missing, it might be large enough to holler for help through.

There wasn't.

Defeated for the moment, she sat back down, jacket draped over her front, legs tucked up.

Just a quick rest, Ellie. Then one more try.

She knew she needed to muster her strength, but fretting over her absent butler's safety won out. Eventually, she slid into another fitful sleep...

She woke with a start. It was pitch-dark. She reached out, her hand touching the cold glass of the oil lamp.

Dead!

How long had she been asleep? And more urgently, what was that sound? Or was she still dreaming? She strained to hear.

No, Ellie. Someone really is drawing the hatch bolts back.

She rose stealthily, grasped the lamp by its base, and flattened herself against the wall.

The hatch eased up haltingly, filling part of the compartment with ethereal moonlight. Then, in a flash, a long dark figure dropped silently beside her. She raised the lamp, poised to bring it smashing down on the intruder's head.

'My lady, wait!'

'Clifford! You're safe? Thank goodness!' She tempered her elation, catching the glint of his service revolver in the shaft of moonlight. 'How many of them have you dealt with?'

'None.'

She frowned. 'But how did you—?'

He cut her off. 'My lady. I feel it is imperative we leave here as quickly as possible.' He kicked over one of the empty crates, leaped up onto it and swung himself nimbly back up out of the hatch. Turning around, he dropped to his knees and thrust both hands down to her.

On deck, she cast about anxiously for her two abductors, but instead spied Angelo waiting alongside the barge in his gondola. She paused, registering sunset had definitely been and gone but a soft glow was suffusing the sky. 'What time, on what day is it?' she whispered. 'And where are we?'

'Six in the morning, the day after you were taken, my lady. And we are somewhere on the north-eastern edge of the city, beyond the Jewish Quarter. Angelo will take us to the security of your hotel suite where I can guard you with my life this time.'

'No,' she said resolutely. 'Unless you're hurt and pretending otherwise?' He shook his head. 'Good. Then you have to trust me. If we're in an unknown part of the city, we must be miles from our hotel. And we can't afford to go back. My incarceration has cost us time we never had in the first place!'

Clifford shook his head gravely. 'After your ordeal at the hands of such a wretch, shock cannot be taken lightly, my lady. You must be—'

'Starving, you're right. Which proves I'm suffering no ill effects, other than bristling with incensed rage that I literally leaped into the thief's trap.'

Clifford eyed her firmly, looking unconvinced. 'Nothing of the like is proven by your robust appetite raising an inappropriate hand at this juncture.'

'Angelo, thank you for bringing Clifford here,' she said, turning to the gondolier. 'We shan't need you for the rest of today. After, that is, you've pointed us to the most discreet café near here that's open at this ridiculous hour!'

The out-of-the-way table the waiter showed them to, in the out-of-the-way café, was perfect for their needs. Eleanor unwound her scarf and slid out of the all-encompassing jacket Clifford had lent her. As the waiter left, their orders taken, she leaned forward, her anger rising once more.

'The whole thing was a set-up, Clifford! Right from when we saw the thief on the other side of that dratted grillework.'

He nodded resignedly. 'Indeed. My own immediate capture on reaching the opening into the walled quadrangle was unforgivable, my lady.'

She tutted. 'Don't be daft. It was my idea to split up. And you weren't the one who took a running jump to land on the very barge the thief had chased me to!' She thumped her forehead. 'So stupid!'

'Hindsight has taught us both a sharp lesson. Notably, in regard to impetuous behaviour never winning over prudent.'

'Hang on, though!' she said in an aggrieved tone. 'I was prudent! After we split up, I ran, rather than fought.' At his look, she shrugged. 'Okay, maybe it was a case of prudence too late, but it's an improvement.'

He nodded. 'I have to admit, yes.'

She sighed. 'For all the good it did me! When I turned around on the barge, I realised the pilot was the same man who had caused the wash that threw the small motorboat and Gaspo's gondola together when Benetto was killed. That was obviously all a set-up as well! And in my case yesterday, the idea, I assume, was for the pilot of the barge to land and get out and cut me off on foot with the thief. But like a fool, I saved him the bother by leaping out of the frying pan and into the fire! So I'm truly sorry, Clifford. Really.'

He batted her apology away with a respectful headshake. 'For my part, I cannot even give a description of the man who dug a gun barrel into my back. All I saw was a flash of black clothing. It could have been anyone. Someone I've never seen. Or...' his brow furrowed, 'Signor Vendelini in that coat of his this morning, or Doctor Pinsky, I suppose. Or—'

'Or even Leonardo?'

He nodded. 'A blindfold was thrown over my eyes. Then I was herded through a nearby door and tied up, amid emphatic threats of what might happen to my mistress if I tried anything.'

'Oh, Clifford, is that why you didn't fight your way out? Because in all our previous scrapes, you've always managed to get the upper hand.' She managed an appreciative smile. 'Usually with a blinding right hook.'

'Your possible safety and several murders already committed kept my fists firmly by my sides, my lady.'

They paused when the waiter returned with a plate of pastries accompanied by hot coffee. Once he'd gone, she leaned forward.

'But you did get free somehow?' she said, pausing in between mouthfuls of both.

He winced. 'Y-e-s. By bargaining.'

She nodded eagerly. 'Top-notch, Clifford. What—'

He held up a hand. 'No, my lady, the bargain was all robbery on their side.'

'Robbery? I don't understand... oh no!' She stared at her butler's crestfallen features. 'You... you swapped the figurine we had for my release, didn't you?'

'Disgracefully, yes. But only after—'

She shook her head firmly. 'Not disgracefully, no. You've saved both of our lives on separate occasions. And mine again today, I believe. But let me guess. You refused to hand over the figurine for as long as possible because an imploring voice, which sounded rather like your mistress', kept pleading that you didn't?'

An inch of concern fell away as his lips quirked fleetingly. 'If pleading is the same as unladylike shrieking of "Don't give it to the wretch, Clifford!", then, yes. But how could you know that?'

She rolled her eyes. 'Because the only reason I didn't try and use my Bartitsu martial arts training on that wretched thief was because I heard your infuriating drone of "Caution, my lady! What would Prudence do?"'

He drummed his fingers together. 'A worrying exchange of influence, yet again.'

She laughed despite their predicament. 'I know. Now, we haven't got much time left. Eat something while we make a plan.' She marshalled her thoughts. 'So, the thief has one of the figurines—'

'Ahem, the uncomfortable notion he may already have secured the other one cannot be ruled out,' Clifford said, taking a sip of coffee.

Her shoulders fell momentarily. 'True.' She looked up. 'No,

wait, that's good news! Because when we find him, which we absolutely will, and soon, we can grab them both back in one go.' She bit her lip. 'Which means, flippancy aside, we've only got until midnight.'

'My lady! The young lady's glass heart. I kept quiet about that because the thief did not ask for it. Do you still have it?'

Her eyes widened. 'Of course! The thief obviously didn't realise we even knew of it.' She scrabbled in her jacket pockets, then stared back at him in dismay. 'Dash it! It seems the rogue is sharper than I thought. And as deftly light-fingered as you can be when the need arises. He must have picked my pocket while tying me up.'

'Nobody ties my mistress up!' Clifford growled. 'Advance notice if I may, my lady. I categorically will not be in control of my fists the next time I meet that unprincipled scoundrel!'

'Good man. Now, you and I have an appointment with a certain Signor Friedman to find out why he led us astray on our last visit. And we're not leaving until he tells us the truth this time. Agreed?'

He held her gaze sternly. 'Only if we agree not to split up, no matter what?'

She bowed. 'You're the boss, my chivalrous knight. Only sheathe your sword long enough to pass another pastry first, please. I'm still starving.'

32

As Clifford flapped a gloved hand, Eleanor jerked to a reluctant stop. She waited as he consulted his mental compass.

'West-north-west, I believe we need to head. Not much further now, my lady.' He pulled his hat lower, gesturing for her to tighten her scarf over her curls and tuck the ends into the jacket he'd insisted she don again.

'Hang on, Clifford. When you gallantly rescued me from the barge, you said we were somewhere we'd never been before. And that café we left just minutes ago was only two streets from there. So how do you have any idea of the way to Signor Friedman's shop from here?'

'Because there is a most unfortunate landmark I have been able to keep on our right behind us.' He waved them onward again. 'Cemetery Island.'

'Oh goodness,' she murmured, hurrying beside him.

'You clever bean,' she cheered under her breath not many minutes later as Friedman's shop appeared. 'I imagine he'll be closed. But we can hammer until he opens up...' She faltered as a hatted figure dressed all in black shot out of the door and vanished into the shadows. All black attire except for the dove-grey neckerchief which fluttered up into his fulsome beard.

'It's Doctor Pinsky, isn't it?' she hissed.

'I think it might have been.' Clifford's brows flinched. 'However, if so, he showed a remarkable turn of speed. Most unexpectedly vigorous for the fiftyish, rather sedentary man I saw you talking to at the contessa's party.'

'True. Maybe it wasn't him then. In any case, if it was, why might he have been here, do you suppose?'

'More to the point, why was he leaving so surreptitiously?'

'I don't know. But chasing anyone in these unlit back alleys is definitely not likely to get us any answers.'

'Hear, hear.'

The sign on the carved door had been turned to say '*chiuso*'.

'Well, that definitely must mean "closed", as it says "*aperto*" on the other side,' she whispered.

'At this early hour, hardly unexpected. Yet the door is ajar.'

'Not surprising, given how much of a hurry the doctor left in.' She pushed the door further open and peeped into the shop. 'It's dark, but there's a glow coming from the end where the workshop is.'

'The element of surprise can be quite disarming,' Clifford whispered, easing the door open just a few inches more.

She nodded. 'We'll catch Friedman unawares and keep him off balance enough so he hasn't the wherewithal to lie effectively.'

Together they tiptoed across the marquetry flooring, and on into the next chamber, keeping their backs against the bookcases of reference tomes to stay out of sight. Just before the threshold into the restoration workshop, she caught Clifford's eye and marched inside.

'A very poor show on your part, Signor Friedman!' she cried, thumping the desk hard enough to make the painting on the easel jump as much as she intended their quarry to. Back turned in his chair at the book-covered desk, however, he didn't flinch from craning over what looked like a weighty reference tome. She thumped it again. 'By ignoring me, you're only convincing me you're definitely up to no good regarding the glass figurine I showed you.' She marched around to confront him. 'And trying to buy a moment to think up another pack of lies! I—' Her hands flew to her mouth at the sight of his puce face set with lifeless eyes, staring into nothingness.

Clifford was immediately beside her. 'Not good,' he muttered, whipping off one glove. He pressed two fingers to the antiquarian's neck, which was streaked with claw marks, his tie hanging loosely, the knot tight, as if he'd tried to wrench it off. Clifford removed his fingers. 'Regrettably, he is dead, my lady.'

She shook her head in disbelief. 'But that's just too awful! I was so busy trying to shock him into being honest with us, I didn't realise.'

'There's no sign of bleeding,' Clifford said, examining the dead man. 'And no weapon protruding from anywhere I can see. I wonder...' He sniffed the air.

'What is it?'

'A particular... odour.'

She breathed in deeply, holding her breath. Then let it out. 'It smells like the mix of things I remember from before. Paint, a bit of grease maybe, brass polish, varnish, and that sort of piney resin smell.' She sniffed again. 'Actually, that last one is stronger than before, now I think about it. Goodness, look there!'

She beckoned Clifford to peer over the edge of the desk as she was. The remains of a tall, stained glass lay in shattered shards across the floor, a short streak of honey yellow staining the pages of the knocked over books.

Together, they quickly stepped over. Clifford sank down to dip the tip of his handkerchief in the sticky liquid lying on the largest glass shard. He held it out for her to smell.

'Some kind of resin. Or varnish? Goodness, that is strong up close. Which feels horribly significant suddenly, but I don't know why,' she murmured, stepping back towards the lifeless Friedman. 'Poor fellow. He looks like he died fighting to breathe. His face is red, but his hands and neck are pale. Save for those claw marks, made by fingernails, I'd say. Not a burn like a rope or similar would leave if he had been strangled.'

'Which he wasn't, I believe,' Clifford said gravely. He leaned in closer to the body and sniffed the dead man's open mouth. 'As I feared. The claw marks were made by his own hands because he died from drinking Venetian turpentine, I think.'

'Poisonous?'

'Very. From my limited knowledge, ingestion can cause a variety of serious consequences. Among them, I remember reading, burning sensations, convulsions, loss of consciousness, and respiratory failure.'

'Though, given his involvement with the figurines in whatever capacity that actually was, this doesn't feel accidental.' She scrutinised the desk more closely, then examined the small tables set with ceramics awaiting repair or restoration. 'There's no real sign of a struggle. The broken glass and books on the floor look more like he knocked them off. During a convulsion, maybe?' She looked around. 'Maybe I was wrong. It does look like suicide at first glance.'

'Or a repeat of a murder being made to look like suicide?'

She nodded grimly. 'Exactly.' The distant, shrill ringing of an alarm bell made them both jerk upright. 'The police, Clifford. Do you think they might be...?'

He pursed his lips. 'I don't know, my lady. Perhaps they are attending a call elsewhere? Who would have contacted them? Unless it was our man in black?'

She shook her head. 'It looked to me like that was the last thought on his mind... oh, my!'

He shot her a look of concern. 'My lady?'

She didn't reply. Instead, she knelt down, her eye fixed on a spot under the desk beside the dead man's shoes. Reaching out slowly as if mesmerised, she picked up a fern-green glove. Standing up, she passed it to him. He took it, both his brows shooting up to his hairline.

'"E.L.S."' He looked at her in disbelief. 'My lady, these are your monogrammed initials! This is—'

'My lost glove. I know. What I don't know is how the devil it got here. And why!'

'Why is easy. Doctor Friedman was forced to drink Venetian turpentine—'

She swallowed hard. 'You think he was definitely murdered, then?'

'Yes. And someone, one assumes the culprit, is trying to frame you for the murder!'

The sound of the clanging bell was now too close to ignore. They stared at each other.

'I would suggest, my lady, this is a case of employing prudence earlier rather than later this time. I know it is not our normal behaviour to flee a murder scene, but in this instance—'

She was already halfway to the door.

33

Outside the bar, Eleanor nodded as her nose tingled with the smell of centuries-old toil, without the luxury of soap. The atmosphere was exactly what she had hoped for; rough and ready, where make-do defined daily life and no questions would be asked.

Let's hope that includes women being admitted, Ellie.

Inside, two rows of stacked beer barrels served as a counter. Despite the early hour, a host of animated games of cards and dice accounted for the coarse-voiced racket. Workmanlike caps and collarless jackets were interspersed with homespun shawls and workaday skirts.

That answers the question of whether women are allowed in, Ellie.

Before she could enter any further, Clifford respectfully blocked her path.

'This is a tavern,' he said in horror. 'The furthest possible place from being a suitable venue for a lady, titled or not.'

'Good. Because to my mind, I'm the furthest cry from being either of those at the moment, given the hideous mess we're in.

In fact, it seems I was only a whisker away from being a fugitive from justice. And might still be for all I know. But I'd love for you to convince me otherwise.'

He shook his head resignedly.

As she settled into the plain wooden seat at the most tucked away table, a white-whiskered man in rolled-up sleeves and an aged waistcoat set down two tankards. He nodded at the amber, froth-topped drinks, plonked down a generous bowl of suspect bread sticks, and shuffled back to the bar. Clifford leaned forward and regarded them askance.

'For heaven's sake, Clifford, do stop behaving like a butler!' she whispered fiercely. 'We need to blend in while we work out what to do!' Realising her worries had made that come out harsher than intended, she grimaced. 'Sorry. While I work it out, I should have said.' She sighed. 'You shouldn't be mixed up in any of this awful trouble, anyway. I so wanted you to come away purely for a holiday.'

'Which it has been,' he said drily. 'In inimitable Lady Swift style; replete with inappropriate venues, danger and, ahem, bodies. However, if you insist on my temporarily relinquishing the duties of your butler, for expediency, I shall not dissent. But never will I do so in regard to keeping you safe.' His expression fell. 'A duty I have failed disgracefully in achieving so far.'

She shook her head vigorously. 'Nonsense. I'd still be locked in that prison of a barge otherwise. Now, get that giant logical brain of yours working. And fast!'

'Very well.' He regarded his tankard with deep suspicion as she risked a sip from hers. 'I suggest we do as we did during our last discussion and stick to one focus only, with purely facts considered wherever possible as before.'

'Good idea. Signor Friedman's death then, since that is horribly uppermost in both our minds.' She ran her hands over her cheeks. 'Now, if it was Doctor Pinsky darting out of the door like a scalded cat, he must have known that Friedman was dead when he ran off.'

'Indubitably, my lady. Because we discovered precisely such only two minutes later. Insufficient time for Signor Friedman to have drunk the Venetian turpentine, forced or otherwise, and for its fatal effects to have taken hold.'

She winced. 'And we're definitely assuming forced, aren't we?' At his nod, she continued. 'Well, your assessment is more than good enough for me. You've proven to know about chemical whatnots and their potentially fatal ramifications many times.'

'Too many times!' he said ruefully.

She nodded. 'And I agree about it not being suicide. I mean, my glove being there, and at Friedman's lifeless feet no less, feels too much like it has to be murder. Otherwise why... try to incriminate me?' she ended falteringly, the magnitude of that notion being too awful to dwell on.

'Distressingly, I can only concur.' Clifford hurried on. 'But, if the perpetrator of this heinous murder was not Doctor Pinsky, why did he flee, rather than call the police?'

She clicked her fingers. 'Because he *is* the murderer! Or at least he's connected with the murders. Clifford, think about it. We saw Doctor Pinsky talking intently with the thief behind that grillework, remember?'

'Most assuredly. And if all three deaths have occurred over the figurine, perhaps Doctor Pinsky wishes the two families to restart the feud? Albeit for reasons unknown to us at this juncture.'

'He's not a member of either family, though.'

'True. He is the only person on our rather tentative suspect list who is not. If you exclude our thief, who may, or may not, be related to either family.'

'You're right. We still have absolutely no idea who he is.' Her fists balled. 'Other than being a sort of evil version of yourself, Clifford. At least as far as your mastery of skulduggery and other associated dark crafts is concerned.'

He sniffed. 'If a compliment was intended, please forgive my having missed it.'

'Oh, you know what I mean. And how much I appreciate your rather dubious talents. I need them now, more than ever, I promise you! But the rogue seems unbeatable, whatever we try. It's like he knows what we're going to do before we know ourselves.' She threw her hands out in frustration. 'If I'm being honest, at this moment I'm completely lost.'

'As am I, my lady.' He inched her tankard closer. 'Italian courage, in lieu of something more traditional?'

'It's really quite tasty,' she said, lying badly. 'Now, if it was Doctor Pinsky who left my glove at the scene, how could he have got hold of it, do you suppose?'

He rubbed his chin. 'You first noticed it was missing whilst shopping with the contessa, I believe you said? Unless that was merely a ruse to distract one from the near decimation of the household accounts in a single afternoon, of course?'

She laughed. 'No, it wasn't. I can only think I dropped it when I bumped into Vincenzo after chasing the thief.'

Clifford arched a brow. 'Which you did, literally. Head on.'

She pointed a breadstick at him. 'And my bag flew open when I fell, yes! The rogue could have surreptitiously returned, found my glove, and then passed it on to Doctor Pinsky. Which could have been what they were passing through the grillework, perhaps?'

'Perhaps. But there is a more uncomfortable alternative.'

She gasped. 'That Vincenzo pocketed it while supposedly helping collect my things?'

He nodded. 'Would that I could refute the possibility, but I was too far away retrieving your hat, as well as his. He may even have bumped into you deliberately to allow the thief to escape. An easy scheme for him to orchestrate because he knew where you would be. On your way to meet him. And thus he could have arranged for the thief to lead you to that very spot outside the *tabacchi* shop.'

She shivered. 'I hope we're wrong, Clifford. I went down to the church crypt alone with Vincenzo!'

He paled. 'Not something you mentioned, my lady. However, let us be thankful that if he is the murderer, it seems he wished to keep you alive long enough to take the blame for Signor Friedman's death.'

'Lucky me,' she muttered. 'Though... I told him I had one of the figurines!'

He raised a brow. 'Before or after he told you Signor Friedman was the restorer and cleaner?'

'Does it matter which?'

Clifford let out a long breath. 'Maybe not, as Signor Vendelini may only have mentioned Signor Friedman's involvement in the affair to ensure you would revisit the gentleman.'

She rubbed her eyes. 'Actually, no, that can't be. I was kidnapped on the way there, so... oh, of course! Vincenzo made sure I'd realise Friedman had lied to me, because he knew that I would go straight back there to have it out with him. Vincenzo then quickly told the thief, who waited and kidnapped me. They then blackmailed the figurine from you, and let you free me. And while we were fleeing the barge, they silenced Friedman because, I assume, he knew too much. Framing me for the murder was just the icing on top of everything else!' She slapped her forehead. 'Oh, Clifford, I feel such a blunt brick about everything.'

'Acting selflessly in a noble cause on the best available knowledge at the time can never warrant censure, my lady. And particularly so in Venice, where nothing seems to run on any recognisable lines!'

'Thank you, Clifford.' She took another swig of her tankard, shuddering as she swallowed. 'But if Vincenzo is behind all of this, what can his motive be?'

He sighed. 'Would that I knew. Rekindling the feud between his family and the Marcellos is all that comes to mind. But for what gain?' He shook his head.

'That's the same for everyone we've encountered since Benetto was murdered, dash it!'

They looked over as a row broke out at one of the card-strewn tables.

The tavern keeper waved a dismissive hand as he passed. 'Is no trouble. No worry.'

Clifford eyed her earnestly. 'I need the same to be true for my mistress. And before my heart gives out with worry. My lady, what can we do?'

His deep concern for her refuelled her resolve.

'We need to work out a plan by the time we've finished our tankards. But one which doesn't involve going to the police. Agreed?'

He nodded with more vehemence than he would normally show. 'Categorically. We have no concrete evidence to give them, and no idea who is truly responsible. Nor, as Angelo confirmed to us, any idea who might be impartial among the police force.'

'The one thing we can be sure of is that if any one of them had found my glove beside the dead Signor Friedman, right now I'd probably be walking over that Bridge of Sighs. To the prison, taking my last ever view of Venice. Or anywhere else!'

Clifford blanched. 'If we might not allude to such, my lady. It sounds like a scene from one of your deplorable penny dread-fuls. Only it would doubtless involve a highwayman or pirate.'

She jerked straighter at the image his words had flashed into her mind.

'Actually. I have been reading something rather more

esoteric back at Henley Hall this last month. In between the penny dreadfuls, of course.'

He shook his head. 'I can only imagine, my lady.'

Her jaw set in a grim line. 'Good. Because, in the absence of any other plan, it might just furnish us with a means to flush out our murderer!'

34

The disapproving flick of Clifford's pristine handkerchief over the array of functional wooden chairs would have made Eleanor shake her head affectionately in any other circumstances. As would the impromptu drinks station he'd set up on the battered filing cabinet in the far corner.

'It's not supposed to be a refined drinks party.' She waved a hand around the third-floor room of the nameless warehouse they were waiting anxiously in. 'We're here to offer someone a shady... low and dirty deal, I think is the expression?'

He ran the tip of his gloved finger along the chipped edge of the impromptu meeting table. 'As so comprehensively epitomised by the chosen setting.'

She shrugged. 'It was the best Angelo could come up with, as well you know. Luckily, his friend knew this warehouse would be empty today. And in case you hadn't realised, Clifford, we're totally backs to the wall here!'

He shook his head. 'I cannot concur, my lady. The flaking plaster would sully the rear of both our attire most unacceptably.'

'Clifford!' she huffed before catching the twinkle in his

eyes. 'Oh, I get it. You've been squabbling to distract me from getting jittery over who, if anyone, will bite at our bait?'

'Perhaps.' He cupped his ear. 'Ah, but someone has bitten. I hear footsteps downstairs. Good luck and remember, you have the upper hand, my lady. Hopefully no one knows it was Angelo who, through the gondoliers' grapevine, spread the rumour that the figurines were being auctioned to the highest bidder this afternoon. Whoever is walking up those stairs is already on the back foot.'

'Right. We both know what to do?' she hissed back. At his reassuring nod, she crossed both sets of fingers. 'It worked in that detective novel I read. And to solve a truly unfathomable crime.'

'Then we'll be fine, my lady.' She slid into the chair at the head of the table and struck a confident pose. On hearing the footsteps on the landing outside, Clifford raised his voice slightly. 'Most definitely, given the potential benefits to interested parties. The asking price should be raised significantly.'

She gave him a thumbs up. 'As I've said all along. And they say women have no head for business!'

Clifford answered a confident knock on the door. A pair of stylish leather brogues strode in.

'Ah, Vincenzo,' she said, realising that of course he'd come, whether he was mixed up in the shady side of this terrible business or not. He had already told her he was trying to find the figurines. She composed her face again. 'How nice of you to grace us with your presence.'

Instead of his customary easy smile, only an agitated frown and an intense stare met her gaze. 'You!' He glanced around the room. 'What is this, Eleanor? Are you working for the enemy now?'

Before she could reply, Clifford gestured discreetly that there were more footsteps on the way up the stairs.

'Looks like we are going to have quite the party,' she said, sidestepping the question.

Dash it, Ellie! This could be more complicated in real life than it was in the book.

And so it proved as the contessa marched in. Eleanor blinked rapidly but before she could say a word, the contessa spoke first. 'Well, of all the... so, you are behind this little joke, my dear? Not a pleasant one, however.' Eleanor caught the corners of the contessa's mouth turn down as she stepped up to Vincenzo. 'No surprise that you are here, of course.'

He smiled thinly. 'It seems, Contessa, we've both unwittingly fallen prey to the English sense of poor humour.'

Time to take charge like the detective in the book, Ellie.

'Oh, it's no joke,' she said. 'Gracious, no. Purely business. So, please, both of you have a seat. Oh, and a drink.'

Looking less than delighted, the contessa folded her elegant curves into the nearest chair, while Vincenzo sat opposite her.

Eleanor waited for them to settle as Clifford served glasses of spritz. 'So, you are both here because of certain information, let's call it, which came your way?'

Vincenzo's eyes narrowed. 'Yes, as well you must know. Naturally, when I heard that someone was auctioning the figurines off, I had no choice but to come. But then,' he said, holding her gaze, 'that is so often the trouble with rumours.'

Eleanor shrugged. 'What makes you think it is a rumour?'

His features hardened. 'Because, Lady Swift, to auction them, you'd have to have them in your possession. Do you?'

She hesitated. The simple answer was 'no', of course. This was all one big bluff. But it was the best, and only, way they could come up with to lure the killer out and trick him, or her, into confessing. The second part of that was rather troublesome as well. No matter how often she recounted to Clifford how the detective had done it in the book, neither of them could quite work out how that would unfold in reality. She was playing a dangerous game.

She smiled. 'Contessa, Vincenzo, only one of you can leave in possession of—'

'The devil take your heart!' Nonno Marcello bellowed, stomping in and waving his cane so furiously, his ivory hair shook. 'I demand to know what is going on!' He glanced around the table. 'Vincenzo Vendelini! You're as no good as all those who have ever been born to your miserable family.' His finely groomed white moustache quivered as he rapped his cane hard on the floor. 'And Eugenia, you of all people! Why are you here, as if I didn't know?'

The contessa smoothed her dress. 'For the same reason you are, Nonno, presumably? I am trying to get my hands on the figurines, of course, for the honour of our family.'

He snorted. 'Eugenia, you have always been a terrible liar.' He turned and marched stiffly up to Eleanor. 'And you. I remember meeting you at Eugenia's party. Now, I don't know what your game is, foolish woman, but hand over those figurines this minute!'

'A drink, Signor Marcello?' Clifford held out the drinks tray. The old patriarch waved him away brusquely.

Eleanor mentally thanked her butler for giving her a moment to compose herself.

'Not even a please?' she said in a sweet tone. Just like when she had challenged him at the contessa's party, his face flushed bright red. Before he could explode, she held up a hand. 'Foolish you may think I am if you wish, but I'm not so stupid as to have brought them with me.'

For a moment, she thought he was going to strike her with his cane as he lifted it above his head. Clifford obviously had the same idea as he hurriedly stepped forward. Then Nonno Marcello brought it down with a thump on the floor.

'Then on your own head may the aftermath be!' He leaned

into her face. 'I have no idea what you are up to. But neither do I care! If the figurines are not handed over to me at midnight tonight, you, and the Vendelini family, will bear the consequences!'

He brought his cane down onto the tabletop with a resounding whack and stormed out.

Vincenzo gestured angrily after him. 'Old mule! When will he realise he cannot rule Venice forever!'

The contessa banged her glass on the table. 'Apologise immediately! Nonno is still the head of my family.'

Vincenzo smirked. 'Why should I? You do not care about your family. And least of all, the grand Nonno Marcello!'

Clifford raised an eyebrow as Eleanor flashed him a look of enquiry.

He's right, Ellie. Let them reveal themselves like the detective did in the novel.

The contessa seemed to struggle to regain her composure. 'I have no idea what you mean! But it appears there is no end to your lack of manners today.'

'Really? Yours is a very tired act from where I am seated,' Vincenzo scoffed. He turned to Eleanor. 'This, you see, is the true reason the contessa has come running to your little party this afternoon.'

Still unsure if he was on the level or not, Eleanor sat back nonchalantly, ignoring the contessa's glare.

'Do continue.'

He adjusted the fine creases of his tailored trousers, a sardonic smile on his face. 'The contessa and her daughter, Regina, worked for years to ensnare Leonardo. But when Catarina appeared on the scene as Nonno's ward, young Leonardo fell madly in love with her. And it was she who made him realise he was being reeled into their scheme like a blind fish.'

'As if I would stoop to snaring anyone, or anything!' the contessa exclaimed. 'Such lies!'

Eleanor decided playing them off against each other looked like it might pay off. 'Matchmaking for mothers seems a common enough pastime?'

'Thank you,' the contessa said, having regained her sangfroid.

'As is revenge,' Vincenzo said darkly. 'Because since Leonardo fell in love with Catarina, the contessa has been determined to ruin his and Catarina's happiness by stopping the marriage. Even if that means starting the feud between the two families again. All her other unscrupulous efforts have failed. And failure tastes very bitter to someone who believes they deserve the world.'

Eleanor nodded slowly, noting the death stare the contessa was directing at Vincenzo.

'You see,' he continued, 'if she had succeeded in marrying Regina to Leonardo, she would have realised her dream. To be the head, the Nonna, of not only the Marcellos but also the Vendelinis as the two would be united for the first time by the marriage of her daughter.'

'Nonsense!' the contessa snarled.

Eleanor waved her down. 'Let me start by saying that the feud between your two families is of no interest, or consequence to me, Contessa. But do tell me, is what Vincenzo said true? Did you kill Benetto Vendelini and Gaspo Secco to fulfil your dreams?'

In the corner, Clifford's inscrutable expression faltered momentarily.

The contessa half rose from her chair. 'I did not!' She bit her lip, and slowly sank back into her seat. 'I might have tried to secure Leonardo as my son-in-law, yes. But I did not, and would not, kill to do so. That, Lady Swift, is slander!' She shrugged. 'I merely took advantage of another's actions to... further my cause as it were.'

To stir up violence and hatred, she means, Ellie.

'Which,' the contessa continued, her voice becoming more and more vitriolic, 'led me to the figurines. If they were mine to dispose of as I wished, I could ensure Nonno carried out his threat. Then I would teach that young boy, and his hussy, a lesson not to cross me and toss aside my daughter as if she were nothing!'

'Now do you understand her motive in coming here?' Vincenzo said to Eleanor.

'Perhaps she does,' the contessa said scornfully. 'But she hasn't heard your ugly tale yet.'

'I do not have one,' he said quickly.

'We'll let Lady Swift be the judge of that, shall we?'

35

'Well, if I must, go ahead.' Eleanor waved her hand languidly, as if the whole thing was becoming an inconvenience.

The contessa smiled cruelly. 'The charming Signor Vincenzo Vendelini cares even less for his family than he claims I do. He has climbed as far up the ladder of nepotism as he can. Now he wishes to obtain those figurines so he can profit from the chaos when the two families, let's be frank, go to war. And in the power vacuum he hopes will result in his own family, he intends to—'

Vincenzo laughed, much to Eleanor's surprise. 'Not "intends to". I will! I am Venetian first and always. Power is the blood which fuels my body! I am not ashamed to say this. Nor to chase whatever will take me there. But I did not kill my relative Benetto. Nor the gondolier. And before you ask, Lady Swift, I am not prepared to leave anything to chance. Especially' – he shot the contessa a disparaging look – 'not by letting a woman obtain those figurines and watching her mess up the job!' He turned back to Eleanor. 'The one thing the contessa and I agree on, however, is that accusing either of us of murder is slander. Half the senior ranking officers in the police force are related to the contessa or myself. Am I making myself clear?'

Eleanor looked between them, only vaguely registering that Clifford had glided away. 'Perfectly clear. But here's my dilemma. If neither of you killed the two men, who did?'

The two stared at each other, then pointed at the door. 'Doctor Pinsky!' they chorused.

The doctor stepped over the threshold with Clifford behind him.

'For a thousand years and more, has that not always been the cry?' the doctor said evenly from the doorway. 'Why? Because the Jew always gets the blame!' He came into the room and bowed stiffly to Eleanor. 'And that is the answer to a different question you must have been asking yourself, Lady Swift. Why did I not go to the police on finding Signor Friedman dead?'

Because the Jew always gets the blame, Ellie. Not for the first time, she found herself unable to refute an unpalatable truth.

'Friedman?' Vincenzo shook his head. 'Dead?'

She scrutinised his features, but couldn't work out if it was genuine surprise or not. The contessa's expression was equally difficult to decipher.

'Yes,' Eleanor said, watching them closely. 'He was murdered.'

'Then Pinsky killed him!' the contessa said smugly.

'There's no doubt about that,' Vincenzo agreed, too readily for Eleanor's mind. She turned to him.

'For what reason? Doctor Pinsky is from neither of your two families as far as I know. Why should he want them to feud?'

'Lady Swift,' Pinsky said through a clenched jaw. 'Unsurprised though I am, I did not come here to be accused of a shopping list of ill deeds these two are doubtless looking to hang on an innocent man. I am not guilty of killing anyone. I am a doctor. It is my calling to preserve life, not destroy it.'

Despite having no motive for him, she was not convinced by his argument. *Sadly, there have been plenty of doctors who killed throughout history, Ellie.* She held her hands out. 'Then what are you here for?'

'I am forced to be here, because I have an interest in the figurines. But that is all I shall say on the matter for the moment.'

She shrugged. 'Then please take a seat with the other interested parties, Doctor Pinsky.'

With a curt nod, he sat at the opposite end of the table to Vincenzo and the contessa.

She shot Clifford another look. The plan had worked to some extent. Possible suspects had been flushed out of the woodwork. And anyone after the figurines was surely a strong suspect for any, or all three, of the murders. But had their plan drawn the true murderer into their somewhat loosely spun web? Or were they still waiting—

At the sound of hesitant footsteps coming up the stairs, Clifford darted out and, a moment later, herded a nervous, but determined-looking Leonardo into the room.

Eleanor didn't miss that Doctor Pinsky started at the sight of him.

Leonardo's eyes shot around the table, resting briefly on each person, then darting away. He ran a hand through his flowing walnut curls, clearly waiting for someone to speak. When they didn't, he cleared his throat. 'I... I came because I heard someone' – he looked at Eleanor and away – 'was... auctioning the figurines?'

Eleanor eyed him coolly. 'Well, maybe you heard right. But what is your interest in them?'

He hesitated. 'I need them so... so...' He sighed heavily and threw his hands out. 'I'm through pretending. So I can marry the woman I love.' He shot a defiant look across the table at the contessa, who scowled back.

Is this all an act, Ellie?

Clifford's face was giving nothing away. She tapped the table.

'Leonardo, before we talk more about the figurines, do you remember a certain night when Clifford and I spoke to you about that very matter?' He nodded hesitantly. 'Good. Then my question is, why did you disappear?'

She caught his eyes slide sideways to Doctor Pinsky and then back to her. 'I... I don't see how that's relevant.'

Clifford coughed from his sentinel's post. 'Then the door is waiting just here, signore,' he said sternly.

Leonardo looked around the room. Eleanor forced a laugh. 'Don't worry. Whatever you have to say will be less... slanderous than we've already heard.' She smiled sweetly, nodding at Vincenzo and the contessa.

Leonardo tugged on the front of his waistcoat. 'Alright. I was about to... to join you, when someone appeared and... and warned me it was a trick.'

'What sort of a trick?'

'One to kidnap me. Or even kill me. I... went into hiding. But' – he pulled himself up to his full height – 'I decided I cannot sit by and let others put themselves in danger on my, or my... love's account. So I have come here to get those figurines.' He glared at Vincenzo and the contessa. 'Whatever it takes!'

The contessa stood up, her eyes blazing. 'Over my, or anyone else's, dead body!'

Eleanor blanched as the room erupted into a barrage of threats, accusations and recriminations.

Clifford slid up to her. 'Amazing, my lady. The plan has gone almost as you described it to me from your novel,' he murmured. 'Bar one insignificant detail. What exactly did your fictional detective do next?'

She groaned quietly. 'I've no idea. I should have stuck to

penny dreadfuls. Dash it, find a makeshift gavel, will you, so I
can call this lot back to order and try again?'

A very uncomfortable hour later, Eleanor trudged
disconsolately beside Clifford towards their hotel, doing her
best to heed his repeated cautions they needed to be stealthy
just in case the police were looking for her in relation to Friedman's murder.

'What a fiasco,' she groaned quietly. 'That ended in absolute
uproar!'

'A most artful ploy on your part to inform each party you
would contact them individually later today and call the
meeting to a close, my lady.'

'Beat a hasty retreat, you mean.' She sighed.

'Yes. But far from it being a complete fiasco, we learned
three new motives, all of which could have given cause for
murder.' Clifford counted off on his gloved fingers as he steered
them onwards. 'Signor Vendelini admitted to wanting to grab
power by pitting the families against each other. The contessa
confessed she wants revenge for young Leonardo not agreeing
to marry her daughter, Regina. And the young gentleman
himself declared he is ardently seeking the figurines so he can
return them and marry young Miss Catarina Marcello.'

'And Nonno Marcello?'

'Hmm, I am minded to think he may have arrived purely as
a smokescreen.'

'To keep up appearances in trying to find the figurines?' She
nodded as he flapped a respectful hand to keep her voice down.
'That would explain why he left so quickly. It seemed odd a
man of his impossible mule-headedness would bow out so readily. Even in a fit of rage.'

He nodded. 'Nevertheless, as I said, I felt the meeting was a
success. Certainly in as much as they all left looking highly

swayed that you do have the figurines. Which means, worryingly, the plan may produce the result we were seeking after all.'

She frowned. 'How? And why worryingly?"

'Because if everyone is now convinced we have both figurines, with Nonno Marcello's deadline only' – he glanced at his pocket watch – 'three and a half hours away, I believe we may soon receive a visit from the very person we were seeking.'

'The killer!'

36

Even after Mrs Butters' second message of reassurance that there had been no police or shady characters hanging around their hotel, Clifford still insisted they took every precaution.

'That's all very well,' she whispered. 'But what plausible excuse have you got up your impeccable sleeves if we get caught sneaking in the service entrance and up the staff stairs?'

'Absolutely none, my lady. So let's not be.'

She tiptoed hurriedly after him, holding her breath until they reached their landing. He gestured for them to hasten to her suite's door, which he unlocked in a trice with his picklocks, the key being down behind the reception desk.

After he'd silently closed the door behind them, she dropped onto the ottoman and sighed. 'It's almost dark outside and I know we're trying to lie low, but let's have the lamps on to dispel at least some of the gloom in the room?'

'If not the lady's uncharacteristic plunge of spirits. Though I am sure she will bounce back after a well-deserved restorative.'

He turned towards the nearest lamp, then stopped, turning instead to close the ivory silk curtains over the double doors out to the terrace first. But as he reached up, he stiffened and pressed himself against the wall.

'Intruder!' he mouthed, waving urgently for her to duck behind the settee.

Already, Ellie?

She shook her head, flattening herself against the wall on the other side of the French windows. 'We grab whoever it is together,' she whispered.

He shook his head in return. 'They might be armed.'

'All the more reason for a joint attack.'

He sighed in resignation and counted down wordlessly on his fingers, 3-2-1!

They flew out through the doors in unison and rounded on the figure, draped in a black hooded opera cape, a Carnival mask obscuring his face.

'Got you!' she muttered, grabbing a shoulder. 'Watch out, Clifford! He's wet and this silk cape's hellishly slippery.'

'You wretch!' Clifford growled, one hand gripped around the man's throat over the neck of the hood. 'I'll teach you a lesson you'll never forget. Or walk away from,' he ended so menacingly, Eleanor blanched.

A plaintive gurgle came in reply.

'Save it!' she whispered fiercely. 'This ends now.'

'I was only sneaking past,' the figure croaked.

'Pathetic excuse, man!' Clifford grunted.

'Bit harsh when a chap knows he is already.'

Eleanor stared at Clifford in confusion. 'Kip? Is... is that you?' she whispered.

'What's left of me,' he wheezed. 'This... this probably doesn't look quite the decent show on my part, I imagine,' he panted, lowering his voice at Clifford's stern shush. 'But it's only the second time I've nipped across your terrace to slide down that pillar at the end, I swear. It's the only way I can sneak along to my room on the floor below, you see.'

Clifford's expression darkened. 'Twice! If you think admitting such will help your case, you are sorely mistaken. I should hurl you off the balcony!'

Kip edged backwards. 'Er, Lady Swift, any chance you might call off your attack dog?'

'That depends.' She folded her arms, overcome by a frisson of mistrust for everyone she'd met in this infernal city. 'Why are you lurking on my balcony?'

Kip hung his head. 'I wasn't lurking. I was eluding the police again, I'm afraid. They're after me with a vengeance this time.'

'After her ladyship vouched for you?' Clifford hissed in disgust.

'Quite!' She shot him a cautionary look. 'However, we don't really want to bring the police here for any reason. They can be rather... bothersome.'

'Inside!' Clifford muttered grimly.

Oh, dear, Ellie. The stress of the last few days is starting to show on both of us.

With the three of them inside, Clifford closed the French windows and then the curtains against prying eyes, which made Kip stare imploringly at Eleanor.

She shook her head. 'It's alright. Though he's positively itching to do so, my butler won't actually snap you in half. But you have some explaining to do. First, Clifford, perhaps you might countenance Kip swapping his wet cape for a dry hotel robe? And then restoratives all round?'

A few minutes later, her pulse had calmed and Clifford had relaxed his stern manner somewhat. The ridiculous figure their supposed intruder cut was restoring her sense of humour. With Kip's aristocratic height, the bathrobe finished just above his knees, so Clifford had insisted a lap blanket, pink at that, be added to the ensemble as a wrapover skirt.

'Mischievous rascal!' she murmured as he held out a glass of brandy on a silver tray. She took a sip and turned to their visitor, who was nervously taking his own glass from Clifford and studiously avoiding eye contact.

'Right, come on, Kip. A few sips to loosen your tongue, and then let's hear the whole sorry tale.' She glanced at the mantel-piece clock.

Not that we really have the time, Ellie.

He savoured a grateful glug before ruffling his blond hair dolefully. 'It's a tragic one, alright. Our illustrious Lord Byron made it all seem so easy from the accounts I've read among Pater's vast library of biographical and autobiographical books. There's no record of him being arrested that I've come across.'

'Although his self-imposed exile from his native England was, perhaps, in part to avoid arrest,' Clifford said.

'But I'm not doing any of the truly controversial things he did!' Kip protested. 'Like courting hundreds of married women under their husbands' noses and scandalously—'

'Ahem!'

Kip held his hands up in apology. Eleanor threw him a more sympathetic look.

'Lord Byron's raft of evidently unmentionable indiscretions aside, what exactly *were* you doing to have incensed the police again?'

'Only swimming in the canals.' At her look, he sighed. 'Oh, I know it's illegal. But well, that's the whole spirit of the romance of it all, don't you see?'

She waved an amused hand over his appearance. 'Not at the moment, but maybe I'm not like your sort of girls?'

'*Girl.*' He held up one finger. 'In the singular. Heavens, what kind of a first-class rat do you think I am?'

'I won't answer that,' she said teasingly. 'So you were swim-ming to impress your latest conquest?'

'My sweetheart,' he said emphatically. 'Of course, we're very new together and all that on account of me only just arriving in Venice, as it were. But it worked for Byron almost a hundred years ago and on first meeting. Girls haven't changed much in all that time. We chaps still have to step up and do the daring knight on a white charger routine, you know. What appeal has a duffer like me to any fair maiden without that?'

'The person he really is, Kip,' she said kindly, thinking he was far too bashful a young soul to be trying to live out his father's unfulfilled adventurous yearnings. 'So, you were what? Swimming up and down manfully while she watched?'

His face lit with animation. 'No! Swimming up to her window with a discreetly burning torch held above my head. Just like Byron used to do to his, well, ladies.'

She glanced at Clifford. 'I can't imagine Byron did anything discreetly?'

'Indeed not. Hence the epithet he earned from Lady Caroline Lamb; "Mad, bad and dangerous to know!"'

She bit back the retort that she was sorry she couldn't have met him herself.

'But I had to be discreet,' Kip said. 'My sweetheart's father doesn't approve. And he's terribly fierce.' He glanced at Clifford. 'Not as fierce as you, though.'

'I shall take that as a compliment, sir,' Clifford said impassively.

Eleanor winced as the clock chimed nine. Time was getting away from her. Wishing she had more hours to idle in Kip's entertaining company, she caught Clifford's eye as she rose. Kip leaped up and put his glass down.

'I say, too good of you not to make a fuss about my stealing across your terrace, Lady Swift. And of your butler not to actually rip my head off my shoulders.'

'Next time,' Clifford said firmly. 'Though there had better not be one.'

As she moved towards the door, she smiled. 'Well, Kip, I hope your sweetheart let you in through her window? Despite you having swapped your shining armour and white charger for soggy striped bathing trunks and a Venetian canal?'

'Actually, no,' he moaned, looking more dejected than ever. 'Own stupid fault, of course. I only went and swam up to the wrong blasted building! Chap felt a right fool appearing at the window. Especially as the police grabbed me on my way back. Luckily, I managed to give them the slip.'

She caught Clifford rolling his eyes.

'Well, if it's any consolation, you probably gave whoever was on the other side of that window a proper shock.'

'Not so,' Kip said. 'The chap inside was far too busy to notice me at all.' He frowned and ran his hand through his hair again. 'Odd thing, now I think of it. When I snuck along your terrace the first time, I couldn't help noticing you were admiring some glass statue affair.'

At her and Clifford's angry expressions, he held his hands up again. 'I wasn't peeping. Promise!'

But Clifford was already propelling a cowering Kip towards the door. As Eleanor opened it to allow him to throw their guest out, Kip swung around.

'All I was going to say was the chap inside the house I went to, the wrong one, had a statue just the same.'

Without pause, Clifford deftly turned him about face and marched him back into the sitting room as she shut the door.

'Another brandy, Lord Kipling?' Clifford plopped the totally confused, and rather scared, Kip, down on one of the sofas. 'Two, perhaps? And do allow me to find you a more suitable change of clothes...'

37

Venice seemed to be on Eleanor's side for the first time since she'd arrived in the trouble-filled city. The streets were bustling with the animated, masked Venetians sidestepping the official ban on the Carnival. Clearly, more than half the houses were holding a private party given the unrelenting kaleidoscope of elaborate headdresses, masks and all-encompassing costumes passing them by. All this activity meant the three of them were practically invisible as they stole along. Though, she thought with a shiver, with every face covered in almost ubiquitously porcelain white there was no telling who was an angel, and who a devil. Her heart thudded, remembering Vincenzo's remark about her not having seen the city in a shroud of white. She thought he'd meant snow, but maybe not?

There was no ignoring the hideous truth, however. They were relying once more on a hastily thought-out plan, reliant on way too many things outside their control. But what could they do with time running out? It was now or never. They'd gone up against their adversary thrice already, and each result had been the same.

So you've already missed the chance of third time lucky, Ellie.

But there was a merciless triple killer to stop. In a city she didn't understand, and where she had no idea who she could trust any more.

Perhaps because you can't trust anyone, Ellie?

She shook her head. No, she could trust Clifford. Her only worry was whether he would lose his nerve and try to lock her back in the hotel room they'd left only half an hour earlier. Glancing at him next to her, she thought, given his... unusual appearance, it was more likely he'd lock himself in and refuse to come out.

Catching a faint smile around her lips, Clifford rolled his eyes. Holding tight to the gold hat which hid her identifiable curls as her mask did her face, she hoisted the skirt of her balloon-hooped gown to one side, and whispered, 'Thank you for being the best sport ever, Clifford. Kip did his best in grabbing the first three outfits he thought would fit each of us. Small consolation, I know. But with that lace-frilled shirt and all the flowing cardinal red velvet of your Regency courtier-cum-highwayman guise, you look positively dashing. Needs must and all that.'

He nodded resignedly under his feather-trimmed mask. 'I will endure the ignominy tonight in the name of a higher cause. But after that...' He sniffed pointedly.

'I hear you,' she said placatingly.

Kip straightened up from adjusting the cape of his diamond-patterned Harlequin costume. 'I say. One thing.' His tone turned earnest. 'Suppose a chap isn't really cut out for this type of caper? It'd ruin everything, what?'

'We'll never find out,' Eleanor said. 'Because you'll be fine. I'd never have asked for your help if we weren't in a serious jam, or if I had a moment's doubt you could pull it off.'

With Kip's chest swelling with pride, she took a deep breath.

'Now, let's hurry before this storm Clifford's barometer predicted arrives early and ruins our plan!'

'Right,' Kip said. 'The best way I know to keep my bearings is to skirt around the back of St Mark's Square. Then keep a street or two off the tourist area, and head straight. So off we go...'

Fifteen minutes later, Eleanor was starting to really fret. There was no denying the packed walkways had been helpful camouflage, but they'd slowed them down to half-speed. Now, the reverse was true. As they'd entered a part of the city that was unfamiliar to her, the crowds had thinned but the three of them stood out like sore thumbs. And worse, the paranoid feeling that they were being shadowed had returned. But every time she spun around or thought she'd seen a shadowy figure, it turned out to be a false alarm. After the third time, she kept it to herself, her eyes darting to and fro, but her lips silent. This area had more canals than anywhere else in the city she'd been, and yet, fewer bridges, which slowed them down even further. The streets weren't playing ball either. Rather than staying relatively wide thoroughfares, they consisted of narrow walkways strung along one side of the canal only. And the few revellers they did encounter seemed to have on even more elaborate costumes than their own. Which made passing without one of them ending up in the canal a task in itself.

Clifford obviously sensed her growing nerves.

'My lady, as long as our Harlequin guide can retrace his steps, we'll have the best chance possible.'

She nodded. 'I know. It's just that the hours, no, minutes, are ticking away! We're—'

Kip spun around. 'A bit baffled for one moment, I shan't pretend.' He herded them both back the way they'd come. She bit her lip, trying not to show her frustration.

'Any landmarks you might remember, sir?' Clifford said calmly.

'Oh, think, Kip, please!' Eleanor blurted out, immediately regretting it.

Kip closed his eyes. 'Yes, there was a stained-glass window of a lion. But I thought I'd turned left there as I did before...' He opened them and looked around, scratching his head. 'But I don't seem to recognise—'

Clifford held up his hand. 'From here, back the way we came, then right, then second left. I noticed one matching that description two streets ago down an alley we did not take.'

'Brilliant!' she said. 'Both of you. Now, please, can we hurry?'

Back at the point Clifford had retraced their steps to, music mixed with raucous laughter echoed across the water from the houses bordering the canal. To Eleanor, it was a reminder that soon, in St Mark's Square, there would be the biggest party in Venice. And if they were late, it might just go with a terrible bang!

Kip nodded to Clifford. 'Bailed a chap out there, old man. Thanks. It's not far now. Along one of the next few canals, I'm pretty sure. Where the backs of the buildings mostly have those balconies one window wide.'

'I can picture them, but I can't see any like that at the moment,' Eleanor said as they hurried on.

'Ah!' Kip abruptly flapped them to a halt and pointed across the canal. 'There! The fourth house. That's it! And there's a light on.'

She stared across at the lower windows barred with grille-work just above the water. A middle-terraced house with no rear exit, the only direct way in would be the front door. Or the second-floor balcony window overlooking the canal.

Clifford slid out his familiar kid leather pouch and flipped the top to reveal a set of picklocks. 'The front, and I assume only, door, must be around the block where a concourse similar to this will allow access. We'll let ourselves in that way.'

Kip gawped at the picklocks. 'I say, who are you two, really?'

'Merely hapless tourists who stumbled into the wrong place at the wrong time,' her butler said smoothly, Eleanor too distracted in scanning the second-floor balconies to reply.

'No lights in any of the upstairs windows,' she murmured to herself, then spun around to tug on the neck closure of Kip's cape. 'Please hurry and do your Lord Byron impression and give the appropriate signal. Hopefully, the one we're looking for!'

'We cannot afford for our trump card to get wet,' Clifford said. 'I shall throw you the packets once you are safely across.'

'I'll be ready!' Kip whispered eagerly as he bobbed down to rip at his shoelaces. Barefoot, he slid silently into the water and struck out for the other side of the canal.

A clock chimed ten fifteen.

'Less than two hours to go! Please, please, don't let us be late. Or on a wild goose chase,' Eleanor murmured.

Kip reached the wall of the house and strained one arm upwards to get a grasp on the bottom of the grillework. With the agility of youth, he pulled himself up. His head cleared the bottom of the window and instantly ducked back down. He braced himself with one hand still holding the grillework and both feet against the wall, raising the other hand to signal twice.

Clifford took a deep breath. 'The thief is there. With the figurine.'

With the deftness of a magician, Clifford whipped a cylindrical parcel from inside his jacket and, nodding to Kip to make sure he was ready, bowled it across the water.

She held her breath. Just as it looked as if the parcel would sail over his head, Kip closed his fist on the prize, waving it triumphantly, but silently, before tucking it under his chin.

The second parcel sailed over. This time Kip was slow, and

it struck the wall and bounced off. She drew a sharp intake of breath, but Kip caught it on the rebound before it hit the water.

'Quick! To the front door!' Clifford said.

'No.' She tugged him back by his jacket sleeve. 'Don't fight me, please. Not this time.'

His brows knitted. 'My lady, why do I feel my heart sinking?'

'Because you're the most wonderful and caring butler ever. But right now, we have to beat a very cunning thief—'

'Who may also be a multiple murderer!'

'I promise to be careful, but with the unknown layout of that house it's going to take every element of surprise on our side.' She held his concerned gaze. 'We know doing the same thing over and over and expecting a different result is madness, but this time we have a, hopefully, trump card.'

He swallowed hard, clearly arguing with himself. Then he gave a resigned nod and produced what looked like a flat, miniature crowbar from his inside pocket. 'Prudence will stay glued to your side?'

'And yours? You're precious too, you know.'

Like Clifford, Kip hurriedly spun around to face away as she hoiked up her gown to wrestle with the fixings of her hooped underskirt. Stepping out of it, she threw it into the shadows.

'Now I'll be able to move. And climb.' She propelled Clifford along to the nearest footbridge and then back to the end house in the row. 'I need a leg up onto that decorative stonework so I can reach the first balcony. Do you see?'

'Reluctantly, yes.'

With his help, she grasped the bottom of the balustrade and pulled herself up and over onto the balcony. She turned and waved down to Clifford to carry on to the front. Jumping across the gaps between the adjacent balconies was easier than she'd dared hope, the capping around the top of each one being wide

enough to balance on. Soon she was on the balcony of the
fourth house. In the water below, Kip was staring up, open-
mouthed. She tried the windows. Locked. She flashed Kip a
signal below. He nodded. Taking a deep breath, she set about
the tricky task of jimmying the windows open.

A few minutes later and she was inside. The room was dark
and smelled of damp plaster. She stayed still, listening. Satisfied
there was no one there, she crossed it swiftly but silently and
gently opened the door. From the sparse furnishings in the
hallway and room she was in, she guessed the thief had rented it
as a hideout rather than a home. An orange glow came from
downstairs. Praying there were no creaky floorboards on the
landing or stairs, she inched along the wall to the top step.
Peering down the stairwell, she recoiled at the sight of close-
cropped dark hair topping a blue suit.

It's definitely the thief, Ellie. Courage and wits to the fore.

She waited, knowing Clifford would do the same.

Assuming he's managed to pick the front lock, of course?

For a second, she panicked. She took a couple of slow
breaths, telling herself not to be stupid. There wasn't a door
made that her butler couldn't open. She slid off her shoes, and
adjusted her mask over her face, trying to quell a new nagging
worry that something had gone wrong Kip's end and the—

The back windows were suddenly illuminated in a blinding, flaring, fizzing light show. Below her an exclamation of
surprise rang out, followed by what sounded like a curse. Then
footsteps hurrying towards the sound of the noise.

She sprinted down the stairs on tiptoe. At the bottom, she
just had time to register the figurine and heart on the central
table as the thief spun back around from the window.

'Bet you can't guess who I am?' she exclaimed behind her
mask, far more calmly than she felt as he moved towards her,
eyes flashing.

'Too much trouble,' he said in a steely tone. 'That is who you are.'

At that moment, Clifford burst through the far door, his service revolver at the ready.

'Surrender your gun. NOW!' he barked.

The thief stopped, looking coolly from one to the other and then out the window where Kip's impromptu firework display was fizzling to a conclusion. 'Very impressive, Lady Swift.'

'Your gun!' Clifford barked again. 'Hand it over.'

The thief turned slowly to face him. 'This I cannot do.'

'As you wish,' Clifford growled, striding closer. 'But it will be the last mistake you ever make. My lady, please go back upstairs. This wretch is about to get a bullet in his chest.'

38

Eleanor walked slowly up the first few stairs. 'Just the one bullet, Clifford, really?' She leaned over the banister rail. 'Surely he deserves more than that after killing three innocent people?'

'A good point, my lady. Three then. Plus one for manhandling my mistress. Which I shall enjoy delivering the most,' Clifford ended menacingly.

'Only I did not.' The thief shrugged, looking as cool and collected as he had during their every encounter. 'Not the killings. And not the rough handling. I was the gentleman always with you. You know that,' he added to Eleanor.

'I can't say otherwise where I was concerned,' she said, coming back down, as he obviously wasn't fooled by their bluff. 'But you'll have a hard job of convincing us you're not the murderer.'

'A very hard job!' Kip said, stepping in unexpectedly.

Clifford caught Eleanor's eye. They hadn't intended for Kip to be in the line of danger.

'Three against one,' Kip said resolutely. 'Better odds for our side.'

The thief blinked as he gazed between them. Up close he was of medium height, his jacket hinting at the muscular form underneath. 'I thought the English were proud to be the sporting types? But just one of you having a gun is more than unfair odds on my side because I do not have one.'

'Lies!' Clifford snorted.

'If you say so.' He held his hands up. 'Check for yourself.'

Training his revolver on the thief's forehead, Clifford stepped forward, whipped open the man's jacket and patted him down.

'No gun,' he confirmed to Eleanor, surprise in his voice.

'None of the murdered men were shot,' the thief said calmly.

'Which does the opposite of convincing me it wasn't you,' she scoffed. 'Kip, grab those curtain ties please and help Clifford pin him in that chair. With both your belts for extra strappings, if you will.'

Her confusion grew as the thief made no attempt to struggle or escape. Evidently, her face gave her away as he nodded over each of his tight bindings. 'So comfortable, thank you.'

'Kip, if you could stand guard at the front door now,' she said, adding in a murmur as he drew level. 'But run at any sign of trouble.'

As Kip closed the door behind him, she marched up to the thief. 'Where is the other figurine?'

'An excellent question. I believe you are supposed to have *both* of them?'

'Never mind that,' Clifford grunted, gun still aimed at their captor's chest. 'Answer, man!'

'I don't like to be made to hurry, thank you.' He nodded curtly to Eleanor.

'And I don't like being kidnapped and held in a metal prison on a barge!' she shot back.

He winked. 'Then we are even.'

As the thief seemed determined to maintain his composed air, she did the same.

'Not quite.' She took a long moment to fluff out her skirt. Then several more to adjust her headdress. 'Perhaps you've forgotten you have an appointment waiting? Or perhaps I forgot to remind you first?'

Clifford tutted. 'I believe you did, my lady.'

'How remiss of me.'

'What appointment?' the thief said guardedly.

'Over the Bridge of Sighs. To prison. But I'll give you the chance to do one good deed in your malicious life before you go... Tell me where the other figurine is?'

He held her gaze so intently for so long, it took all her resolve not to be the one to look away. Finally, he nodded slowly. 'Alright. I will answer. But only if you answer my one question first. Those are my terms.'

She folded her arms. 'Alright. What is your question?'

'Where is the other figurine?'

That pulled her up short. 'What a lame trick. You blackguard!'

He tutted. 'You should look in the mirror. Then you would see what I see!'

She turned to take a deep breath, no longer able to trust herself not to let fly the rage burning inside her.

The thief, however, was looking thoughtful. He nodded to Clifford. 'Why don't you just shoot me? Why this charade?' His brow furrowed. He shot her an enquiring glance. 'Time is running out. For both of us, I think. So, one more exchange. If you tell me exactly what brought the two of you here from the beginning, I will do the same. Or we stick with the stalemate. Your choice.' He looked pointedly at the wall clock.

Less than an hour and a half to midnight, Ellie!

Clifford's puzzled glance told her he was equally confused as to their captive's game.

She held her hands out. 'I've nothing to hide!' She quickly filled him in from her arrival in Venice, through to unwittingly getting caught up in Benetto's murder, as well as Gaspo's and Friedman's. 'And as you know, we recovered the figurine on the table there from the canal. That's why I am here now.' She flexed her fingers. 'To take it back. Because, unlike the merciless wretch you are, I would never forgive myself for not doing whatever it takes to save the last chance for two young lovers to be happy. To say nothing of preventing more deaths and bringing a killer to justice.'

The thief's brow furrowed. 'Lovers?'

'Yes. But I shan't waste time appealing to your better nature, because I honestly don't believe you have one.'

He shook his head. 'Oh, but you are wrong.' His eyes were scrutinising her face. 'Maybe I have been wrong too?'

She felt the merest flicker of hope but kept her expression sceptical. 'Only the truth will help you now.'

'That is all I have,' he said evenly.

'Then tell me the truth,' she shot back. 'Because if your plan is to keep stalling until it's too late—'

'It is not!' he said sharply. 'Now, it is my turn. My friend, my dear friend Benetto Vendelini uncovered a plot to steal the figurines and hand them over to the Marcellos' Nonno tonight at the annual get-together of the two families. But they would be given in pieces. Smashed to crushed glass. As the greatest insult to ever be thrown at the Marcellos and their Nonno.'

She frowned. 'To restart their feud?'

He nodded. 'But I do not know who is the one behind this plot.'

She was confused. 'Obviously, Benetto.'

'No! I said he uncovered it and told me of it. Because he wanted my help to stop this terrible thing from happening.'

'Sounds too convenient,' Clifford barked.

The thief shrugged. 'To you, I can see this. But I was Catarina's father's long-time friend and confidant from his military days.' At the mention of the young woman's name, Eleanor's face gave her away. 'Yes, Catarina Marcello,' the thief continued. 'I owed her father a great favour. One I was eager to repay. This is why I have been looking out for Catarina since the day he died. So, when Benetto came to me, we came up with a plan to steal the figurines ourselves before anyone else could. We planned only to keep them safe and to return them intact at the reunion of the families. I, and a friend, assisted, but Benetto was the one who actually stole them. As a Vendelini, he had the most access to them. I am not related to either family.'

Desperate though she was to believe him, the stakes were too high and the creeping cynicism that had taken hold of her in the last week refused to let go.

'You need to learn how to lie more convincingly. Because that does not fit with Benetto hurling one of the figurines to the bottom of a canal and the other to who knows where!'

The thief shook his head. 'You do not understand Venice at all. It is a miracle you two are not at the bottom of a canal yourself!'

'Are you threatening her ladyship?' Clifford growled.

The thief shook his head again. 'If I had wanted to do that, would I not have done so when she was tied up on the barge?'

Neither of them could deny that.

'Stick with your explanations.' She was acutely aware time was not now ebbing away, but racing on. 'Why did Benetto dump one of the figurines in the canal, then?'

'I never knew he had until you found it. It was not what we had planned. We were to keep safe one figurine each. But I assume he was interrupted when he stole them. So he took the precaution to first post the heart to Catarina. This I found out later. And he obviously hid one figurine in the canal when he realised he was being followed. The other, I have no idea.'

Trying not to look too intrigued, she waved a laconic hand, coaxing him on.

'I waited at the meeting place for Benetto,' the thief continued. 'The friend I spoke of was on the barge, coming to pick the two of us up.' He let out a long breath. 'I could see nothing from where I stood. But my friend saw Benetto was in danger and tried to save him by making a big wash to upset the killer's boat.' He hesitated. 'Unfortunately, it had the opposite effect of that he intended. It threw the two boats together.'

She jumped in. 'Then you know who the killer is! Your friend must have seen him?'

'Yes, but like yourself, I believe, all he saw was a man, or woman, dressed in a long cape with a scarf and hat. Similar in fact to the disguise my friend likes to adopt. Many people in this city wear such things at this time of year.'

She could tell that Clifford was thinking the thief's statements over, though his impassive expression gave nothing away. 'Then why did you steal her ladyship's bag and ransack her suite?'

The thief looked confused now. 'Why do you think? I watched you drag Benetto's body into your gondola, but when I searched him and the gondola, there were no figurines.'

Eleanor rolled her eyes. 'You want me to believe you searched his body while we were all waiting for the police? Impossible!'

Clifford cleared his throat quietly, his coded message that his sleight-of-hand skills would have let him do so, she knew.

Not so coded evidently as the thief nodded.

'What else, then?' she said coolly.

'My friend then told me that at the contessa's party, the very lady who pulled Benetto dead from the canal was talking to Vincenzo Vendelini, one of the people, along with the contessa, that we suspected of being involved in trying to steal the figurines.'

He's right, Ellie. That was something we found out from our little get-together earlier.

He nodded, as if reading her mind again. 'Yes. When my friend overheard you talking to Vincenzo about Benetto's murder, it was obvious to us. You are working with them. Then you found one of the figurines in the canal, with little trouble too. As I said, my friend and I did not even know Benetto had hidden it there. So, what else is there to say?'

For a moment, she didn't know what to say. 'What about Leonardo? Who warned him off talking to me and Clifford?'

'My friend made sure to do this. We believed you were attempting to kidnap him. Or worse!'

'And what exactly was your friend, Doctor Pinsky, doing leaving Friedman's shop? Just after he was murdered, incidentally?'

The thief bowed his head. 'So you have worked out who my friend in this is.' He shrugged. 'At this point, it does not matter that I tell you. He was looking for the other figurine that was still missing.'

'And planting my glove at the scene of Friedman's murder?'

'Ah! That was a stroke of luck. I passed the spot where you and I collided some time later. I was on my way to meet Doctor Pinsky and I happened on your dropped, initialled glove. I passed it on to the good doctor in the hope he might be able to make use of it somehow. And so he did!' He shrugged again at her disbelieving look. 'I have nothing more to say to make you believe me. And we are all running out of time. Doctor Pinsky and I searched high and low for the other figurine. Every place we could think of.' He glanced at the clock. 'Time and tide waits for no one, Lady Swift. Particularly in a city of water!'

Her breath caught. Where had she heard that recently?

Of course, Ellie! Benetto's favourite phrase.

'Clifford, over here!' she said, hurrying to the furthest corner of the room.

He was immediately at her side, his gun still trained on the thief's chest.

'Listen. I think I know where the other figurine might be,' she murmured.

Clifford's eyes widened. 'Let's go!'

She waved a hand at the thief, who was staring not at them, but still at the clock.

'But I don't know if he is telling the truth. Or if we can trust him?'

'Would that I could be sure either, my lady.'

'Exactly. We can't risk leaving him tied up alone, especially as he didn't try to struggle as you tied him up. He's as wily as you and you'd get out of that chair in a flash, I'm sure.'

'Most assuredly. But what other choice is there?'

She jumped as Kip's face appeared between them.

'I can guard him,' he whispered. 'I've come this far and not let you down.'

For a split second, she was tempted. But she shook her head as she gestured for him to give her his cape. 'It's not that you aren't capable, Kip, but this isn't your battle. Though I do need you to do something else. Go to this boarding house' – she ripped a strip off the newspaper on the table, scribbling the name and address down – 'and ask for Mrs Butters or Trotman. Tell them you need their help to create whatever diversion you can think of between you to stop the two families meeting in St Mark's Square. You have to buy us some time.'

'Got it. I'll find the boarding house, no problem.' Like an unleashed hound, he shot out of the room.

Clifford made to move. 'I'll double-check his bindings.'

'No,' she said resolutely. 'We can't chance anything. You need to trust Prudence is with me one more time tonight.'

He closed his eyes. 'My lady, no. Never. I cannot permit you to go alone.'

'Then all of this will have been for nothing,' she said firmly.

'The feud, almost certainly, more murders and a young girl's broken heart will be the result.'

He hesitated, then nodded. Throwing the hood of Kip's cape over her head, she grabbed the figurine and the heart lying next to it, and ran.

39

'Left, then right,' she murmured as she dithered in confusion at yet another junction of canals. She took a deep breath. 'All you need to do is keep your head,' she muttered. 'The clock's been against you before in tight spots.' And it had. But this time it felt more monumental. Because what was at stake was not just catching a killer. Or even stopping a bloody feud re-erupting. Not just life, but also love. And without that, what could a life saved ever hope to be, except empty?

She took a dash of comfort that the streets were getting wider. And busier, despite the late hour. That meant she had to be nearing her destination.

Soon enough, St Mark's Square stretched out before her, the lights in the centre of every one of the hundreds of arches illuminating the immense space. All she could do now was pray she was right.

Before her, the heavyset wooden door of the Torre dell'Orologio greeted her like an ancient guardian, tasked with keeping intruders at bay.

But not government officials like Benetto, Ellie. They have access to the tower, Vincenzo told you. And he also told you 'time and tide' was a phrase of Benetto's .

She scrabbled in her cloak pockets for Clifford's picklocks, then stiffened at the sound of voices behind her. Darting into the darkest shadows of the arch, she held her breath as a flurry of partygoers passed, noticing nothing but their own laughter.

Returning to the door, she calmed herself.

Remember what Clifford taught you.

She willed her fingers to copy her butler's dextrous touch, but the sturdy lock wasn't going to give up that easily. She stopped and took another couple of deep breaths. This time, she tried to block all thoughts out and concentrate only on the task at hand. A few moments later, she was rewarded with a dull clunk as the door swung open an inch.

Inside was eerily dark, the only light filtering down weakly from the few windows set high up. The coolness she had so appreciated on that humid day of her visit with Vincenzo was now making her shiver as she closed the door behind her. The realisation she was alone in the tower, looking for an object three men had already been killed for, hit home. She gripped the figurine tighter and took a second to lie back against the door to rally her courage.

Creeping up the first flight of steps, she froze before the top. It felt as if someone's breath were brushing her cheeks. Could someone be waiting for her? Waiting close enough that she could feel their every exhale? She tried to swallow down a wash of fear. She shook her head.

Don't be silly, Ellie. No one knows you're here except Clifford. And the thief. But he could hardly have escaped and made it here before me.

Then it dawned. It was the air disturbed by the clock's pulleys rising and falling that she could feel.

She steeled herself. She could only focus on where the figurine could be hidden, or her adrenaline-fuelled imagination would have her conjuring up danger lurking in every shadow. Ignoring the echo of her footsteps pounding up the spiral metal staircase, she reached the next floor.

It was brighter, being lit by larger windows. Her optimism soon faded, however. She'd forgotten how vastly tall and complicated the clock's workings were with its tangle of moving chains, cogged wheels and rods filling the twenty-foot space in front of her. The enormity of her search dawned. The other figurine could be hidden in any of a hundred places only feet away, its exquisitely sculptured glass face watching her at this very moment.

Think, Ellie, think!

No matter what she tried, however, the only thing she could think of was that she'd never find it in time.

But the clock keeper would have! He'd told her keeping the mechanism working took up most of his day. Surely he'd have discovered the figurine by now if it had been there?

Nodding to herself, she pounded up to the next floor, and stifled a scream.

Glaring back at her were the life-sized three Magi and angel statues, looking for all the world like real people. She chided herself for being so jumpy as the barrel bearing the Roman numerals that told the time ticked around. She checked the other barrel.

Eleven thirty! She was going to need a miracle.

She snapped her fingers. The Virgin Mary! The statue was watching silently over the square where shortly a drama would be played out with, or without her.

She squeezed her slender frame past the right-hand barrel and out the door the Magi passed through on the two processional days. Immediately she had to flatten herself against the Madonna and Holy Child, the blustering wind threatening to blow her over the edge of the balcony.

Reverently bowing her head to the two figures, she searched

the folds and recesses of the Virgin Mary's robe and cloak. Dropping to her knees, she felt around the base of the stone seat. 'Nothing!' she muttered. 'Sorry to have troubled you.' She squeezed back inside the tower.

'Benetto, talk to me!' She rubbed her face, and then groaned. Of course! Benetto had been far too heavyset to have squeezed through the gap she just had.

She closed her eyes, wishing desperately Clifford was there with her. He would have wisely pointed out her mistake before she'd made it and saved her five wasted minutes she couldn't afford.

Wait! Wise! The statues of the wise men, the Magi, wouldn't be moved until Ascension Day. Vincenzo had told her that. Which would make it the perfect place for Benetto to have hidden the figurine.

She sprinted back to the statues and searched each one, then the surrounding area. Nothing. Refusing to give up, she next checked the angel and the area around that. Again, nothing.

That left the next floor up. But like the clock mechanism, the keeper would surely spend a lot of his time on that floor, as all the spare parts and tools were stored there. Benetto would know that. It would be too likely he would have discovered the figurine.

It has to be on the roof, Ellie!

She hurled herself up the last two staircases and threw open the metal hatch. Stepping out onto the balustraded stone terrace, she made sure to keep away from the edge as the wind gusted around her, even stronger and more spiteful than below.

She scanned the roof. It was much smaller than she remembered, and with nowhere obvious to hide anything as large as the other glass figurine. She ran up the last few steps to scour the two muscular bronze statues of the Moors, who chimed out the time on the giant bell with their hammers. She shook her head. The figurine was glass. The reverberations from the hammers striking the bell would almost certainly shatter, or at least crack it. Benetto would never have risked that.

That left two possibilities. The only thing which could save Catarina's happiness and stop the most influential families in Venice feuding was hidden at the furthest end from the bell. Or she was wrong. And the murderer had won.

Her heart sank as she stared over at the far side of the roof. There was no space to hide anything. Unless...

A moment later, her fingers grasped a sackcloth parcel tied to the back face of one of the supporting balustrades. Only if one could fly around the outside of the three-hundred-foot-high tower, would it have been visible. The irony that Vincenzo had told her only a yard from that very spot he wished he had wings made her smile grimly.

Whatever Benetto had tied the parcel with cut into her fingers with the viciousness of piano wire. Praying she didn't drop it onto the flagstones below at Nonno Marcello's feet as he entered the square, she wrenched it free.

Scrambling up with her prize, she ran towards the stairs. Just then, the moon slipped out from behind a cloud and cast an eerie light on the bell and the two Moors with their hammers. Her heart missed a beat.

'Hammers!' An image of a blade being hammered into Benetto's back flashed into her mind. Followed by the same image again. But this time, the weapon wasn't hammered into a man, but—

She turned and stared down into St Mark's Square, her mouth dropping open. Even with the figures below seeming as small as clockwork toys, there was no mistaking that two distinct groups of people were amassing, like warring clans. Kip must have somehow failed to alert the ladies. Or they had failed to stop the families. Either way, she'd run out of time!

She sprinted for the stairs. She now knew who the

murderer was, but she had a job to finish. At the bottom of the first flight, she clattered on to the second, but before she could start down, the hairs on her arms stood up as if electrified. She stumbled to a halt, a menacing figure blocking her way.

40

For a moment, neither of them moved. Then a strange calm descended on Eleanor.

'Hello, Tomaso,' she said slowly. In the shadows, his face resembled the gargoyles on a church. 'Have you brought me a present? A chisel, perhaps?' She cocked her head. 'Or maybe some Venetian turpentine?'

He said nothing, his gaze transfixed on the figurines she clutched in each hand. She looked down at them. 'So these are worth three men's lives, are they?' At his silence, she continued. 'I know you killed Benetto. You were the man on the motorboat. And you killed Friedman. And' – she shook her head in disbelief – 'your own nephew, Gaspo.'

'No!' he cried out in a strangled voice. 'I did not mean to kill him! He was my brother's son!' He looked down, wiping his face with his hand. When he looked back up, his eyes were sad. 'I saw in horror Benetto was on his gondola. I wanted to stop, but... it was too late. Then Gaspo was arrested. He came straight to me when the police release him.'

She held his gaze. 'He came because he knew it was you who killed Benetto, didn't he?'

At Tomaso's nod, she couldn't hold in her disgust. 'He could have told the police the moment they arrested him. But he didn't. He never even mentioned your name to them, did he?'

Tomaso shook his head slowly. 'Gaspo was a good boy to me. I say again, I did not mean to kill him. But he told me I had to confess. And that... if I did not confess... he would tell the police I was guilty.'

'So what happened then?' she said quietly, keeping him distracted while she worked out how to get past him.

Tomaso ran a hand over his brow. 'I had drunk too much grappa when he came. The worry of what I did to Benetto was eating at my insides. Gaspo and me had a big argument. I was too angry and... and I pushed him away. This is the last thing I remember.' His jaw shook. 'Until I woke up the next morning lying on my workbench. The sun had not yet risen. And I found Gaspo outside, lying with his face in the water between his gondola and the posts it is tied to.' He let out a ragged breath. 'I had pushed him so hard he had hit his head on the stones.'

'And drowned while he was unconscious,' she said sadly. A thought struck her. 'But I found his body floating in a canal by the Venice Arsenal?'

He nodded. 'I took little Gaspo's body there. To hide that it was me who killed him.' His chest constricted. 'I cried all the way like a baby. And all the way back.'

He clamped a hand over his mouth as he bowed his head. But when he looked up, there was murder in his eyes. 'Why did you have to interfere? You should have stayed playing the tourist.'

She retreated back up a step. He was so thickset there was no way around him on the narrow stairs. And, even if he was unarmed, she was doubtful she could overpower him.

'I tried, trust me. But seeing one man killed practically in front of me, then hauling another from the canal, rather changed all that. The third murder convinced me I couldn't go back to postcard shopping.'

His face turned thunderous as he raised his right hand, a long-bladed tool in it.

Another from his squero, *Ellie?*

He jabbed it at her. 'You should have done just that. Not dig up dirt which was none of your business!'

She shrank back.

Stay calm, Ellie.

She managed a shrug, trying not to look intimidated. 'Well, I did. And guess what I found? A murderer.' She shook her head. 'It's so obvious now. Who would be welcome to wander in and out of every *squero* in Venice? Only another respected gondola builder, of course. Which made it easy to steal that chisel from another yard to throw suspicion off yourself. You see, it was when I saw the statues of the Moors up there on the roof with their hammers that I knew it was you. From the way you hammered that chisel into your workbench.'

As he lunged forward, face contorted, she stumbled back two steps.

'Stop! At least tell me why you killed Benetto? Was it for the figurines?' She tried again to work out how she could get past his strong, stocky frame. Running upstairs wouldn't save her. The only other door on any of the floors was the hatch up on the roof, but she'd seen herself it had no lock or handle on the outside. She'd only be inviting him to follow and throw her off the top. 'Well?' she coaxed.

For a moment, she was convinced he was going to rush her. Then he shifted the chisel in his hand.

'Benetto Vendelini was on the council, like his cousin Vincenzo. But Benetto did not care about his city. My city! He had only plans to kill it. Always he brought in new rules, new ways, that destroyed the traditions of his, and my, forefathers.'

Ah, Ellie! That links up with what Angelo was saying about Benetto supporting progress against tradition.

Tomaso was becoming more and more agitated, the veins standing out on his neck. 'Already these changes were destroying the way of life of the people who have kept this city alive. The gondola builders like me. And the gondoliers. It was Benetto's doing that I got an official notice to tell me my *squero* was to close!'

Her brows rose. 'Why?'

'Benetto, he wanted only new shiny motorboats to go on the canals! Progress, progress, progress! Venice was built one thousand years ago by men hammering poles into the mud. With their tools and hands. Not with motors! So, in the last years, because there are less and less gondolas, I have not made enough money to pay the rent on my yard. Benetto used this debt to send me notice. Like many other *squero*.'

'But how can he do that?'

He laughed bitterly. 'Because the Venice Council owns the land.' He raised his hands. 'The gondola in my workshop you see being built by these hands when you came? It is the last one I will ever make. Because of him! After my whole life has been dedicated to the craft, the skill and the love that my father taught me. Like his father did for him. And back many generations.'

She blanched. 'So you killed him with a tool used especially to build gondolas?'

'Yes!' he sneered. 'He died by the symbol he wanted to destroy! And I used a motorboat. Stolen, of course. There are plenty to choose from on the canals now because of Benetto. More sweet justice, eh?'

She tried desperately to keep Tomaso distracted long enough for him to drop his guard.

'So, apart from deadly tools among the confusion of jars and tins crowding your workshop shelves, you've also got a supply of equally deadly Venetian turpentine. I remember the smell now from when I first visited. For varnishing the gondolas once they're built, isn't it? And for killing people. People like Friedman. What exactly had he done to deserve to die?'

'Nothing. But I had no choice.' His cold-blooded statement sent chills through her body. He grinned smugly. 'The gondoliers. You think they just row the gondolas, take the money and go home for their supper? But they listen too. Everyone takes the gondolas, from the lowly to the high and mighty! And they talk!'

She groaned. 'Venice's grapevine. Angelo too?'

He nodded. 'He told me about you. That you were working to catch Gaspo's killer.' He shrugged. 'He thought it make the sad old uncle feel better.'

'He told you everything I've done? And where I've been?' she said, feeling betrayed.

'No.' Tomaso held up a finger. 'He did not tell me the details. Then I heard from one gondolier that he passed an English lady with the red hair very early one morning with some swimmers. I realised you were searching for whatever Benetto had thrown into the canal. I thought it must be worth a lot of money, otherwise, why would an English lady be interested? And then when I asked among the gondoliers, one told me you took it to the antiques specialist in the Jewish Quarter.' He held up a triumphant finger. 'Then I *knew* it was worth a lot of money!'

She shuddered. 'So that's when the last piece of your plan for revenge fell into place, was it? If you could get hold of the figurine and sell it, you could pay off the debts on your yard with money taken from Benetto himself. The fact he was already dead by your hand probably made that idea taste all the sweeter?'

'Now you understand,' he sneered. 'This was to be justice for all Benetto did to me! I went to Friedman's shop to get the figurine because I believe you sold it to him. I demanded he gave it to me or tell me where it was. But he insist he did not buy it and you still have it—'

'You didn't need to kill him, though,' she interrupted angrily.

He shrugged. 'He knew I was looking for the figurine. I could not risk him connecting me to Benetto's death.'

'So you forced him to drink Venetian turpentine.' She shivered. 'It's a truly awful way to go, you know?'

'I did not stay to watch...' He paled. 'Not to the end. Then I hear through the gondoliers that the figurine, no, *two* figurines were for sale, so I know it was you selling them. I follow you everywhere.'

Then you weren't paranoid, Ellie. The thief and *Tomaso have been shadowing you!*

He frowned. 'Only tonight I lose you in the Carnival costumes after you leave your hotel. But then.' His eyes glowed with malevolence. 'I passed the clock tower on my way to watch the Marcellos and the Vendelinis meet in the square. I looked up at the time and I saw that red hair on the balcony with the Madonna!'

'Lucky you! Only the figurines are—'

'In. Your. Hands,' he said menacingly. 'As is your life. Now, hand them over!'

She thrust the packages behind her back. 'I can't do that, Tomaso. They aren't mine to give.'

'I will take them!'

She jumped as the bell tolled above her. Midnight! Her heart constricted.

There's nothing you can do now to save Catarina's happiness, Ellie. Or stop Nonno Marcello declaring war on Leonardo's family. If you rush Tomaso, it will be suicide. All you can do is try and save yourself.

As if on cue, a closely cropped head of dark hair appeared behind Tomaso.

Her heart sank further. *The thief, Ellie! He was working with Tomaso all along. He must have escaped!*

Tomaso advanced another step. 'Give them to me or I will take your life in their place!'

Before she could act, Clifford's commanding voice rang out. 'Actually, I think we'll take yours, you mongrel!'

Tomaso swung around in surprise, to be met by two blinding uppercut punches. He crumpled to the floor. The thief shook Clifford's hand with a grin.

'Boxing champion of my division in the army. I still fight occasionally, Signor Clifford. As I see you do. Mostly for the lady, I imagine.'

'Don't worry, my lady, this gentleman is with us,' Clifford said to Eleanor as she looked from one to the other in astonishment.

The thief looked down at Tomaso, then up at Eleanor. 'I'll deal with him.'

She let out a breath she never knew she'd been holding. 'Thank you. I'm very confused, but very grateful.'

She stepped over Tomaso. The thief vaulted over the other side of the stair rail so she could pass.

Taking another deep breath, she looked questioningly at Clifford. 'But... how?'

'Suffice to say, this gentleman' – he pointed to the man they'd been referring to as the thief – 'repeated his story to me a second time without the delicacy he had included in your presence to spare your sensibilities. I taxed him with more questions and that was when I heard my mistress in my thoughts.' His lips quirked as he folded his arms the way she so often did and mimicked her voice. 'Oh, for heaven's sake, Clifford, what's the point of intuition if we can't trust it?'

She stifled a sob of relief as she nodded to the thief where he was tying the unconscious Tomaso to the staircase railings. 'I'm sure Clifford delighted in telling you on the way that actually sensibilities are one ladylike department I often fall short in.'

The thief laughed. 'He may have mentioned that. And thank goodness, because you have replaced them with the courage of a lion, like the winged lion of Venice! And you have the full set of figurines.'

'But too late!' she cried as the bell finished tolling the hour above her.

'Not quite!' Clifford said, darting to the window. 'But if you are to prevent war and save our two star-crossed lovers, run, my lady, run!'

41

Eleanor flew out of the Torre dell'Orologio into St Mark's Square, the figurines clasped tightly in her hands, the glass heart in her pocket. Within half a yard, however, she stumbled to a stop. While she'd been busy inside the tower trying not to die, the whole city had descended on the square.

The air was charged with anticipation, the usually loud and demonstrative Venetians, silent. The tense expressions on the crush of faces made her realise the outcome of the meeting mattered as much to Venice herself as to the two families. This was all very well, she thought, as she attempted to force a way through the lines of onlookers, but no one was moving out of her way.

A hulking, dark-featured man in a long black coat raised an imperious hand. 'Sta' fermo!'

You can't fail at the eleventh minute of the eleventh hour, Ellie!

'He said, stop!' She spun around to see the thief hurrying up. 'No worries, Lady Swift,' he continued, reaching her side. 'Mr Clifford will be here in a minute. He is just waiting for the police to arrive to pick up Tomaso. In the meantime, follow me.'

The thief strode up to the hulk. After a brief, urgent exchange, the man's eyes widened. Like an unleashed bull, he tore into the crowd, shouting she knew not what in Italian. The crush of people parted like the Red Sea, allowing her to finally make progress towards the centre of the square.

A moment later and she was standing at the front of the crowd watching the Marcello and Vendelini families marching from opposite ends of the square. Even knowing how momentous this meeting was to both sides, somehow she hadn't expected there to be so many relatives striding determinedly behind the head of their respective family.

As the Marcellos arrived, led by their Nonno, she caught sight of a face she knew. Dashing out of the crowd, she slipped the heart into Catarina's astonished hand and retook her place.

A moment later and the Vendelinis joined the Marcellos, led by the head of their family. An even greater hush fell on the crowd as the two patriarchs faced each other. As Nonno Marcello started speaking, she caught the threatening tone in his voice.

The thief stepped up next to her. 'He just asked the Vendelini Nonno if he has the figurines.'

The man spread his hands as if in disbelief. 'Non è stato possibile trovarli!'

'He says "no, they could not be found!"' the thief translated. At Nonno Marcello's barked reply, the thief winced. 'He is holding his counterpart responsible!'

A further angry exchange broke out. Suddenly, Nonno Marcello raised his cane as if to bring it down on the head of his counterpart.

'STOP!' she cried, running out of the crowd into the centre of the square.

Nonno Marcello's ivory hair shook as his expression blackened. 'You again! You have no business here, foolish woman. Leave!'

'Certainly. But not before I have given you these.' She held out the two figurines.

'Un miracolo!' he breathed, taking them reverently. 'But I did not believe you had these after the meeting in the warehouse.'

She shook her head. 'I didn't. You really are too shrewd to be hoodwinked, you know.'

He nodded sharply. 'Of course.'

For the first time, she noticed that, at the sight of the figurines, both families had broken ranks and crowded around her and the two heads of the families.

Nonno Marcello shook his head. 'Never have I met a woman like you. But...' He dropped his gaze to the figurines and then fixed his counterpart with a stony gaze. 'Without the heart, the symbol of unity is not complete.'

'Then take this, Nonno,' a soft-spoken female voice said. 'And unite our two great families again.' Catarina stepped forward and held up the glass heart, her amethyst-blue eyes shining.

Eleanor watched with racing emotions as her grandfather held the figurines with the palms of their hands almost touching, then nodded to Catarina. The glass heart trembled as she reached out and placed it between the outstretched hands, where it slipped down to the centre, locking both figurines together.

Eleanor felt an overwhelming rush of relief.

For a moment, Nonno Marcello gazed at the figurines. Then he hoisted them high above his head. The square rang with a wild cheer. 'This,' he cried in his arresting rich baritone, drawing an instant hush. 'This has been the symbol of unity between the Marcello and the Vendelini families for generations.'

He stepped back, letting go of the figurines at the same time.

Eleanor's heart stopped as they fell in slow motion and then shattered on the flagstones, the feet, bodies and then heads exploding into a shower of a thousand glass shards.

Out of the corner of her eye, she saw the contessa throw Vincenzo a triumphant look. Then all hell broke loose. The crowd erupted as the head of the Vendelinis grabbed Nonno Marcello by the shoulders, letting forth a barrage of rage.

Clifford had now arrived at her side and his brows met as he held Eleanor's horrified gaze. For once, he seemed as upset as she was.

You failed Catarina, Ellie. And Venice. It was all for nothing.

But then she realised Nonno Marcello was... smiling? And shaking hands with his counterpart? She blinked twice, but it was true.

Nonno Marcello looked around the crowd, who had seemingly magically fallen silent. His voice boomed out. 'We no longer need a fragile symbol of unity, friends! We have all seen in these last days how easily a symbol can be manipulated. Or destroyed.' He beckoned to Leonardo, who was standing close by, mouth still agape. 'Leonardo Vendelini, the marriage between you and my beloved Catarina will cement our two families' friendship forever. A bond and union far more secure than a heart of glass and the figurines of two old men!'

'Nonno? You... you knew?' Catarina gasped.

He nodded. 'Of course, I am Nonno! Now, kiss your soon-to-be husband or everyone will think the wedding is off!'

Leonardo spun Catarina around and she fell into his embrace, both of them lost in a passionate kiss. The crowd erupted into a cacophony of raucous cheers and whistles, so heartfelt it wrought a sob from Eleanor's exhausted chest.

A few yards away, she caught sight of Clifford handing out handkerchiefs to her four ladies, streams of tears coursing down their cheeks.

'Young woman!' Nonno Marcello brought Eleanor's attention back to what was happening in the centre of the square. He gestured at the two families following behind Catarina and Leonardo as they entered Florian's café opposite. 'Our annual tradition is not yet complete. None of this would have happened without you. Please, you must join our two families in the Room of Illustrious Men. And tonight, Illustrious Women!'

She shook her head, failing to swallow the lump in her throat. 'It would be an immense honour and I'm sorry to have to say no, but' – she beckoned Clifford and the ladies closer – 'I have my family waiting for me.'

42

Any masked ball in Venice, one of the most vibrant and unique cities on earth, was going to be an unforgettable spectacle. But this one, in a palatial Renaissance ballroom with just a single couple dancing before a vast assembly of elaborate costumed watchers, was so much more than that.

It was nine days after Eleanor's fateful encounter with Tomaso in the clock tower. And nine days since Leonardo had kissed Catarina in public for the first time. Now here he was, passionately waltzing her for the first time as his wife of only an hour before. It was the last day of the Carnival and the night had only just begun, but it was already etched into Eleanor's heart as testament that love always wins. Something, she mused, her beaming smile had likely given away to her butler. She laughed as he nodded, guessing her thoughts, the fine feathery fronds adorning the brim of his courtier's hat fluttering.

'Clifford, you really didn't have to dress up again, you know. You're probably squirming at attracting so much attention of the female variety as you look extra dapper and handsome tonight. You could star as the dashing hero in my penny dreadful novels if you wanted, though?'

He eyed her sideways. 'Not a notion which had sprung to mind, my lady, until it was pointed out by yourself. So, thank you. However, with Master Tomkins and Gladstone stealing the show...' He gestured down at her excited bulldog and cat, side by side in his arms, both proudly sporting matching lace black masks over their foreheads and miniature soft-trimmed hooded capes. 'I believe I am...' He tailed off at the excited giggles of Eleanor's four ladies approaching.

'You lost, Trotters!' Mrs Butters said animatedly.

Her staff looked every inch the delighted belles of the ball in their simple, but bright Cinderella costumes Clifford had organised as a surprise the day before. Eleanor had accompanied him to deliver the gowns, along with a raft of reassurances the invitation had expressly invited them too. Along the way she'd met the sketcher, now back in his usual spot, and thanked him profusely while insisting he took generous payment for the second sketch.

As the bright-eyed ladies curtseyed to Eleanor, their firmly linked arms made her heart squeeze with affection.

'And what did you lose at?' she asked her cook with a chuckle.

'Our bet, my lady. That Mr Clifford wouldn't join us women in dressing up.' She shot him a sly glance. 'Not that he knew we had a book going on him, mind.'

'I wouldn't be so sure.' Eleanor laughed at her butler's wink. 'You should know better than to try and trump him. I've been trying since the day I inherited Henley Hall and he's had the last laugh every time. Haven't you, Clifford?'

'If you say so, my lady.' He gently placed Gladstone and Tomkins on the ground, swished his coat-tails out, then blanched as his arms were grabbed by two eager-eyed women who steered him determinedly off to the dance floor.

Eleanor and the ladies were still laughing as a Harlequin costume topped by a bouncing head of straw-blond hair joined them, a petite-framed, dark-haired young woman holding his arm.

'Kip!' Eleanor cheered as the two of them lifted their masks. 'And?'

'This is Felicita, my sweetheart. I found her window at last. But then I went to the front door like a decent chap and told her father how I felt about her.'

'Not in soggy bathing trunks, I hope?' Eleanor turned to the girl, thinking she had the prettiest face ever to be set with such determined eyes. 'Hello, Felicita. It's lovely to meet you.' She leaned in to whisper. 'Kip here is a very rare find, you know. I should keep him close if at all possible.'

Felicita beamed. 'I think this too. I already have a plan to make him stay in Venice, do not worry.'

'What?' he crowed. 'Really? Wait until I write home to Pater about this!'

'One moment, Master Kip!' Clifford reappeared, scrubbing in horror at his cheeks with a handkerchief. He slid an envelope from his inside pocket and handed it to Eleanor.

'It's a fearful cheek, Kip.' She held it out. 'But if you don't mind, I'd love you to include this with your next missive home to your father. It's my account of how an incredible young man wowed Venice with his extraordinary talent in a single night. Just by being himself.'

'But... oh wickets!' He shook his head. 'I failed you at the last minute. I never reached these ladies at their boarding house. Bally police recognised me as I ran over one of the bridges, right smack into their arms.'

'And took the rap like a gentleman, sir,' Clifford said.

Eleanor nodded. 'Besides, Kip, our team still won.'

'I say!' he stuttered, his cheeks flushed. 'You're the best brick ever, Lady Swift.' He took the envelope. 'I might have to dash home so I can see Father's face when he reads it.'

'Oh no, you don't!' Felicita said with Venetian vehemence. 'Not without me!'

A waiter appeared and drinks were taken all round, two non-alcoholic cocktails with all the trimmings clearly having been organised for her maids by Eleanor's ever-thoughtful butler. As they toasted Kip and Felicita, a man approached dressed in familiar blue, albeit now in a baroque courtier's doublet and matching trousers tucked into highwayman's boots. Eleanor saluted as he lifted his mask up over his close-cropped hair.

'Hello, er...?' She tutted. 'You know, I can't go on calling you "the thief". It sounds so rude.'

His eyes danced with amusement as he bowed. 'My name is Salvador dal Zio. And I think the title "the thief" is now yours, as you have stolen the heart of my city.' He bowed again. 'It is an honour to know you, Lady Swift.'

'Likewise,' she said genuinely. 'I've never met anyone who could get close to my scallywag butler's dubious skills. But you, you're like his rascal twin from Italy! Please, to stop my curiosity eating me up, tell me your background—'

Clifford's quiet cough halted her words. She mimed buttoning her lips, which Salvador acknowledged with a grateful nod. 'I'll leave it to my imagination instead,' she murmured as he gave Tomkins a quick ear rub before gliding away, Gladstone looking rather put-out until Kip ruffled his.

The first waltz ended amid vivacious cheers and applause for the newly-weds. They all joined in, Eleanor loudest of all. As the orchestra struck up the next dance, heralding a veritable flood of elaborate costumes onto the floor, Leonardo and Catarina came over to Eleanor.

'Lady Swift,' the clearly besotted groom said, pulling Catarina into his side, 'we are forever in your debt.'

She shook her head, smiling. 'The only thing you two need be forever in is each other's arms. Now, go enjoy your night.'

As the couple left, surrounded by well-wishers, she caught Mrs Trotman and Mrs Butters bumping hips as three good-looking Italian musketeers appeared, resplendent in red, gold and green velvet costumes.

'Ah, ladies! Angelo and his diver friends, if I'm not mistaken.' She waved at them. 'Grab a drink and join us, won't you?'

In reply, they whipped off their fine-feathered hats in unison, held them across their chests and bowed to her four female staff with a synchronised courtly flourish. Still bent over, Angelo grinned up at Clifford. 'With your permission, signore, may we take the ladies for a dance?'

Eleanor's shoulders rose with delight as the two divers led a wide-eyed Mrs Trotman and Mrs Butters onto the dance floor, Angelo following with a giggling Lizzie and a goggle-eyed Polly. Clifford raised a brow.

'Since my mistress is betrothed, and therefore dancing with an unknown gentleman is far from acceptable, would the lady care to...? He offered her his gloved hand.

She laughed. 'Will I waltz with you? And deny all Venice's females the treat? Which you are merely trying to have me save you from? Tsk! No, you terror, you're on your own!'

'Traitor!' he quipped weakly. 'In that case...'

She opened her mouth to reply, but stopped abruptly as he slid a telegram from his inside pocket. She tore it open. 'Oh, Clifford! It's from Hugh!'

Darling Eleanor,

Blasted telephone makes me stick foot in mouth! Know that whatever you are doing, my heart surges with joy that you're happy. I'll never think of asking more of you. Ever.

I love you.

Forever yours,

Hugh

Eyes swimming with happiness, she pressed it to her heart, then slipped it into an inside pocket.

As the waltz finished playing, a woman in an outrageously feathered costume stopped in front of her horror-struck butler, giggling as she lunged for his hands. 'Signore, may I have the next dance?'

Before he could reply, Eleanor smiled and shook her head. 'I'm sorry, but you'll have to sit this one out. Clifford?'

He passed Gladstone and Tomkins over to the four ladies' outstretched arms as they arrived breathless from the dance floor, bowed and took Eleanor's hand.

'When in Rome, my lady.'

She laughed. 'Let's go there next. For another holiday.'

'Let's not!'

A LETTER FROM VERITY

Dear reader,

I want to say a huge thank you for choosing to read *A Death in Venice*. If you did enjoy it, and want to keep up to date with all my latest releases, just sign up at the following link. Your email address will never be shared and you can unsubscribe at any time.

www.bookouture.com/verity-bright

I hope you loved *A Death in Venice* and if you did I would be very grateful if you could write a review. I'd love to hear what you think, and it makes such a difference helping new readers to discover one of my books for the first time.

I love hearing from my readers – you can get in touch through social media or my website.

Thanks,

Verity

facebook.com/veritybrightauthor
x.com/BrightVerity

HISTORICAL NOTES

VENICE

Eleanor is quite right, Venice is one of the most fascinating cities in the world. Over a thousand years old, it is built on a series of lagoon islands, some of them tiny. And as Angelo tells her and Clifford, the foundations of all the incredible buildings you see are hundreds of thousands of wooden poles driven into mud. Despite what Tomaso tells Eleanor, however, it has always been a progressive city, laying claim to a disparate collection of firsts, including the first woman to ever graduate and the first casino to ever open to the public.

GONDOLAS

One thing Tomaso and Angelo were both right about was the decline of the gondola. In the eighteenth century there were around ten thousand in Venice. Today, there are around four hundred. Each gondola is built from eight different woods to match a particular gondolier down to his weight. And, as Eleanor noted, they are mostly funereal black. This is due to a decree passed in the sixteenth century to stop noblemen spending a fortune on them in one-upmanship with their peers.

GONDOLIERS

After a ride in a gondola, Eleanor fancies her hand at becoming a gondolier. Angelo, however, tells her it's hard to become one, and impossible for a woman. A hundred years later and it's much the same. The right to be a gondolier is still passed down through families and only after four hundred hours of training is a new gondolier qualified. Unsurprisingly, only three to four new gondola licences are issued each year, and even now, there is only one woman gondolier.

VENICE FESTIVAL

Before it was banned in 1797, the Venetian Carnival was an annual event held for around ten days, ending on Shrove Tuesday, the day before the start of Lent. It soon became an extravagant affair with the entire city dressing up, always masked, with lavish private parties and general merry-making. When it was at its height, the Carnival was taken so seriously, it was forbidden to work or to disrupt it. So much so, when the Doge, the ruler of Venice, died during the Carnival, his death wasn't announced until afterwards. When Eleanor visited, the ban was still in place in public places, but not strongly enforced, and certainly nothing the vivacious Venetians weren't determined to sidestep. In the 1970s the ban was finally lifted, and the Carnival is now one of the most famous in the world.

THE JEWISH GHETTO

Most people have heard the word 'ghetto', but few realise the term actually comes from Venice. The area near the Venice

Arsenal that Eleanor and Clifford visit was used to cast metal and the term 'ghetto' is believed to have derived from the Italian word for 'casting'. The Venice Ghetto was created in 1516 to separate Jewish people from the mostly Christian inhabitants of the city. At night it was forbidden for anyone to leave the ghetto. The canals were patrolled and bridges barred to make sure no one snuck out. The Ghetto was abolished when the city fell to Napoleon in 1797, so Doctor Pinsky would have been free to live wherever he pleased. Unfortunately, Doctor Pinsky's claim that 'the Jew always gets the blame', was quite valid, so even after it was abolished, most Jewish people stayed living in the Ghetto.

LORD BYRON

The Romantic English poet, Lord Byron, certainly lived up to his reputation, which Clifford mentions, of being 'mad, bad and dangerous to know'. While in Venice, apart from challenging all and sundry to swimming races (despite having a club foot), he also womanised his way through half the female population of the city (he claimed to have had over two hundred lovers). Oh, and he also had run-ins with Italian soldiers and kept a menagerie of animals in his house including horses, dogs, monkeys, cats, eagles, peacocks, guinea hens and an Egyptian Crane. And yes, *in* his house!

MURANO GLASS

Since 1291, the little island of Murano in Venice has been famous for its glass. Glass at this time in history was a luxury item and became a huge source of prestige and income to the city. So much so, divulging the secrets of how Murano glass was made was punishable by imprisonment and even death! Glassmakers were revered so highly that they enjoyed immunity from prosecution for most crimes and their offspring were allowed to marry into blue-blood families.

VENETIAN TURPENTINE

Venetian turpentine is actually a varnish, traditionally used by some gondola builders and painters. It can be used to thin oil paints and also to clean brushes. It is obtained from the European larch, and if swallowed in large enough quantities can, as Clifford noted, cause burning sensations, abdominal pain, nausea, vomiting, convulsions and respiratory failure, among other symptoms. In the nineteenth century, however, ordinary turpentine was generally used as a medicine in small doses for colds, sore throats, rheumatism, pneumonia, toothaches and other assorted maladies.

GOLIA CANDY

The sweet wrapper Eleanor finds on Benetto's body is a brand you can still buy today. Golia is probably Italy's favourite liquorice candy (I love liquorice!). It was, in fact, not really popular until a few years after Eleanor was in Venice, but I allowed myself a little artistic licence.

ACKNOWLEDGEMENTS

Thanks to the fabulous team at Bookouture for all their individual and collective efforts in making this book so much more fun to write, and to read.

PUBLISHING TEAM

Turning a manuscript into a book requires the efforts of many people. The publishing team at Bookouture would like to acknowledge everyone who contributed to this publication.

Audio
Alba Proko
Sinead O'Connor
Melissa Tran

Commercial
Lauren Morrissette
Jil Thielen
Imogen Allport

Data and analysis
Mark Alder
Mohamed Bussuri

Cover design
Tash Webber

Editorial
Kelsie Marsden
Jen Shannon

Made in the USA
Monee, IL
26 March 2024

55807475R00173